This
Plague
of Souls

ALSO BY MIKE McCORMACK

Getting it in the Head
Crowe's Requiem
Notes from a Coma
Forensic Songs
Solar Bones

This Plague of Souls

Mike McCormack

CANONGATE

First published in Great Britain in 2023
by Canongate Books Ltd, 14 High Street, Edinburgh EH1 1TE

canongate.co.uk

1

Published simultaneously in Ireland by Tramp Press

An extract from this book was published in
Reading the Future: New Writing from Ireland (2017) edited by Alan Hayes

British Library Cataloguing-in-Publication Data
A catalogue record for this book is available on
request from the British Library

ISBN 978 1 83885 932 9

Typeset in Van Dijck by Palimpsest Book Production Ltd,
Falkirk, Stirlingshire

Printed and bound in Great Britain by Clays Ltd, Elcograf S.p.A.

Country Feedback

Opening the door and crossing the threshold in the dark triggers the phone in Nealon's pocket. He lowers his bag to the floor and looks at the screen; it's not a number he recognises. For the space of one airless heartbeat he has a sense of things drifting sideways, draining over an edge.

The side of his head is bathed in the forensic glow of the screen light.

'Yes?'

'You're back.'

'Hello?'

'Welcome home, Nealon.'

'Who am I talking to?'

'Only a friend would call at this hour.'

The voice at the other end is male and downbeat, not

the sort you would choose to listen to in the dark. Nealon is aware of himself in two minds – the voice on the phone drawing against his immediate instinct to orient himself in the dark hallway. He turns to stand with his back to the wall.

'You know who I am?'

'That's the least of what I know.'

'What do you want?'

Two paces to his left, Nealon spots a light switch. He reaches out with his spare hand and throws it, throws it back, then throws it again. Nothing. Half his face remains shrouded in blue light. He takes five steps to open a door and passes into what he senses is an open room. A swipe of his hand over a low shadow finds a table; he draws out a chair and takes the rest of the phone call sitting in the dark.

'I thought I'd give you a shout,' the voice says.

'You have the wrong number.'

'I don't think so.'

'I'm going to hang up.'

'There's no rush.'

'Goodbye.'

'We should meet up.'

'No.'

'Not tonight, you're just in the door, you need some rest.'

'We don't have anything to talk about.'

'I wouldn't be so sure.'

'I am.'

'In a day or so when you're settled.'

'Not then, not ever.'

'We'll talk again. One last thing.'

'What is it?'

'Don't be sitting there in the dark, the mains switch is over the back door.'

And with that the phone goes dead in Nealon's hand.

Nealon pushes aside his immediate wish to dwell on the phone call: who is it from; what is it about? He needs to orient himself in the house so that is what he sets himself to. After a quick scan through his phone, he finds the torch app and sweeps the room with the light at arm's length.

To his right is another small room barely six feet wide, with a fridge and cooker, shelves along one wall. There's also a solid door over which sits a junction box with a complex array of meters and fuses. The mains switch is at the end but it's too high to reach so he drags a chair from the table.

He steps up and throws the switch; light floods from the hallway into the kitchenette and living room. The table sits beneath a large curtained window and beyond it is a sink and worktop with white cupboards overhead. Everything is flat-pack melamine, all the units date from sometime in the eighties. Against the left-hand wall sits a three-seater couch over which hangs a picture of the Sacred Heart with its orange votive light now glowing beneath.

He reaches out and flicks the switch. The walls come up in a cool green glow against which the pine table seems warm and homely.

There are five doors off the L-shaped hallway. The first is a bathroom with a shower cubicle tucked behind the door and a toilet beneath a small window which looks out from the back of the house. Behind each of the other doors are three bedrooms of equal size with a double bed and built-in wardrobes. Pillows and duvets are stacked on the beds, but all the wardrobes are empty.

Back into the hall.

There is something coercive in the flow of the house, the way it draws him through it. These are doors that have to be opened, rooms that have to be entered and stood in. He catches himself looking up and examining the ceiling. What does he expect to find there?

Inside the front door is a sitting room where a laminate floor runs to a marble fireplace with a low mantelpiece. To the left and right of the chimney breast, empty bookshelves reach to the ceiling. In the middle of the floor is a single armchair, angled towards a large television. Its shape and plain covering make it an obvious partner to the couch in the living room.

Empty and all as the house is, it still has the residual hum and bustle of family life. It feels clean and it has been carefully maintained. Not the raw cleanness of a last-minute blitz before visitors arrive but that ongoing effort which keeps it presentable to any sudden need.

Nealon becomes aware of a low vibration throughout the room and stands listening for a moment. He lowers his hand to the radiator and finds that the heat has come on. The house is beginning to warm up.

★

Over the front door, a globe light illumines a stretch of gravel frontage closed in by a pair of black gates. Outside lies the main road, the small village to the right, less than half a mile distant and the coast road running to the left. Lights are visible in the distance but all is quiet. No cars at this hour.

An uneven grassed area flows into the night, darkening at a tall hedge that leans towards the gable of the house. A cement walk takes him around to the back door where the rear garden runs about thirty yards to a sod fence at the end of the site. He passes by the garage, locked and lightless, and moves deeper into the darkness where the shadowed outline of a small car sits hunched beneath overhanging trees. It has the shape and sheen of a giant armoured insect sheltering for the night. Beyond the trees the looming outlines of the hayshed and the cow barn are visible. Light from the living-room window reveals the central-heating pump on the far gable and he returns once more to the front door through which he re-enters the house.

A glance at his Nokia confirms that he has been here twelve minutes. He punches in a ten-digit number and listens. After several moments the call goes through to voicemail. Nealon speaks.

'Hello Olwyn. If you get this, I'm home. Give me a ring. Love to you and Cuan.'

He is tempted to sit for a while and gather his thoughts, but he knows that if he does he could be up for hours. The phone call still nags at him but he had better get some rest. He goes into the first bedroom and kicks his boots off, strips down to his t-shirt and pulls the duvet over him.

He is asleep before his eyes close, drifting off like a man with a long, hard day behind him.

And if the circumstances of his being here alone in this bed at this hour rest within the arc of those grand constructs that turn in the night – politics, finance, trade – it is not clear how his loneliness resolves in the indifference with which such constructs regard him across the length and breadth of his sleep.

He makes breakfast the following morning.

Scrambled eggs on toast is a simple task, but having his meals handed to him on a tray for so long has thrown him completely from the flow of these things. And even though the cupboards are well stocked, his efforts involve much opening and closing of doors and return trips to and from the kitchenette before the food eventually sits on the plate at the end of the table.

In all, the ten-minute task has taken closer to twenty.

He listens to the radio as he eats. A mid-morning talk show is developing the news stories of the day. There is no mention of his name and he is thankful for that. Has the world forgotten him already? That would be a mercy. Voices and stories unfold across the room and Nealon is happy to feel no part of them. There is a war on terror and a financial crisis enveloping the globe. Nationally, there are employment and health-policy issues. At one time, these stories and themes would have interested him greatly – he took seriously the obligation to stay abreast of such things. But he does not relate to them now, they do not affect him in any way whatsoever. He does not belong to them, nor they to him. They are birds of a different sky, tracing different arcs through this blue day. The engaged tone of the speakers now baffles him. How can you be so involved, he wonders, as a correspondent quotes figures on hospital overcrowding and underfunding. Does this really affect you? The voices drone on as he eats and while his detachment is total he is not inclined to turn them down or off.

From the head of the table he has a clear view out over the back garden. In the darkness of the previous night he missed a few details. Off to one side, a galvanised shed butts up against the sod fence at its end. From this distance he sees that the padlock on the door is hanging loose. Running from the corner of the house is a clothesline which is fastened at the end of the garden to the crooked limb of a hawthorn bush. This is Olwyn's work, he remembers – one of her improvisations on a task he never got around to doing properly himself. Beyond the hawthorn bush looms the hayshed.

The day outside is wet, this weather given to sudden gusts of rain that drift by and swallow the distance. This is one of those days, the light saturated, time itself congealed in its bleak hold. Looking out the window,

Nealon feels like a child, kneeling on a chair with his nose pressed to the glass; whatever plans he might have had are now on hold as long as this rain comes down. He has to be careful of this mood. If it deepens in him he knows that he is fully capable of sitting here for hours, content to stay looking out the window at nothing at all.

What time of year is it? The question flummoxes him for a moment. One end or the other? God knows, it is not something he will have to answer to.

A quick glance at his phone tells him that no one has called, but he decides against phoning Olwyn. Not at this early hour. Wherever she is, she's likely to be busy with Cuan and Nealon knows how difficult he can be in the mornings. So, he sits there with his hands flat on the table and allows himself to drift off in a vacant reverie that might lead anywhere. At that very moment the phone on the table rings.

'So, how does it feel to be a free man?'

The voice from the night before, the same unmodulated croak.

'What do you want?'

'Good man, straight down to business. I forgot that you have a lot of time to make up. Have you given any thought to my proposal?'

'Meeting you?'

'Yes?'

'I did, it won't be happening.'

'I'm sorry to hear that.'

'You'll get over it, goodbye.'

'Before you go . . .'

11

'I'm gone. Goodbye.'

Nealon ends the call and turns off the phone. A bite of adrenaline clasps his veins, a sudden rush of pins and needles to the back of his hands.

Home so soon and a small victory already, he says to himself.

He fills another mug of coffee and goes outside.

At the gable of the house, he stands and looks out over the garden that runs down a shallow incline to the sod fence at the bottom – the property's boundary between the fields and sheds beyond. In the middle distance, the Sheeffry hills throw down pale light over the lower ground and the white homesteads scattered along the roadside. To the right, Mweelrea thrusts up its blunt head, darker and drawing all distance towards itself.

There's more rain on it, Nealon says to himself; there's always more rain on it.

The house looks shabby in daylight. Two hard winters and a hot summer have taken their toll since it was last painted. A shadow of moss has begun to bleed down the wall from under the soffit. Paint has begun to blister, lifting away in dry flakes, showing all the layers that have gone on over the years. Nealon runs his hand up and down the wall. It would be no use putting more paint on top of that, he reflects. Better to take a power hose to the whole thing and clean it down to the cement. But that would be a job for the summer, let the walls dry out properly before putting on an undercoat.

He remembers a recent summer when Olwyn went

through a sudden mania for refurbishing. It followed Nealon's casual mention that she was the first woman to have crossed the threshold since his mother's death.

'Your whole life together,' she exclaimed, 'just yourself and your father.'

'Pretty much.'

'The two of you all alone?'

'We didn't think about it like that, it was just the way things were.'

'Your father must have felt alone.'

The thought had never crossed Nealon's mind. The intimacy of shared feeling was not how they lived.

'A man returns home without his young wife but with a babe in arms. How lonely that must have been. He must have talked about your mother's death?'

'No, that's not how we lived our lives together.'

Olwyn drew back from further questioning. Whether it was to spare Nealon's feelings, or her own bafflement, he could not say. Either way, he realised for the first time just how much of his life he had taken for granted and how much more of himself Olwyn appeared to see than he did.

The conversation sparked in her a vivid need for change.

He woke the following morning to find her at work with a cordless drill, having already removed two of the flush doors from the other bedrooms. He stood in the hall watching her but knew better than to question her too deeply, because in those days Olwyn frequently operated to an energy and impulse all her own. More often than not, her purpose and designs went over his head, sometimes taking considerable time to resolve into any recognisable form. That's how it was with this. He stood back and let her at it, and she did not stop till all the doors and carpets from every room were piled in a heap at the sod fence, and she was standing over them with a can of petrol which had been set aside for the lawnmower.

Nealon watched the whole lot go up in a blaze from the kitchen window.

The house sounded hollow now, and with all its separate spaces flowing into each other there was a lawlessness to the place he could not abide. He found it impossible to sit in any of its doorless rooms with their echoing concrete floors.

But she did not stop with carpets and doors.

Now that she'd started, she was going to change everything. She moved all the tables and chairs into the garage, sweeping everything ahead of her in a tidal wave through the house up against the farthest wall. Then she took off to buy new stuff. Nealon stood in the garage looking at all the stacked furniture. Something about chairs tipped upside down and standing on tables filled him with unease. The fact that he had grown up with these pieces – and that most of them had been in this house since his parents' marriage – filled him with a sense of betrayal he would never have expected to feel.

A sullen impulse goaded him to pull the two-seater couch out to the grass slope behind the house, where he faced it towards the fields and the distant mountains beyond. He pushed the cushions in and then threw himself into it and this was his station for the rest of the summer. On weekends he would spend hours sitting there, gazing out over the small fields beneath blue skies and letting the sweep of rolling space clear everything from his mind. By rights it should have been time spent planning his next move – there had to be a next move – but all that summer, under its blue sky, Nealon was pleased to discover his mind was an empty space in which nothing of any worth or importance took root.

'Thank Christ,' he breathed, 'a bit of peace at last.' And he settled back to enjoy his rest.

Even when the carpenter came to replace the doors and put down those laminate floors Olwyn wanted throughout the house, Nealon had stayed on the couch, gazing into the distance at some vanishing point visible only to himself.

And if Olwyn had thought the presence of this burly tradesman who went about his work whistling through his teeth would provoke some sort of jealous reaction from him, she was mistaken. For two full weeks, while the house vibrated with the sound of saws and hammers, Nealon grasped the opportunity to vacate the house almost completely – going so far as to take all his meals on the couch, balanced on his lap, and drinking bottles of beer while staring out over the hills. Come evening, when the sun went around the front and spread its shadow over the couch, Nealon pulled a blanket over himself and closed his eyes to put up a silent barrier between himself and Olwyn. He maintained the same blunt silence when the removal van came to take away the stacked furniture in the garage. Nealon had opened his eyes to find Olwyn standing over him with her arms folded.

'No,' he'd said, 'the couch stays.'

And then he closed his eyes again and imagined her turning on her heel to stalk back into the house.

But that was then.

Different times under different skies.

Out in the middle distance now a huge, bruised cloud moves across the sky, with leaden sheets of rain peeling from its underbelly. Dull light glances off the galvanised shed which gables onto the sod fence. This shed houses the lawnmower, the shears, the strimmer and all the other garden tools Olwyn had bought when she had tried to put some shape on all the overreaching growth that was encroaching on the house. This was a side to her Nealon had found unexpectedly attractive – Olwyn the gardener, the tiller of the earth. Several times he had come upon her in unguarded but focused moments, standing with a trowel or shears in hand, streaked with dirt but wholly attentive to the work at hand. Where the passion came from, she could not say. Her upbringing in a tower block with nothing around it but concrete and waste ground may well have been the very thing that nurtured a wish within her to make things grow. Olwyn had an instinct for it, and if all her efforts expressed themselves in a chaotic blaze of colour around the margins of the house, it was more than Nealon had expected. And judging by her own delight, more than Olwyn herself had hoped for also.

He had marvelled at how quickly she had taken to

country life. It heartened him at the time to see her put down such sudden roots. Standing there looking at her among her shrubs and flowers was one of the few moments in his life Nealon had allowed himself to feel good about something he had done. And if he could take no credit for her new passion, he could at least congratulate himself on bringing her to this place where she had discovered it herself, this small, west of Ireland village with its distant hills and clear skies. Nealon dared to think she had come into herself properly, grabbed the opportunity to become the person she might fully be. Sometimes he thought he could explain it to himself. Something about her being at peace with herself at last. Her having found her authentic self, and that self stepping forth to find her own willing imagination. Something like that. He was not inclined to worry about it too much.

But that was then also.

Different times under different skies.

The beds and borders around the house are layered over now with a dense mat of dead vegetation and exposed roots. The lush grass of last year's growth has turned onto the concrete walks in thick skeins. All this wildness comes as a shock to Nealon. Apparently, some part of him believed that such growth might have ceased in his absence, the normal rhythms of decay and renewal suspended themselves with respect to his plight.

Time itself should have stood still or moved to a slower measure in his absence.

The idea embarrasses him. It comes from a part of him that is ever prone to such nonsense; a soft place in which he has often lost his footing. He flings the dregs from his mug onto the grass and turns into the house.

It is coming up to one o'clock and there is now a steady fall of rain spreading from the west.

So where is Olwyn? Where is she?

His wife of three years, Olwyn the fair. Where is she now in these brittle hours? Nealon senses her. She is out there now, alone and pale-skinned in the middle of some complex circumstance beyond even her own devising.

Nealon has always seen her as someone from the end of days, some pale functionary with a specific role to play in whatever way the darkness will come down. Among his visions of her is one where she is taking the sacrificial lead on some sort of cosmic altarpiece. He has a single sketch of her — charcoal on cardboard — in which he depicts her adrift in some inky void, trailing IV lines and catheter, naked but for the raised bush of her pubic mound. Nealon remembers nothing about the sketch. There was no thematic precedent for such an iconic representation in his work. The cardboard medium suggests something hurried, something reached for on a sudden inspiration.

This is how she presented herself in the early days of their courtship — something sacrificial about her, even if it was never clear to what hungry god she was being offered or by whom. The clarity of her skin hinted that if she had put some illness behind her, it had also scoured her in a way that left her clean and lighted but with a ready inclination towards flight. So pale now that neither weight nor colour could snag her, flight ever latent in her long limbs.

There was something fitting about all that. Being raised in a high tower had given her a light touch on the earth. Her proper element was surely somewhere in the middle light, with the ground always receding from her as she rose higher and higher. To what purpose she would rise like this Nealon could not say, but that is the way he sees her, always ascending.

He looks at his phone again. Nothing. Where the hell is she? *Where are they?*

Later that evening, another call.

Nealon is standing in the middle of the floor when his phone lights up on the table, turning around itself in vibration mode. A sudden prayer bursts from him.

'Please Jesus, let it be her.'

He pounces on the phone but sees the private number notification. He is about to hurl it across the room in exasperation, but something in him deflects his intent and before he can check himself, he has the piece already jammed to his ear.

He is beaten to the first word.

'Don't hang up,' the voice says.

'Fuck you,' Nealon replies, slamming the phone to the table.

The phone starts to ring again before the sound has died in his ears. Nealon stands for a drawn-out moment, knowing clearly that this hesitation is all part of a desperate waiting game. But, right now, this is all he has – this dangling moment twisting in rage and frustration before he decides one way or another.

He picks up the phone.

'You're disappointed,' the voice says. 'Of course you are. Why wouldn't you be? You thought it was herself, but here you are listening to me. How long is it now since you spoke to her?'

'What's it to you?'

'It's nothing to me, but it's everything to you, I would imagine. You slept well, I hope, the sleep of the innocent?'

Nealon does not rise to the bait. The voice continues with no change of tone.

'So, you're fed and rested now, it's time for some work.'

'I'm a free man,' Nealon says, 'I hadn't planned on working.'

'You're not a man to sit around doing nothing, stop codding yourself.'

Nealon does not respond. He has no wish to push this moment beyond what it already is.

'So, about this meeting,' the voice continues.

'I'm not moving from this house if I don't know who I'm dealing with or why. A name would be a good start.'

A long silence falls. When the voice resumes it is with the same guarded fatigue as before but this time with the slippery note of something finally moving on.

'My name is neither here nor there — it won't make you one bit wiser knowing it. All it will do is add more to your own cluelessness. I'll put it this way, it's not a question of who I am but what I know; the breadth and depth of what I can tell you, that's the important thing here.' There follows another silence before he resumes.

'Let's assume that each of us knows certain things, me and you. Not everything we know is the same, but there are similarities. And sometimes, while we may be talking of the same things, we might have a very different telling of them. So, in order to make sure, we need to compare our stories and arrive at a single version we can both agree on. Now, you can make of that what you will, but I have made this call in good faith and all I want is for us to have a meeting.'

'Why should I go to a meeting with a man I've never met or know anything about? More to the point, why would I meet a man who talks in riddles?' Despite his belligerence Nealon is relieved. Something solid on the table at last, something to focus on. 'In case you haven't heard I *am* innocent, a free man. I want to be left in peace.'

A dry guffaw blurts down the line. 'You're a man of habit, Nealon, the plea to innocence doesn't suit you. You're too long in the tooth for that.'

'I was never convicted of anything. Read the papers.'

'Yes, the collapse of your trial. I was there, I saw it coming and saw it happening. You can always rely on some cops to fuck up these things. A ten-month investigation, thousands of man-hours and god knows what amount of taxpayers' money set at naught by bad grammar and poor spelling. The wonder was that it took so long for your counsel to point it out. If I didn't know better, I would have thought you let the whole thing go on just so you could pull the rug out from under them at the optimum time. A fine sense of timing and drama, no doubt about it.'

'People have forgotten the basics. The old curriculum, the three Rs, you can't beat them. Besides, there was more to it than that. Neither dates nor documents were in accord, the whole thing was a shambles.'

'Let's cut to the chase,' the voice urges. 'We need to talk. Both of us are in agreement about certain things.'

'What things?'

'We don't have to be specific just yet, not over the phone, but it would be interesting to compare notes.'

'That's no assurance and no one in their right mind is going to rise to bait like that. Especially someone just out of prison with his name cleared.'

Nealon feels himself getting cocky now, a risky note of levity giving his voice a bounce it does not need. He curses inwardly. The worry now is that he has given something away, spilled something essential from his hand and revealed some chink. Focus on the present moment, he tells himself. Follow the ball that's in play, not the one that's passed over your head.

If the man on the other end has picked up on any slip, he does not reveal it. Nealon appreciates the tactic – file it away for a moment of greater need down the line when the stakes are higher. This thought worries Nealon further. Any slip at this point might come back to haunt him.

'But there's no rush,' the voice amends suddenly. 'You have a lot on your mind, I understand. Think about it, sleep on it. I will give you a call tomorrow sometime and we can talk some more.'

The phone dies in Nealon's hand and the longer he holds it the colder it gets.

All this while four miles away in the adjoining townland, three men have gathered to dig a series of trial holes for a percolation test on a plot of land for which one of them has posted a planning application for a domestic dwelling with septic tank. The men are confident of their project. The geology of this surrounding area is primarily alluvial gravel over Ordovician limestone.

Boredom gets the better of him, the house with its empty rooms and the phone lying silent on the table. He decides to walk across the fields. He might run into Shevlin, his neighbour.

Shevlin has rented the land off Nealon since his father's death and the lease will be up in a couple of months. It would be no harm to show the face and let Shevlin know he's around. That said, it's the need to stop listening to the churn of his own thoughts that compels Nealon now more than the prospect of haggling with Shevlin over the terms of the lease. Besides, Shevlin is going nowhere. His tongue is hanging out for the forty acres that make up this holding if it ever comes to market. With no sign of any income anywhere on the horizon, Nealon has a vague notion that he might raise the possibility with Shevlin. Just dangle the idea in front of him. Coming out of the blue with it might flummox him and that, Nealon felt, would be worth seeing in itself.

There's a pair of wellingtons in the shed, standing inside the door with their twin bores gaping up at him. A rivulet of sand drains away in a thin feather when he turns them upside down. The cold feel of them rises into his spine so it takes a moment standing there in the damp smell of the shed before they warm up and he moves off.

The sheds around him stand empty with the desolate air of structures that have lost their true purpose of men and animals moving through them. Light falls like dust in the narrow space between the barn and the dairy. The door of the calf shed is shut, the right-angled hasp on the jamb browned and smooth against the lead paint. It opens with that burred groan of metal and wood coming apart. The sound is a beacon from an age when things were simpler, when locks and doors were fitted with maximal regard for what they were about and nothing else. He lowers his head to duck inside. The interior is gloomy, the barred window blocked up with a sheet of galvanise held in place with a length of four-by-two wedged diagonally into the narrow recess. A plastic dosing bottle stands on the sill, yellowed and speckled like a small effigy in its own commemorative grotto. Overhead, there's a hay fork wedged between the rafters and the corrugated roof.

The smell of the place – dried cow shit, hay and timber – fills him with his whole childhood. The years fall away and he is now a child moving through these outbuildings. The old smells, the old light. Any moment now he will hear his father call his name, see him come around the corner, walking towards him.

He steps back out into the yard and walks through the hayshed, the curved space over his head holding the still air within. Old hay is banked against the far wall — grey and mouldy now. A wad of black silage cover lies deflated in the middle of the floor. The whole assemblage looks like a carefully staged memorial — a site-specific installation — to a way of life gone completely, a way of life which would never evolve beyond these parts.

How many times has he stood in this hayshed with his father to shelter from a passing shower? Standing together and listening in silence to the rain falling on the galvanised roof, hearing the whole structure hum in a single continuous note. Such moments always seemed to hang outside of time, suspended intervals within their lives together on their small farm. And as the rain fell, the young Nealon sometimes wondered if this same rain might have fallen through the same angle and light across his life from the day of his birth. And if so, was it a sorrow or a consolation? And he remembers also how this mood moved him once as a child to an embarrassing tautology. Watching the rain rolling towards them across the fields in thick swathes he was startled to hear himself say out loud

'That's wet rain.'

Spoken as if there was a chance there could be any other kind. And his voice hung in the soft light, invoking some in-finite foolishness until his father, apparently seeing nothing redundant in what he had said doubled on it with

'That *is* wet rain,' and then added for good measure, 'and never an end to it.'

And, for whatever reason, this is one of the moments in their lives together that Nealon holds dear and that comes back to him most often. A moment with a weight of understanding which reaches across the years.

Now he is overtaken by a feeling of shame at the depth of stillness and silence throughout these buildings. In his early teens he had become aware that he would be heir to all this – this homestead with all its land and cattle – and that realisation had filled him with dread. The prospect of a life amongst these sheds and everything they entailed frightened the shit out of him. This could not be his whole world, he raged, these sheds and barns, these fields and livestock. And the death of his father a couple of years later compounded that fear – now he was stuck with the place and there was no way out.

But whatever fears he had about life as a small farmer had been offset by the fact that he was at bottom his father's son and he could not rightly see this place fall to someone else's name. The problem was solved for him when, shortly after his father's month's mind Mass, Shevlin knocked on his door and proposed renting the land off him, adding solemnly that he would give him as good a price as the next man. In those stunned days after his father's death and with the house still ringing from his absence Shevlin was the last man young Nealon expected any favours from. So startled was he by the proposal he could hardly gather his thoughts to think properly, but when Shevlin named his price Nealon calculated right there on the doorstep that his offer would provide a small income for the next few years while he studied and worked through what shape he might put on his life.

Nealon had a lease drawn up and Shevlin came over the following week to sign it on the kitchen table. Shevlin in his great coat and wellingtons filled the kitchen with the smell of cow shit. He was canny enough to gloss over the mood of embarrassed opportunism with a slew of thin words about a young man having to live his own life and not get tied down to something if his heart wasn't in it. When it was done, Shevlin folded the forms into his coat pocket, shook his hand and walked from the room. Nealon watched his broad back filling the doorway, like a cowboy moving off to some ready destiny. But whatever scorn Nealon might have felt towards him was offset by the contempt he now reserved for himself. How quickly he had taken the soft option and enabled Shevlin to move on this opportunity.

'Two months dead already,' Shevlin said suddenly, turning in the doorway with a fine sense of dramatic timing. 'You never feel the time passing. And such a shame for a man who had been given a taste of life.'

And then he walked from the kitchen, having scored some obscure point on the young Nealon, leaving him with something to think about.

Nealon's memory of Shevlin goes back to childhood. He was one of those men who were always reliably present at those frequent bawling crises that mark out the rhythm of livestock and farm life. Calving and sculling and castrating, wherever there were bawling animals with bloodied mucus and liquid shit, that's where you'd find Shevlin with his castrating tongs or hacksaw or stick of caustic, directing operations from a boss's distance while Nealon's father and neighbours wrestled with the animal until he was tied and secured. Shevlin would step forward then and go down on one knee, gripping the massive testicles between his hands before leaning into the beast to clamp shut the tongs and there would follow that awful strangled roar as the animal buckled down on its back legs with shit pouring from him.

And he was a man of one joke which he never tired of repeating. Holding up the stick of caustic to the child Nealon he would say

'You wouldn't want to get a rub of this on your lad.'

And then he'd back off with a sour grin.

Nealon's accommodation with him was that he knew such men were necessary to rural life, men who went about their work without disabling sentiment. Later, in his student years, he would come to a different respect for Shevlin when he found himself surrounded by watery vegetarians and animal lovers of every stripe. Nealon found their oversensitive regard a sickly denial of all the shit, blood and pain in which life itself is sourced. There was a pallid squeamishness about them, and he found himself quickly distancing from it in distaste. Farm life was not some pastoral idyll populated by saintly shepherds and warm animals, strewn with homely implements smoothed by venerable use. Farming was a glutinous realm, throbbing with pain across cycles of death and renewal that were tinted with green shit and blood-veined mucus.

30

It was around this time Nealon found himself filling his canvases with rich aortal and cloacal colours that took their hue from life's under-realm where blood and shit had their proper communion.

Beyond the hayshed, in what used to be the haggard, Nealon stands over the axle of the old horse cart. It is set aside in one corner of the enclosure, separated from the body years ago and now crusted with rust. The shafts stand as gateposts to the outlying fields, a five-bar gate hanging between them. Nealon remembers how all these gates were hung and balanced differently, and how the opening and closing of them was specific to each one. Some swung back easily, some had to be lifted and carried. With others it was easier to leave them closed and climb up over them. And knowing this was all part of your being on the farm.

These gates were the focus of an exercise Nealon returned to several times during his studies. Year after year, in pencil, charcoal and pastels he sketched them one after another around the farm. Composition was the same in each case. Timber, wrought iron, five-bar or makeshift pallet constructions, all were centred in the blankness of a white sheet with no sky or landscape to give them context. Each of them looked as if they had been excised from the world to stand without purpose in the middle of an otherwise blank terrain. Nealon filled entire sketchpads with these gates.

This one opens easily, swinging smoothly towards him, lightly hinged on the shaft gatepost. It was years old, but Nealon could still see his father's hand in it – the neat and resourceful way he was with such jobs around the house and sheds. He prided himself on being tasty in his work and leaving no waste. And of course there was a use for everything, if not now then sometime in the future. A frugal man who saw a natural continuance in things, no matter how decrepit they might seem, and a master of those incidental skills for which there is neither name nor accolade.

Nealon pulls the gate behind him. The ground is heavy underfoot, a full month's rain rising up through it. The fields are empty, the land too soft to have cattle ploughing it up.

Shevlin's house is nested on the far side of his own barns and outhouses. With a clear view down the hill as far as the main road and banked around with conifers, there is something of the fortress about the whole set-up. He'll miss nothing from up there, Nealon's father had often said.

In the distance, sheeted clouds brush down to the horizon. There is no one around as far as Nealon can see, no car pulled into the gable, nor smoke from either of the two chimneys. Not only does the house appear deserted but it lends Nealon the uncanny idea that this same emptiness is leaking out into the wider world.

Nealon passes a decrepit shed. There's a line of hollow-core blocks along the edge of the flat roof, weighing down the sheeted galvanise that is eaten with rust beneath. The sky is visible through the blocks and it has been that way for as long as Nealon has known Shevlin. Rough as fuck, he says to himself, remembering his father's judgement of his lifelong neighbour.

He raps on the door and stands back on the thick rubber mat. It must be there to give visitors a space upon which they might gather and compose themselves. Nealon has the impression that anyone seeing him now would think him an apparition, a ghost from their own past. His lank hair and the putty weight he's put on during his time inside adds a further degree of transparency in the grey light which has gathered here between these sheds and the back of Shevlin's house.

He knocks a second time and stands back.

There is a single grey stone on the windowsill beside the back door. A sea stone worn round and smooth. Why it should be there Nealon has no idea, but it gives the impression that this is where it belongs, that somehow it has found its proper place in the world, like a small meteorite which has crossed the universe to settle on this narrow perch.

No one is coming to the door and a part of Nealon is relieved. He's not sorry. He has done his duty, and if some part of it remains unfulfilled it's not his fault.

After a few moments he returns home across the fields. A dog barks in the distance and a rook saws across the evening light. It is easy to believe there is not another soul in the world but himself.

Except among others, a young mother whose child has gone down for a nap, and who is now taking a moment to herself with a cup of coffee in her kitchen. She is scanning a Boots catalogue that came through her door this morning with all its pages of healthcare and beauty products pressing a claim on those loyalty points she has amassed over the past twelve months.

This is where Nealon lost it. In this house, this home and this holding.

Not so much lost it as experienced it turning away from him. He'd returned a few years ago with a genuine ambition to do great work. His years of wandering were now behind him. They'd given him experience and broadened his technique; now he would settle down to do the work his gifts demanded from him. He gathered his tools, rolled up his sleeves and started refurbishing the garage, putting in shelves and a broad worktop. He plumbed in a sink. And even if this studio was short on natural light there was no doubt it was a broad enough space in which imagination could take flight. He lined up his paints and pencils, his canvas and brushes. He was sorted. He had money, time and space; there was nothing to stop him now.

But that's as far as he got.

Whatever impulse had driven him this far was now exhausted — it would go no farther, nor give any more. In the neatness and order of his new studio, Nealon recognised not a new beginning but an end, a memorial to everything he had already done and a lament to all those things his imagination now refused to reach for. That was how he experienced the moment. A colossal refusal from within to pursue his world in shade or colour. This studio, with all its order and neatness, was a line drawn in the sand.

It took him a long moment to acknowledge his own feelings. There was nothing simple about the relief that engulfed him. All he had known about himself up to this was borne away in that churning surge and it took a long time before he recognised what it was that replaced it. At the precise moment he had wished to move forward decisively and bring his gifts and ideas into working focus, something turned in Nealon. He stopped seeing the world as a composition of light and line. The rhythms of colour deserted him. Habit and practice fell away and the years of accumulated scholarship with all its references dissolved. Something else supervened, a shadow for which he had no name but which would not be denied. The whole experience left him dazed.

'So this is where you are, I've been looking everywhere for you.' Olwyn had come into the studio with Cuan in her arms.

He lifted Cuan from her and held him to his shoulder. 'Are you going to stand here all day?'

Nealon took a last look around him. 'No, not a moment longer. I think I'm done,' he said.

With the child still on his shoulder he picked up a bag and threw a hammer and a saw and a set of chisels into the bottom of it. He would spend the next few years working with lengths of four-by-two and sheets of plywood as a first-fix carpenter.

Come nightfall, his mind defaults to Olwyn.

And as ever she comes to him suddenly, but with no clear definition. Of course, this is the time of night and the type of light out of which Olwyn is always likely to loom: a creature of gloom and shadow, always keeping late hours.

And all her arrivals echo their first meeting. She had materialised out of a fog of dry ice and strobe lights, disentangling herself from a sway of bodies. Suddenly her face was in front of him, wearing an expression pitched at an angle between crazed and querulous. The first thing he noticed was that her pupils were so dilated there was no colour in her eyes. To confirm that impression, she then stuck her tongue out to show the pill clinging to its tip. And this was a time in Nealon's life when he did not need twice telling. He leaned in and covered her tongue with his mouth and took whatever she was offering. In keeping with the turmoil of that night he has no memory of what happened after that but when he woke beside her the following morning with his jaw aching and his mouth

37

tasting as if he had been chewing metal, he sensed that something had been settled between them. When she turned towards him her eyes were fully open.

'Grey,' he said.

'What?'

'Your eyes, they are grey.'

'I thought they were blue.'

'No, I'm a painter, I know these things. They're grey.' And for a moment he regretted how adamant he was in declaring this.

They arranged to meet up later that evening where they found themselves at a cultural event of some sort, an opening or launch, the whole place packed with that bohemian element which was Nealon's milieu at the time. Olwyn surveyed the room quickly and appeared to frame it smartly within some damning context. Nealon's need for information had him asking more questions.

'What do I do?' she said, as if repeating the question broadened out the available options. 'In this room it would be more enlightening to say what I don't do.'

'OK, lets go with enlightenment,' Nealon replied.

'I don't write, and I don't sing. I don't paint or photograph. I don't dance or act or meet the world in any of those ways.'

'All that sets you apart from everyone else in this room.'

'I would think so.'

'It still does not tell me what you do. I'm still in the dark.'

'I'm a listener,' she said. 'I listen to people's stories.

I turn up at your door or maybe sit opposite you in a coffee shop or on the side of your hospital bed. I smile and put out my hand and tell you that I work for a government research project on values and attitudes and would you like to talk to me. So I listen to your story and eventually they all mount up and reach a critical mass. Next thing we have a government white paper, legislation . . .' She ended with a shrug.

'And people respond to that?'

'This is the age of testimony; everyone wants to speak.'

And even if that answer left so many questions hanging, Nealon still recalls how her standing before him, so still and full-faced, lent the moment an openness that felt like the beginning of something he had not previously encountered.

But he has no clear idea where she is now. This too is typical Olwyn. Nealon was never sure out of which direction or circumstance she might appear beside him. So fleet in appearance, he was often given to believe that she had no past at all but that she could suddenly materialise on his shoulder from one stuttering moment to the next, forever in the present. All he knows now is that she is out there, a distant spark in the infinite night, filing for divorce and sole custody of Cuan, the child she has kept from him for the past few months.

During his period on remand Nealon learned all the finer nuances of what it is to beg and implore. Over time Olwyn revealed herself to possess the tight focus of one who would not be shifted. Nealon's understanding was that in their shared life together she saw something in Nealon that she needed to protect Cuan from. Her regard for Nealon changed so completely that she drew Cuan into her exclusive care. Nealon was at a loss and his hurt went deep. Olwyn was unwilling to explain herself.

'You can't keep him away from me.'

'Yes, I can. And I will.'

'Why would you do this?'

'You ask that question in a supervised meeting in a prison! If you can't see it then I can't make it clear to you.' And she walked away from him then, leading by hand the child who did not even bother to glance behind him.

Nealon's keenest memories of Cuan are of them sitting together on the couch outside the house, soaking in the warmth of that summer's sun, both of them leaning into each other, the child moulding himself to Nealon's side. The warm days had brought Cuan some respite from those pains that lanced through his body from time to time, pains that doubled him over mid-stride and were so deep in their reach that they would leave him wrung out on the floor. This was where Olwyn shone again, stepping forward before Nealon knew what was happening, and already down on one knee beside Cuan with her hand on his face to soothe him before scooping him up into her arms, completing the drama. Her possession of the moment was so complete it left Nealon standing hopelessly to one side, aware of some failing on his part that he could not put a name to.

Where the hell is she now, he wonders.

The longer this wait goes on the more Nealon comes

to believe she may have taken herself and the child back to her parents' place, smoothing her way with lurid tales of how she'd been wronged by a bad man. Nealon has no doubt that she could play the part of the injured wife if called to it, the strong woman driven to the edge of endurance by a bully. There was a part of her that remained traumatised by that midnight flit across the country which had brought her to the west. She'd spent that three-hour journey lying in the back seat of a Honda Civic, trussed up in the duvet which was taped around her body.

'A rescue mission,' Nealon explained after.

'An abduction,' Olwyn countered, without dropping a beat.

'Some people have to be saved from themselves.'

'That's how you see things? The whole world needing to be rescued?'

'Not everything, but some things are so far gone, someone has to step up.'

And the expression on her face was so knowing that sometimes, in the white set of her rage, Nealon would see there was a part of her that had never forgiven him.

The following day has hardly begun when the phone goes again.

Christ, will this man ever give up? Nealon does not want to be listening to him at this hour of the morning – or any hour for that matter. But there is no argument in him any more about this. How did that happen? Why is listening to him so inevitable?

'I've been thinking,' the voice begins, 'you're there

now – what is it, four or five days – all alone in that house. It would do you good to get out of that house and talk to someone. Socialise a bit.'

'That's your advice?'

'You need to get out and mix with people. Too cooped up in yourself, that's what's wrong with you.'

'And you'd know?'

'I'm only for your good.'

A blurt of genuine mirth explodes from Nealon. 'A proper comedian.'

'I'm only saying. It's no use being there all alone. Talking to yourself, listening to your own voice.'

'My health is my wealth, you're saying.'

'There's a lot of truth to that and the older you get the more you realise it.'

'I'll take your word for it.'

'Even if you only got out for a spin. The car is there at the gable, you could hop into it now and take off. A change of scenery would do you good.'

'Not right now.'

'On the other hand, if you were to get in that car and point it out the road we could be sitting and having a proper conversation with each other in a couple of hours and not beating around the bush like this.'

He will not give up on this, Nealon thinks. This is about patience, the lengths to which he can go. His time is his own and no one or thing has any other claim on it. It runs to no calendar or schedule but is gaining steadily on some appointed end.

It is not hopelessness that fills Nealon as he mulls

this. Nor is it the vain sense of having met some sort of worthwhile adversary, a genuine test of his own wit and resolve. What fills him is a sense of wider issues beyond the demand for a meeting that needs his attention.

That conclusion is so vivid and banal that it takes him a moment to grasp it fully. Nealon is tired now. Early and sudden as this conversation is, it has drawn on all his abilities to keep abreast of it. All his instincts and reflexes feel blunted.

Before he can speak the voice resumes.

'That was some stunt you pulled at the trial. The whole identity thing.'

'I don't follow.'

'It beggars belief that in a country so intimate you managed to smudge your identity. That was a masterstroke right enough.'

'That's what good counsel is for.'

'It was a slick piece of lawyering all right. I'd be interested in hearing how exactly it was done.'

'I won't be giving seminars on it.'

'There are people out there who would give a lot to know how you did it. They see it as a significant security threat – not to mention a judicial and legislative chink. A close analysis is needed.'

Looking out, Nealon sees that the hills are nothing more than dark blurs in the distance. Cloud cover is low and heavy. Nealon is aware of a scooped-out hollow in his belly and he remembers that he has not eaten any breakfast. He will get something from the freezer. A pizza maybe. One of them would go down well now and give him time to think while it heats in the oven. Now that his mind has turned to food it has also by association turned to Olwyn. But before he can draw up a full image of her the man interjects once more.

'Anyway,' he says amiably, as if conceding some point of minor importance, 'we'll leave it there. Have a think on what I've said, and we'll talk again. You can take it from me that it will be in both our interests to do this thing together. The world will be the better for it.'

And with that the phone goes dead.

The sudden concession surprises Nealon, wrong-footing him for a moment. He finds himself scrabbling within himself to make sense of it. Why so sudden? What exactly has he conceded? What threshold have they crossed together? He gazes at the dead phone in his hand which is now slicked with sweat before leaving it on the table and drawing his palms over his thighs.

He stays in the seat for a while feeling the tension of the last half-hour drain from him, the silt in his whole being settling down. A few moments to piece the head and heart back together again. Then he will do what has to be done, whatever that is.

He goes into the kitchen and throws open the lid of the freezer, drawing up an icy cloud of condensation. When it clears, he finds a frozen pizza and a bag of oven chips, some chicken nuggets. Kiddy food, he realises, but the only evidence anywhere that there was ever a child in the house.

He puts them in the oven and spends the next fifteen minutes sitting at the table mulling over the phone call.

That disembodied voice — he can't get a proper hold on it. Its dull patience and unquestionable presence set against Olwyn's absence. Also, the lack of any facial image on which to pin it has his mind slipping on something ghostly and evanescent. A face would give definition and direction.

A wild impulse drives him to his feet. Nealon raises his hand and worries the air in front of him with a few short swipes. Whether he is attempting a curse or a blessing he does not know. And whether it is directed at his own immediate situation or the wider world he cannot say either. That part of him that would blacken the room with curses leaves him standing in a tangled rage.

And even if he were to draw breath and calm himself it would come as no solace to him that ten miles away an endocrinologist in the county hospital is looking forward to lifting the phone and telling a woman in her early thirties that elevated levels of thyroxine in her thyroid is the likely cause of her fertility problems and that she will recommend to her a course of hormone treatment for which she is very hopeful.

Like every origin story or creation myth, it needs a full telling for it to make complete sense. It does not work in bits and pieces, and leaving it incomplete might admit some dangerous uncertainty into the whole thing. So, even alone in his kitchen, Nealon feels compelled to tell it complete.

And of course, it begins with a bang.

Nealon bursting through the front door with such sudden violence it gave those inside no time to react before he was already up the stairs and in her room where she lay on the bed with the needle and tinfoil beside her and the tourniquet still looped on her upper arm. Nealon was glad to have caught her in the euphoric upswing of her hit. She would surf that for the next twenty minutes or so. And then rolling her into the duvet while she giggled through her bliss, smiling up at him as if he were a big child inventing some new game. She thought the roll of duct tape an interesting diversion as he looped it around the duvet, tightening in her arms, her legs and ankles. Down the stairs then with her slung over his shoulder, to that encounter inside the front door that would make his name among those who lived by their reputations.

Then the long cross-country flit, skirting through the city itself till he found his way onto the motorway, beyond the toll plaza, heading west. Three hours with her trussed up in the back seat and three hours checking the rear-view mirror for anyone following them.

When he had finally arrived in this house and stripped the duvet from her, her face was swollen with rage, her thighs and hair matted and sweat-filthed. Her focused anger had driven the corroded blood into the shallow flesh over her cheek bones so that her face was gorged and livid. He wrestled with her in the darkness, this flushed wraith of a woman with a scent coming off her like a fug of burnt plastic, before dragging her towards the shower, losing their footing on the slippery surface, falling under the cascade of warm water from the showerhead. They sprawled together on the tiles with Nealon trying to keep hold of her as she tried to twist from his arms. He lost his grip and she scuttled into the hall, slipping away before turning to face him at the end of it, naked now but not so far gone in pain that she did not feel her own acute humiliation. She came towards him then with her hands outstretched and her teeth bared, some creature native to a child's nightmare, barrelling onto him with the full force of her angled body. He grappled her to the floor again, holding tight so as to keep her arms and legs from flailing. This drove her to a deeper rage; with a sudden heave she drew her head back and let her forehead fall with a crunching smash on his cheekbone. The sickening impact rose through the back of his head, and he felt himself plunge through a sudden darkness. She freed herself from his embrace and, with a jagged shriek, turned and retreated to the end of the hall where she tried to fold herself into the shadows.

And somewhere between her tears and sobs she realised what was happening.

He saw it dawn on her like a black sun and he was never so proud of her. The terror of it drew her off the floor with a livid energy and she came at him again, closing the short distance between them with her elbows flashing, something beyond teeth-grinding anguish and stretched sinew driving her on. She fought now as if she were a being of pure light and pain, driven to such flurries of speedy aggression that it became clear very quickly to Nealon he was going to become exhausted before she did, and that there was a real possibility she would be the one standing alone at the end of this fight which was the very outcome neither of them could risk. And where did such desperate energies come from? Nealon's gamble that those three hours trussed up in the back of the car would have exhausted her and sent her to sleep appeared to have done nothing but pressurised a rage which she was now determined to expend on him.

Her white body was now the only source of light in the hall, all its angled kinetics generating a glow that held to her. She bounced from her sitting position on the floor as the walls seemed to throb in sympathy with their struggle. Thinking about it afterwards Nealon believed that, despite the horrible intimacy of these moments, they had never been so distanced from each other. Every scream, every blow she tried to strike seemed to traverse some gigantic arc before it registered in his ears or landed on his body. And this was all the more uncanny as she was coming at him with such incessant speed. Nealon knew it was easy to square these distances and time lags with a woman who at that moment was her own frenzied crisis apparition.

And that smell.

In his confusion Nealon had the impression that some aerial substance, possibly the ethereal element of her very soul, had ignited and caught fire.

And now she was coming the full length of the hall again in the naked glow of herself, before she walks flush onto the punch which glanced through the bottom of her chin to throw her head upwards as her knees buckled and she fell forward where he managed to catch her under the armpits before she hit the ground.

He gathered her up and carried her to the bedroom at the front of the house. For a long moment he stood over her with his fists clenched – the chemical surge of the night's drama and violence coursing through him. When he finally calmed a little, he lay in beside her and stayed with her all night as she slept. He drank mugs of coffee and listened to William Byrd's *Mass for Four Voices*, an old favourite that had never failed him.

Olwyn lay full length beside him, so still under the covers that she gave the impression she was filling an empty space that extended from the centre of her being.

She woke after about seven hours.

Nealon lay on the covers beside her, a cigarette in one hand and a full ashtray balanced on the flat of his chest. She rose suddenly from the depths of her sleep, broke the surface with a wild flaring of her arms and legs, which spilled the ashtray and rucked the duvet to the floor. She stared down on him for a moment and when her gaze had focused, she set to him again, throwing herself once more into the fight with a renewed vengeance, dragging the earphones from his ears as Byrd entered into the Agnus Dei once more.

This second bout lasted ten minutes, Nealon meeting every blow with blunt reprisals of his own, her bouncing off the ash-streaked bed and the walls. He was proud of this livid energy she had dug up from the core of herself, the way it replenished and sustained her. He drew her onto himself, urging her to more vicious attacks, playing to that inner core of shamed dignity which he knew was now nearing its shallow depths, draining from her and possibly leaving the dried-out husk of her. Ten minutes of flailing and punching and wrestling came to an end with both of them lying on the floor gasping and retching for breath. She turned on her back.

'I'm hurting,' she rasped.

'Yes.'

'Please.'

'No.'

'Fuck you.'

'I have no answer to that.'

And she drifted off among the ash and cigarette butts, naked in the grey dawn and with whatever dynamo that spun at the core of her being, humming in a frequency accessible only in the depths of sleep.

Morning rose on the other side of the house. Nealon could hear the plastic guttering along the roof beginning to creak and flex itself in the gathering heat of the day. Olwyn lay flat out beside him and her stillness told him that she would sleep for a couple more hours.

He went to the kitchen to make coffee and stood in the living room drinking it with his back to the sink. Something in the house had adjusted during the night. There was a different resonance around him. Had it picked up on their fight and absorbed already the memory of it in its walls and ceilings? The sense of granular change was real and ran throughout the whole structure.

It took Nealon a long time to realise that this was the first time he'd had someone stay overnight since the death of his father. Ten years and no person other than himself to warm it. For some reason this realisation gave him confidence, something in him reached into the room and expanded the light within it.

This is the house in which Nealon and his father had made their lives together. A house without women, it had gathered itself around them in the dark shades of furniture and cabinetry that dated from before Nealon's birth. Over the years fashions and fads had left so many of these pieces trailing behind, leaving them without even ironic virtue. But not once in all the years had Nealon himself felt the wish or desire to throw away any of it.

When Olwyn woke in the early afternoon, she looked up at him through eyes as dry as sea stones. She now moved as if there were some viscous impediment in the air.

Her eyelids scraped down over her eyes before she laid into him one final time.

Now, with the end within reach, her rage renewed itself once again. Seeing her come towards him with the effort of this last godawful attempt evident in her eyes, Nealon had the sense of her grasping hold of the glowing, numinous core of herself and having found it, thrusting it forward one last time. She swung at him out of a blinding headache, her arm flying in such a torpid arc that Nealon saw it coming a mile off and blocked it with his forearm; the stunted impact torching through the white noise of pain which was her whole being now. Her face disappeared behind an open-mouthed howl as she tried to hold on to consciousness before her body buckled over and drew her to the floor once more.

She looked up to see Nealon above her. She would taunt him with this moment later on.

'Your finest moment,' she would say. 'Standing over the woman you love with your fists clenched and your knuckles skinned.'

53

'So I have not improved?'

'There's still time.'

'I have no answer to that.'

'I think that is wise.'

Nealon now bent to ease her, placing his hand in the small of her back. But with his chin over the back of her head, she lifted it suddenly and gave him the full force of it into his mouth, which instantly filled with a jagged mixture of pain and blood and teeth fragments. The impact tipped him sideways onto the bed from where he looked up to see the heel of her elbow come down once more onto the bridge of his nose. And now she was screaming above him.

'Get up, get up and fight! Don't leave me like this!'

The new pain in her shoulder scored a bright path through her mind. Once again, she had a clear sense of their collusion. Now her terror was that Nealon might black out and leave her in this shimmering world of pain when she was within touching distance of the redeemed self that had lain inside her all these years.

He managed to roll off the bed, crashing onto the floor as she hung off his neck. She was coming forward once more, and Nealon sensed she was fully conscious of what she was about now and how narrow and improbable a chance this was. And she was willing to use the full range and fuel of her humiliation to lay claim to it as if it were a bargain struck with her own soul. And some part of her must have wondered in what mood and at what hour of the night did this bargain seem like a good deal, a fair exchange with no robbery on either side.

She was so maddened with anxiety now that Nealon

found it difficult to hurt her carefully, to honour the unspoken rules of this engagement. He reined himself in, shortened his blows so as not to unleash that vengeful part of himself that would have been gratified by the full impact of his fist along the side of her face, that part of him that would exult, *Take that, you cunt!* So they fought on to the end of their strength, in gasping fits and starts until she was finally exhausted, collapsing beside him on the bed. She tried to struggle up out of the immense weight of herself before eventually giving up to lie sprawled across the full width of the bed.

She lay like that for a long time, and when she finally set her feet on the floor outside the bed she stood up with such a smooth motion it was as if she were drawn up into herself from on high. Ash-streaked and bloodied, she looked down on him in that shambles of a room and she was finally clean. She stood there for a moment, a wraith from the other side, before she walked from the room.

Christ, he was tired!

An inrush of fatigue began closing his eyes, drawing with it a hopeless wave of terror. Sleep was about to claim him, but he fought against it for fear of what he might wake up to. He tried rising from the bed with some distant idea that if he could gain his feet, he would be able to stay awake. But in the next moment he was swept away as a wash of blood surged through his head and pushed him back into the filthy bed. For a split second he was above himself and saw how he went down.

He looked pleading and stricken as he went under.

★

How long he slept he could not say, but the glow on the curtains told him that the sun had moved round the front of the house so it must be late afternoon. The bed was stripped, no sheets or pillows around him, nothing but the bare mattress. He rose to his feet and made his way up the hall. There were scuff marks along the walls, signs of their struggle.

She was not in the living room or the kitchenette. He found her sitting on the concrete walk with a mug of tea in her hands, staring into the distance at the Sheeffry hills. She had showered and was wearing an outsize sweater over blue jeans and a heavy pair of socks on her feet which were pushed out in front of her on the grass. With her hair pulled back, her face looked so exposed and raw that Nealon thought surely the slightest breeze glancing across it must be a painful abrasive.

Any hope that she might be at peace now, calm in the wake of all she had endured, was short-lived. She was a bag of nerves, her teeth chattering, her body a taut discord of anxiety. When she looked up at Nealon something like relief crossed her face. He noticed that smoke was rising from a pile of stuff in the corner of the garden, a fire that hadn't yet caught.

He lowered himself down beside her, aware of a throbbing pain in his ribs – he should have known better than to think he would come away unscathed from any battle with her. The pile of stuff in the corner caught flame and went up in a sudden orange bloom. Now that his eyes had adjusted to the afternoon light he recognised that the flaming pile was made up of the bedclothes and pillows from the bedroom. Olwyn turned and examined his face. He flinched from her touch when she examined his swollen nose.

'I did that?' she said.

For the first time Nealon was aware of himself as the one who was bloodied and covered in filth. 'It couldn't be helped.'

'No.'

He drew her towards him, choking down a lump in his throat. An expectant rush of feeling within him hoped that their ordeal, all the pain they had levied on each other, contained something of love they could build on.

In the weeks and months that followed, he watched Olwyn return to something like full health. Reared her whole life in some twilight concrete kingdom, she now bloomed like a pallid stalk brought out into the clear light of day. She became a miracle of careful nurturing and that salty air which blew in from the sea.

Her body thickened under the outsize clothes, prompted by an appetite which returned with such sharp ferocity that his lasting image from those days is of her walking around with some piece of food or other in her hand – her teeth clamping down over a piece of toast, her mouth open to devour an apple or spooning something from a bowl as she crossed the floor. All this eating gave her a cusp of a belly over the belt of her jeans, something she found hilarious and never tired of checking, front and side in the hall mirror, giggling and chuckling at it. Nealon was happy to see she took it as a sign of renewed health.

The longer he looked upon her in this new light, the

more Nealon became convinced that it was him and not her who had been saved. She had been delivered to him by whatever providential forces had finally wearied of the life he had led up to this. She was the gift in which he surpassed himself and finally put behind him all the trivial shit of his former self. But the terms of their togetherness meant they should come to redemption in different ways. She had merely to reclaim herself. A difficult but not complex job, the essential Olwyn lay waiting to be uncovered under sedimented layers of experience. Time, with all its corrosions, would bring her to the surface. Nealon's task was more nuanced. If he were to make anything of their lives together, he would have to slew off a lot of ingrained habit and prejudice. A life lived exclusively in thrall to his own appetites and instincts, without commitment to anyone, would have to be unlearned. It was hard work, and Nealon realised he could not start soon enough.

So Olwyn's recovery was swift and smooth. She fell in with the change of seasons and as the days lengthened into that first summer she gained in strength and vitality. With her face and limbs bared to the sun, her skin took on a glow that Nealon shied from seeing as something spiritual. His was not a life to which such lustrous beings were drawn. Too ordinary, too thwarted in its energies. And yet, there she was. She could not be denied, the way she picked up the elements of summer light and made them her own. But Olwyn kept this radiance to herself. It did not illumine the more shadowed parts of Nealon's own soul and a time would come – not so far into the future – when her radiance would take on a metallic sheen.

Now, sitting at the head of the table he has the feeling their impending divorce will be the proper end to their time together. In the last months of his remand, Olwyn's visits had tapered off from the weekly penance of desultory conversation under supervision to a monthly apparition in which she would spend the hour glancing at her watch and fitfully answering Nealon's queries about their son.

'Yes, he's fine,' she repeated week after week, 'he keeps asking about you. I don't know what to tell him. What do I tell him? What do you want me to tell him?'

And not for the first time Nealon was stuck for words.

Less than a quarter of a mile away the passport of a man he went to school with is lying in the bottom of a chest of drawers and this document will expire in less than a couple of hours when the clock turns midnight and prevent him from travelling to his niece's wedding in Rome.

Every call now begins without salutation, as if each moment, regardless of whether they are talking to each other, is part of a ceaseless conversation.

'I was just thinking . . .' he might begin. Or, 'Do you know what would suit you . . .' The tone is that of a man who is relaxed in himself and certain of his hand, in no rush whatsoever.

'Do you know what I was thinking today?'

'I have no interest in what you were thinking.'

'I was thinking that you are a man who knows a lot of things a lot of people would be interested in hearing.'

'Who would have any interest in what I know?'

'There are people out there who would pay good money.'

'I didn't think I was that clued in.'

'I'd well believe that. Sometimes we don't know the things we know or the worth of the things we know. But I'll tell you this: there is a great shortage of imagination out there, you couldn't underestimate it.'

'I wouldn't know about that. I have noticed that there is no shortage of foolishness.'

'No, there is never a scarcity of it, not as long as men and women draw breath. But that's not the same as imagination. It would be easy to confuse the two, but I can tell you they are very different things entirely.'

'And you think I have an antidote to all that?'

'As I said, there are things you know.'

'Tapping me for information that will be fed on to some security agency? I have no interest in that.'

'No, we're not talking about snitching or an information trawl. This is about something deeper, it's about fundamental pain, a basic lack of well-being. A summary of the facts is exactly what it is not.'

'You could expand on that.'

'Not over the phone, you wouldn't thank me.'

'Always a mystery with you, always talking in riddles.'

'Half an hour face to face and all of this will be clear. Context is everything, all these elements will come together.'

'It would be a lot clearer to me if I knew who I was talking to. A name would be a help.'

'I understand that. I sympathise too, but again, it might not be in your best interest knowing such a thing. My name might be Tom, Dick or Harry but that would not shed one more bit of light on the situation. Be careful what you ask for – not everything is worth knowing. Being in the dark is no bad thing if the alternative is being blinded by the light.'

'None of this is making me feel good.'

'That's easily solved,' he says. 'Get into your car and we could be face to face in a matter of hours.'

'I don't know who I'd be meeting, what sort of a set-up?'

'It would be exactly as I say: me and you, face to face. Two men having a talk. No seconds or proxies, just the two of us.'

This last exchange gives Nealon to believe that a line has been crossed. Things have been settled now and every word between them is a final fixing of events into their proper place. Expectations have hardened.

When Nealon puts the phone down he is unable to sit still in himself. A nervous jitter runs through his arms and hands.

There is now a pale continuum stretching between the voice on the phone and the quiet it leaves in its wake. This following silence is an essential articulation of its timbre and resonance.

The sense of being dangled is real but this is not what worries him. That's all part of the game, the move and countermove of these things. What grates is the feeling that he is being pre-empted in everything he does, that this man is forever two steps ahead of him, knows so much about him. That is an intimacy Nealon cannot abide and wants no part of.

Nealon walks through the house and turns on the light in every room. There is an immediate sense of the whole place expanding around him. The structure of the house has not changed since it was put up in the early seventies, built shortly after his mother and father got married. And the changes Olwyn had brought about were mostly cosmetic – new timberwork and cabinetry, which did not alter the layout of the house itself. After his initial scepticism Nealon had welcomed the changes. He appreciated the way light swelled off the new colours and how it sifted into himself, lifting him also.

But that is not what he is searching for now.

He is trying to attune himself to something deeper, some presence that may or may not be there. It will be concealed wherever it is, high up in the corners or in one of the light fittings. Nealon trusts himself here. He stands in the centre of each room and opens himself to all the possibilities of the room, all his nerves strung and exposed. He sheds all interference, everything that is not essential, leaving nothing but his raw self to grasp whatever is hiding here. With no time to do a close-up, fingertip search he takes in the resonance of each room, one by one. But there is nothing, no sense of anything looking at him or crawling towards him. No sense of anything, organic or electronic, sucking up his rhythms and pulses, nothing but smooth walls and static furniture.

The house is clean.

He goes back to the kitchen and stands replaying the phone call to himself for a few moments. Moving or sitting still now present equal opportunity for failure. After a few minutes he goes into the bathroom, leaving the door to the hall open. Fully lit, the small space glows blue within its tiled walls. He takes off all his clothes, shaking them out separately and searching them carefully with his fingertips along the seams and collars before laying them aside on the floor. He takes off his shoes and raises them into the light, parting the laces and spreading the tongue so that he can see into the toes.

Nothing there.

For the first time in a long while, he has a clear look at himself in the mirror. He is startlingly pale, a kind of subdermal milkiness which he cannot be sure does not reach into the core of his viscera. He has become slope-bellied and round-shouldered, the lanky frame of his youth which at juvenile level had made him a better than average footballer – good enough in fact to go for county trials – is now sheathed over with a layer of fat and wasted muscle. So long under lockdown with a maximum of one hour a day aimless loitering in an exercise yard has brought on the doughy contours of middle age. Nealon is surprised at how disappointed he is in this – he would never have guessed he was so vain. Standing at six foot three and never properly filling out beyond the lankiness of his early twenties, he still gives the impression of a small man dropped into a bigger frame. In the glaring bathroom light his bones jut beyond their proper measure, his shoulders finishing in great knobs above his arms, giving him that loping balance that had served him well as an athlete, but which today lends the impression that he is lagging a heartbeat behind himself, out of sync with his own driving mechanism.

But he is glad to see that the face is still fit for purpose.

He retains the tapered jaw and the gaunt cheekbones that top off his height. And his eyes still radiate a degree of confidence that is almost physical in its presence. He touches a finger to his nose. It is still sensitive and misshapen since the fight with Olwyn; it has never properly reset. His hair lies low on his neck.

A quick scan of his whole body in front of the large mirror over the sink fails to reveal any recent scar tissue or suspicious lumps. A hand mirror, held high over his shoulder, allows him to scan the plane of his back, tilting it away from him like some topography tipping away to the horizon. With this preliminary search completed he then settles down to a careful fingertip search of his whole body, starting with the farthest extremity of his feet, prising apart the toes and inspecting the nails before working up the sloping flesh of his calves and thighs, front and back, all the way up to the warm juncture of his groin. As he works, he has a curious sense of dislocation, of himself as a separate entity, the object of his own regard. His fingertips locate his body at some crucial distance from himself, offset beyond the normal focal length which brings it into proper focus.

What is he searching for? He cannot rightly say. It may be more an idea than a thing in itself – an embedded idea. But he will get no peace if he does not go through with this, if he does not examine himself as someone who might be his own betrayer. Every moment alone would gradually become more anxious without the assurance of this search no matter how hopeless it may turn out to be.

And while everything about the voice on the phone convinces him that the man and whoever he represents would not be so crude as to resort to such blunt technology, he still perseveres.

Parts of his body now twitch under his fingertips. The pale area behind his knees, the humid crack of his arse down to the tight muscle of his anus, they flinch and shrink from his touch as if he is violating himself. He is incapable of duping his own flesh, it shies away from him. It will not buy the idea that this survey is a normal examination, that this is a check for some medical malignance like testicular cancer or some lumpish melanoma – one of those things which come with the years, and which puts an end, good and proper, to what passes for youth.

He probes his ears and nose, his anus to the knuckle of his index finger. He runs his tongue over the corrugate surface of his inner mouth. How strange those textures are now, all its gradations and rhythms, veined and mucused. His own body is a whole new continent with an infinite number of hiding places and refuges. By now his fingertips have become sensitive to the rhythmic bumps and striations of muscle and pooled fat. If the beacon is secreted within the softer parts like his arse or thighs or love handles it will surely rise in sympathy to meet the tips of his fingers. While working he has refined his image of the tag. It now resembles a red pulsing diode, gripped to his bones by a fibrous tissue which has made a cosy nest for it. From there it calls out to the mobile phone or the broadband network with a ceaseless aortal pulse.

He works on in this over-lit bathroom. With his white

body twisted and contoured for access, his skin and hair take on an electric charge. Time and space focus completely at the tips of his fingers.

For some reason an article from the *National Geographic* comes back to him, one of hundreds he read in his cell. He remembers how mine sweepers in Bosnia and Angola had developed such crippling sensitivity in their hands and eyes that they would have to sit alone in their huts for several hours to rid themselves of the extreme cautiousness they had developed while moving over broken ground with their nose pressed to the earth and a knife held in their mouth.

He is not at all sure why he should remember that now.

His search continues for a further twenty minutes. Progress becomes slower on the upper part of his torso, with more terrain to cover, more time scanning over his shoulder in the mirror behind him. Over his man-tits now, and shoulders. Into the recesses of his armpits and up his neck till he gets to the top of his head. The search has aggravated him, but he knows that he must make it complete. He walks naked through the hall – something he could never remember doing before, not even with Olwyn – and finds kitchen scissors on one of the shelves over the cooker. They are both heavy and sharp, with short powerful blades. When he gets back to the bathroom, he cuts away his hair which falls in soft hanks to the bathroom floor. He doesn't stop there; he cuts away his pubic hair also with a few deft clips and then reaches for the shaving cream and razor. Five minutes later he is running the tips of his fingers over the dome of his head, paying special attention to the trough at the back of his neck where his spinal column softens and enters into the base of the skull; this is where a transmitter might be placed, it would nestle right in there. But nothing beyond a normal boniness reveals itself, nothing which might extend him and his body into the wireless network.

He finds nothing, nothing at all. And that gladdens him.

So he stands there in front of the large mirror with the cold air swirling round his raw head and shorn balls feeling more naked than he would ever have thought possible. If there is some sort of electronic tag or beacon in him it is buried deeper than his fingers can probe. It is probably drifting on some subdermal tide in his guts, a strobing pill pushing along his digestive tract and lighting up the surrounding viscera with a dull glow. He has an impulse to turn off the light to see can he spot it in his lower belly.

But the search has done him good. Something in him has been put at ease for the time being, the anxiety of the phone call momentarily set aside.

He stays awake a few more hours, lying on the bed and listening to a small radio he found in the press surrounded by tins and jars – one of his small offerings to Olwyn. In truth he had bought it for himself because its warm analogue sound returned him to his childhood when his father had listened so religiously to an old valve radio with deep sonorous tones, most especially at those times during the day when the news came on, and his

69

father, sitting sideways at the head of the table, would listen with his forehead tipped into the palm of his hands and his eyes closed. For a long time, young Nealon mistook this pose as his father's anguish at the state of the world; it was entirely possible that his feelings ran so deep. In reality he was trying to relieve the pain in his head from the tumour that pressed on his temporal lobe and which would carry him away eventually.

Now Nealon finds that the radio is tuned to a late-night request show on MidWest Radio with a playlist of country-and-western songs and old showband numbers singing across the night. He lies in the darkness, listening to the sound of lost loves and lonesome souls.

Sometime after midnight he sets the alarm on his phone before he settles back to sleep. He has made his plans. Or they had been made for him. It's all the same one way or the other.

And there is a woman out there who has just put her son's name on a waiting list for a limited-edition diver's watch that will be released in Milan in time for his twenty-first birthday. This is his wish, this diver's watch with its outsize dial and luminous numerals, a tough but elegant marriage of industrial design and horology. And it is engineered beyond human endurance, water-resistant well below the depth at which the wearer will have lost consciousness if he keeps descending. Her son has assured her of this. And she wonders, as she closes her laptop, what comfort would it be to the wearer at such depths to know that his watch is intact and still marking time while the darkness closes over him.

No Traffic and a Dry Road

The car is a twelve-year-old Peugeot, the little hatchback he'd bought for Olwyn when she'd announced herself pregnant. It was more of a flustered gesture than a gift on Nealon's part, something to cover his own shock and gratitude. But it was precisely the sort of extravagant impulse he was prone to at the time.

Once she'd got over her own surprise, Olwyn had taken to it eagerly. Within a couple of days, she had learned to drive and would then take off on sudden, solitary jaunts around the county during the early months of her pregnancy. Nealon would often wake to find the bed empty beside him and a text on his phone saying she was visiting some tourist spot or historical site. Sometimes in the afternoon he would get a phone call from her when she had parked up.

'Guess where I am,' she would say, 'guess.' As if this was all part of a child's game.

'Tell me what you see.'

'I'm standing on a small bridge over a pretty big river. To my left I can see a broad waterfall – not high but wide, and to my right I can see a narrow sea inlet. In a kind of valley. Do you know it?'

'Yes, I know where you are, you are very close.'

Towards evening she would return with thoughtful news of this new world she was discovering.

'I seemed to be driving for hours,' she exclaimed.

'Probably not for hours, that's a narrow, twisty road.'

'And so many moods and different landscapes. Little towns and villages and bogs and mountains stretching away to the coast.'

'You enjoyed yourself?'

'Oh yes, this is the real Wild West. There's space here to lose and find yourself.'

Nealon was not sure what she meant by that, but he appreciated how she always returned in the brightest mood after these adventures, her idea of the world happily enlarged in ways she had not expected. He was relieved. A part of him lived in mortal fear that she might return to him some evening strung out and unreachable. Being so far from an urban centre was no barrier to getting a personal supply. But that never happened. She held true and Nealon began to breathe easier as the weeks passed. If this was all it took, these solo adventures, for her to deepen her feel for the place so that she might call it her home, then that was good with him. He set aside the idea of buying a map and showing her the spread of the county on the kitchen table. She was doing well enough on her own.

And now the same car that had brought with it such an energising independence sits with the rooted look of something that has not moved in the longest time. And with over a hundred and eighty thousand miles on the clock, Nealon wonders if it is up to the journey ahead. The keys were over the holy water font inside the front door.

He sits in and switches on the ignition. The engine turns once, twice on a rolling lurch then holds on a short cough. All her levels come up on the dash, and Nealon is glad to see there is a full tank of juice in her. The heater throws down a blast of cold air around his feet which, after a moment's fiddling, he manages to redirect onto the windscreen. Country-and-western music from the local music station pours from the radio.

He turns onto the main road and down the hill. Then through the crossroads and over the bridge before going up the lighted main street of the village. Moments later he is passing the grotto outside the church and then watching it fade in his rear-view mirror.

Quicker than he would have thought, Nealon settles into the journey ahead. For the moment he resolves to rid his mind of everything except the vacant pleasure of driving, the selfless feel of putting miles behind him and the landscape passing in the darkness. Somewhere up ahead he will turn to thinking about the reason for this journey but for the time being Nealon is content to settle back and let the miles flow by. He pushes back into the seat, lowers the heater which has now warmed the car and turns the radio down to an ambient hum.

It is six a.m. and with no traffic and a dry road he should arrive before eight o'clock.

Nealon has long considered driving in the dark to be an almost occult pleasure, especially when the sky behind the ragged clouds is lit by a cold moon. Somewhere in his reading he has come across the word 'noctilucent' and he is inclined to think that it is as good a way as any to describe the metallic edge to this darkness. He cannot say exactly where he read the word, but it was most likely in one or other of those journals he immersed himself in during his detention.

The miles go by.

He slows down for a newly resurfaced section of the road that runs through a neat little village. The approach is marked with traffic lights and the soft margin along its length is lined with a series of small lanterns. Like hallowed ground, Nealon thinks. The surface is so frictionless that the car seems to rise up off it, edging on flight.

Within half an hour he has passed through a couple of small towns and villages, all gathered around the usual pubs and supermarket, all bookended by speed limit and lotto signs. There is a real sense of trespass in driving through the empty streets at this hour. Nealon is aware of himself trailing some disturbance behind him, a fugitive spirit drawing some black voltage through their dreams.

★

Even if his life with Olwyn and Cuan came to little over six years it makes little coherent sense to him now as he drives.

Six years is a sizeable stretch of time. Long enough for a relationship to deepen and cement itself to its final shape if things are going well. Or long enough for one side or the other to find out that they have taken what they need from it and leave, pulling the door behind them. But Nealon's sense of this six years feels nothing like that. Olwyn and himself were there, they were together and that was all there was to it, the arrangement needed no more explaining.

After the initial drama of their cross-country flit they settled quickly into the home place. Nealon was glad to put the head down and try making a family life around Olwyn. The plan was simple. He was going to use the various skills he had gathered as an artist and art handler to work on construction as a steady earner, while all the time conserving his best energies for what he would do in his garage studio. Once and for all he was going to meet his own gifts head on and apply himself to his brushes and canvas.

Looking back now, he can see little of those early years together. It is as if they have gone by in a smear of colour, nothing definite, nothing specific on which to build a detailed picture of their time together, nothing but an abiding assurance of their togetherness. And even if he would not reach to say that they were happy – although there had been happy times – he is certain that those years were not spent in sorrow either. How is it possible to have so few memories of them? He can only believe that those days he spent as a remand prisoner have smoothed away all the detail of their lives together, time passing in a way that left nothing in its wake but their lives as a contoured blur.

And then there was Cuan.

Cuan standing in his own light, all elbows and shoulder blades, always summer around him. Made to generate memories, colour and drama crowding around him. And so vivid was this child that now everything about Nealon's life with Olwyn is remembered in the light of this small boy. He was the bright spirit that drew things to him, Olwyn and himself included. And while Cuan was everything a child should be, he was also Nealon's proof that he himself really was of this world. Not that the child had inherited anything of his features, his skin colouring or eyes, and nothing, thank Christ, of his filthy temper, which too often in its heated vehemence had him saying things he would later have no memory of. None of these things mattered to Nealon; he had no wish to see any paler version of himself replicated anywhere. What mattered was that this child had reached in and pulled something from him that was new and lasting, some thread of connect-edness with this world. In truth there was a part of Nealon that saw Cuan as his proper investment in this world, his true eternity project.

It was a bold idea but too often it was betrayed by Nealon's own doubts. Anyone seeing him reach out and leave his hand on top of the child's head in passing would easily have mistaken it as an absentminded gesture of affection when in truth it was Nealon's way of seeking proof. The feel of the child's head under his hand was his assurance that he was real and not some construct of light and wishful thinking, some being who had come to stand at the intersection of his own longing and life in the world. And there was not one of these moments that was not crossed with shame; the idea that he needed his child's head beneath his hand to allay something so crude as his own lack of faith in this world.

Nealon now prefers to dwell on those rituals that evolved so heedlessly over time that they had become the stuff of their lives. Sometimes, in the darkest hours of the night, Cuan would climb into the bed between himself and Olwyn, wriggling down between them and pushing Nealon onto the cold edge. At first Nealon wanted to wean him off this habit, but Olwyn would not hear of it. She told him tartly that she would take all the hugs and cuddles she could get while they were going, he would not always be a child. So, for as long as it went on, Nealon would find himself pushed to the edge of the bed with Cuan star-fishing, knees and elbows between them. Soon enough however, this visitation reached such a point of refinement that Nealon in his sleep could anticipate his arrival at the bedside, waking just in time to see him materialise on the floor beside him while rising in the same moment and tucking him in beside Olwyn before crossing the hall in the dark to the single bed where he would lie face down in that small pool of warmth that Cuan had left behind him. And there could be no more vivid testimony to the child's existence than that warm glow reaching up into his own bones. That is Nealon's preferred memory now and he is glad to set it against the last image of him invoked by Olwyn on her final prison visit when she told him that his specialist finally had news for them.

'So they've found the cause for all those headaches?'

'Yes, his X-rays are back. Cuan's bite is out of alignment,' she told him in the prison visiting room. Nealon's initial sympathy for her on these desperate visits was burned away over time by the anger that radiated off her from across the table. He would never erase the memory of her standing in the doorway of the house with Cuan in her arms and that look on her face as she watched him being led away and put into the back of a squad car. In the following months the shock of that incident had turned to outright rage within Olwyn, a vehemence that had its source in her genuine sense of betrayal.

'You promised to look after us,' she had said blandly. 'That was your promise.'

And it was only then that Nealon has a proper sense of her hurt and how something implacable lay at the heart of it. Now both were glad to move on to a theme they could both work on equally. This too was part of Cuan's function – to be the point of agreement between them. Anything was better than Nealon protesting his innocence to her again and churning over the tired old ground of a trial date that seemed to move further into the future with every passing day.

'That's no big deal,' Nealon said now, so smartly that even as it was coming out of his mouth, he knew it was a mistake of some sort or other. 'It will give his face character,' he persisted.

'You understand nothing,' she hissed. 'It will cause him a whole lot of pain. By the time he reaches the growth spurt in his teens it will be pressurising the top of his spine and his headaches will get worse. He is likely to develop a stoop.' Olwyn raised her hand to the back of her own neck as if she were already in sympathy with whatever her child was likely to suffer.

'And this doctor . . .'

'He's an orthodontist.'

'An orthodontist!' Nealon blurts. 'He can tell what's going to happen the child?' Nealon could not believe his own foolish persistence.

'Stop talking nonsense,' Olwyn said, pressing towards him across the table. 'I did not come here to argue this with you. I came here to tell you that this is what we are going to do.'

'What are we going to do? It sounds to me like you have made decisions already and are going to go ahead without me whatever happens.'

'And I wonder why that is – I don't know if you have noticed, but you are not so readily available for parental discussions. Cuan is going to have surgery, he's going to have his jaw reset, we can't have him going around in such pain.'

'What does reset mean? I don't like the sound of it.'

'It means he will have his jawbone broken and reset so that it fits more comfortably.'

'He's only a child, for Christ's sake, why does he need to have his jaw broken?'

The look on Olwyn's face was proof enough that he

was responsible for some further idiocy. The visit ended shortly after, and he has not seen her since then. For days afterwards he was plagued with the image of Cuan floating in some global anaesthetic while a masked surgeon stood over him with a coping saw.

The small incidents of family life, that's what he remembers now as he drives along. Lying in bed each morning and hearing Cuan cross the hall on his way to the bathroom to have a wee. His small feet hitting the ground in a soft rhythm, the sound of him raising the lid of the toilet and the trickle of water, one of those small pleasures he has no word or context for. The memory comes to him now as pure loss, as pure a loss as he can imagine.

And Cuan was also prone to nosebleeds. He would appear suddenly in the small hours, standing in the middle of their bedroom door with his hand up to his face and bleating with fright. Nealon marvels now that he could be out of bed and halfway across the floor towards him while still partly asleep and not at all sure what he was doing. Then the little drama in the bathroom with the cold tap running and the facecloth and all the soothing words he could muster, making light of the whole thing so that he could pull Cuan back from his own fear. And then carrying him back to their bedroom where Olwyn was sitting up to take him into her arms and lay him down beside her. He would tuck them both in before stripping the sheets, pillowcases and duvet cover from Cuan's bed, throwing the lot into the bath, and standing over them while the cold water rose over them.

And that was his life at the time. His sleep broken and sitting on the side of the bath in the small hours of the morning watching the water rise up over the folds of material before turning pink with his child's blood. And he was grateful for it because that too was part of a good life.

He drives on, but as yet there is nothing in this journey or its destination that allows him to feel he ever had a proper part in all of it.

Through another sleeping town with its empty main street and its doors locked against the darkness. Farther on, the corporate citadel of Allergan Pharmaceuticals sits back from the main road in its own rolling demesne.

Lit from below, it rests like a spaceship in its own bowl of light, drawing attention to its own unlikeliness. When he had his first summer job there as a student Nealon could hardly believe this complex research facility with all its pristine labs and production lines stood within such easy distance of his own village with all its fields, stone walls and small herds of cattle. It seemed to him like something spliced in from a science-fiction scenario. It did not chime with such a rural hinterland but there it undeniably was, this polished construct dropped in from another version of the world. Nealon still finds it hard to believe that half the world's supply of Botox is now made here; manufactured and shipped from this facility by men and women from the outlying towns and villages, sons and daughters of the soil whipping up that cosmetic corrective from some botulism derivative.

Nealon has fond memories of this place. He had spent a happy summer working for a developer who had the contract to extend the shipping warehouse. Nealon drove a dumper for three months, tearing around and tipping loads of hardcore into the stepped foundation, raising clouds of dust. He returned the following summer to work in the same warehouse where he proved to be an able forklift driver, navigating with confidence the narrow aisles beneath towering stacks of boxes and pallets. Nealon had shown a sure instinct for height and balance which enabled him to raise and lower crates and drums of solvent from the highest tiers. This was a skill he would repurpose a few years later in a different country and to a different end but for that summer he was happy that it earned him a rightful place among the other warehouse operatives who kept the whole operation running smoothly. Here, among the camaraderie of fellow workers and canteen slagging, Nealon had found his place. He was there by rights, a man among men. And it was most certainly the last time he had felt so at home in the world's indifference.

The facility recedes into the distance. Twin plumes of vapour rising from roof vents over the lab annexe are the only sign that the whole thing is not some sort of mirage within the surrounding lights.

He has driven this road thousands of times. Rain, hail and shine, coming and going to college and other places. But there is a special feel to it in these hours. It would be good to think that things settle to their proper heft and balance in the darkness, but Nealon is not so sure this is the case.

He is aware of himself cut through with some narrow interference, some malignant jitter having got into the more finical regions of his being and affecting the most sensitive part of himself.

On the outskirts of another town two water towers rise in the distance like enormous chimneys. These too are lit from beneath, a tide of green and red light climbing up the concrete stems to the domed reservoirs on top. They look like some fifties conception of what the future will look like, a dream of futures past.

Farther along that same road a huge DIY and tool hire centre sits behind a broad car park, the empty parking spaces clearly lined out in the artificial light. There is something devotional about the arched frontage, the way it rises to a peaked spire above the entrance. No doubt there is some hungry god within, crouched in some dim grotto behind the tiers of hammers and saws and chisels.

The whole edifice slips behind him in the darkness, and Nealon reflects that its presence with all its tools and instruments is no surer sign that the world is still a work in progress.

First word of the security alert comes with the seven o'clock news; Nealon hears it going through The Neale.

Hard information is scant, but there are reports that all airports are closed with outgoing flights grounded and all incoming ones returned to origin or rerouted to airports in England and Wales. All shipping is being held in dock and there will be no maritime traffic until further notice. People are urged to travel only if absolutely necessary and to carry picture ID; all schools are closed for the day. Beyond that there is little else, no indication of what exactly the threat is, whether it is biological or chemical or explosive, and no indication of who is behind it. A government spokesman will only confirm that all security agencies are on maximum alert and that they will continue that way until further notice; more information will be released to the public when it becomes available.

There is a note of incredulity in the voice of the newsreader as she delivers all this. As if she can hardly believe the terms of her employ would ever stretch to something like this. Not just the world and its persistent drama, but she herself has reached a limit. She sounds relieved to move on to what she calls 'other news', even as she surely knows at this early hour that there is no other news; every other story from now on is already nested within the arc of this one defining narrative. Even at this early hour it is already huge and all encompassing, bringing its own horizon and a different kind of certainty with it.

Nealon turns off the radio and the heater, shearing away all distractions so as to get a clearer focus on what he has just heard. Something in him is already attuning itself to a higher order of disturbance, a twitch in the ether to which it is sensitive. There is now a sharper edge to everything. Things are differently fixed before the day has properly risen into itself.

Nealon opens his mind as far into the situation as he can. The global context is obvious; with its far-flung locales and shadowy principals, the war on terror is the sprawling narrative of this age. It lies across the world as a vast unease, the defining narrative under which entire nations have come to live. There have been attacks on Madrid, Bali and London, but so far this island nation has avoided or escaped a direct strike of any sort despite the well-documented lapses and gaps in security procedures at ports and airports. Shannon, with its rotating schedule of American forces stopovers, presents itself as the most likely focus for any kind of attack or as the launch point for a strike on the bigger and more telegenic targets in our neighbouring country. Analysts warn that it is only a matter of time before our tacit compliance with the US makes us a target for some sort of retaliation. And no one is confident that existing security measures are capable of dealing with any kind of serious threat.

So how acute is all this, he wonders. What exactly does maximum alert mean and how is a citizenry supposed to react to it? Has someone been killed – a cabinet member, possibly? Has a suspect device been discovered? It must be wider than that, a nebulous incident with such broad circumference that it warrants the closing down of all ports and airports, all commercial traffic. An event with both impact and spread.

Now that our time has come, Nealon wonders how the country will acquit itself. Where will it look to for guidance and precedent? What will be the communal response? The nearest thing Nealon remembers by way of comparison is from a couple of years back when the whole country almost came to a halt when BSE arrived like a medieval visitation. Everyone had stepped up to their civic duty and worked together, taking seriously the injunction against needless travel and assembly, everyone acutely aware of themselves as a possible disease vector. Every doorstep and threshold in the country was saturated with Parazone and Jeyes Fluid so that any possible transmission routes were broken up. The whole response was little more than window dressing, but in the absence of other effective actions people embraced these measures as shared commitment to a common cause. After a week the whole country stood and turned to gaze across the Irish Sea where a dense wall of smoke rose over Wales as whole herds of cattle were culled and bulldozed into massive windrows and hosed down with benzene before being set alight to send waxy columns of smoke rising into the air that were visible one hundred miles away . . .

Nealon shakes his head to stall the drift of his own thoughts. This is something he is prone to, these lateral segues from the present moment into the abstract, lurid reaches of imagination. It's a throwback to those other phases of his life when he lived by his wits and such digressions were part of what made his reputation as a man who skilfully came at the world from a different angle.

But now is not the time for free association.

He needs to clear his head and concentrate on what all this means for him and his meeting. He has that nagging feeling of linkage, of obscure connections coming together and webbing into the coming day. His own appointment is somehow woven into the broader reach of this event, it has that feel to it. He needs to clear an open space in his head so that these two things can have free play with each other and reveal the true nature of their connectedness.

If he weren't driving, he would lie back and close his eyes. A couple of minutes adrift in himself would make all the difference.

A rise in the road and beyond that a right-angled turn that looks out over a broad stretch of bogland. In the distance, a range of low hills. Nealon counts six or seven homes scattered along the road, each house marked against the black hills by yard lights over barns and haysheds.

He pulls over to the side and gets out. There's no cold but a light breeze brushes across his face. Nealon sits back on the warm bonnet. This is something he has often done in the past, not because these journeys are long or difficult but because this darkness is a pleasure in itself; the sky above with its ragged cloud cover while up ahead the road disappearing till it comes up against those lighted homesteads. The silence is fitting also, an expansive waiting which places him at its centre. The only sound is the cooling tick of the car engine behind him.

This is where Nealon is good. Any silence that swells like this would normally enable him to focus on disparate elements and see the complex pattern of their coming together. Art and politics, light and dark, past and future, he can see the links between them all. Somewhere along the way he has mastered the trick of demarking opposing forces while holding them together in his mind's eye, separate and apart. Then their electric weave is given free play without interference from himself or anything in him which might give bias or slant to their eventual coherence.

He can spend hours at this, marshalling a flux of converging forces and possibilities, hardly daring to breathe for fear of affecting the whole assemblage with some sullied part of himself. These were hours of brittle enchantment. There is no proof, but he is certain that he's never aged during these fugues, this total absence of himself lifting time itself out of his body. And as always, he is filled with a sense of trespass, an acute privilege which has never left him. There was nothing else so peaceful or achieved in his life and it was as if the whole thing had little to do with him but was something bestowed from on high.

But nothing comes to him now, nothing on the edge of this bog spreading out into the darkness.

This does not surprise him. For the moment he is not jacked up on the proper sense of anxiety, not quite at that frayed peak. Furthermore, he is bound to be rusty considering the length of time he has spent lying in his cell leafing through library magazines. Blunted intuitions are a predictable side effect of such torpor. Feeling his way into this delicate scenario will not be rushed so he is content to let it rest within him. The old sensitivities and intuitions will return in their proper time. Keeping sharp and vigilant, that is his task now, not allowing himself to be thrown wide of his best reflexes. Small as it is, this guarded resolution assures him. It feels good, a vote of confidence in himself.

A wave of relief courses through him. He had feared

that being laid up for so long would have atrophied such delicate gifts. Days scanning through volumes of *National Geographic*, the only publication within the prison which enabled him to reach into the outside world. Weeks spent grazing through long articles and photo essays on the Borneo rainforest or Liberian blood diamonds. With his whole world closed down to a ten-by-seven cell, he'd felt a gradual slackening of his mind and metabolism. As the weeks went by and the haggling over the exact nature of the charges being brought against him were tweaked and sharpened, he had felt certain impulses within him begin to wane and refuse access, leaving him sluggish and without willpower. It had frightened him – he will admit that – left him vulnerable in ways he had not foreseen. He had tried to offset that in the small prison library by reading certain texts in philosophy and politics, pitting himself against the arguments of phantom opponents. But he gave up after a couple of weeks; he could not fully convince himself of anything meaningful at stake or of a worthwhile adversary.

His error became clear. It had been too easy to mistake it as a simple waning of his faculties, the narrows and channels of his mind silting up from so little use. In truth, the grey necrosis spreading within was clear proof of how much a creature of context he really was. In the dullness of prison life there was a complete lack of mind-sharpening engagement and without it there was always the likelihood that Nealon would turn in on himself and close down around his own pulsing core.

The sudden ringing of his phone startles him back to the present. The noise is gratingly narrow. He pulls it out and raises it to his ear. There is no mistaking the voice, he is used to it by now.

'Get back in the car, you need to keep going.'

It took him a long time to recognise it as chaos and he wonders now how he could have mistaken it as anything else.

Every day the same routine. Turning out the cell, breakfast and then back standing at the door for inspection and headcount. Then the desultory conversation on the landing with the other inmates, whiling away the time till the one-hour's exercise in the yard. Day after day the same routine, rinse and repeat, repetition lending the whole thing the appearance of structure. Rhythm was everything, and the way it gathered up a legion of men into its daily shuffle was its own justification, the machine in its inexorable mission of purging guilt. Men of all backgrounds and failings processed through its cleansing mechanism till the day they left, blinking in the light with their souls shorn and shriven.

And it got into his soul too. Not in the way it swept him up to become another lathed component of its apparatus, but the way it wiped so many things from his attention. During his time there he no longer gave any thought to his work or to his studio with his brushes and paints now abandoned. Nor, during daylight hours, did he give any thought to either Olwyn or Cuan. They were out there, and he presumed they were safe, and so he could set all thoughts of them aside. And it was not just an effect of the pink walls and rubberised flooring that he had no conscience on any of this. This was no place for new guilt, no place in which to gather new sins or failings.

He found it hard to pass the time. Waiting for word of his trial, having it stalled time and time again on technicalities and points of law. His initial impatience and optimism quickly waned and Nealon took up a defensive, embattled posture in his head which would not allow him to register for any of the educational classes or courses offered. Nor participate in any of the reading groups that gathered in open-doored cells along the landing. For that first month he lay glooming on his bunk.

One afternoon he made his way to the small library. This was a chamber behind the farthest end of the landing, a lighted place set up like a children's classroom. There were single desks scattered across the middle of a room that was ringed around by wooden bookshelves which reached floor to ceiling. And it was immediately obvious to Nealon that the handful of men who were there, bent over books and magazines, were of two types. There were those, like himself, who had slunk away from the tension of the landings for some space and time to sit alone by themselves. Many had no interest in their open books or mags, they had enough reading to do of their own souls and their lonely efforts drew down a thin light on top of their heads. Theirs was dark work and Nealon knew instinctively to leave them alone.

The other type was forbidding in a different way. These men were avid with the idea of books as repositories of wisdom and learning, men desperate with the need for this same insight, scouring texts and magazines for that chink in the legal system that would enable them to rewrite history and establish themselves as wronged or worthy of a second chance. And even with their heads bent they reeked of anxiety; it rolled off them in a sibilant hum that grated on the nerves. Nealon did not have to spend too much time appraising them either to see that he wanted no part of their endeavours. He felt closer to the first cohort, those who put their heads down and quietly did their time.

He took up a desk at the back of the room, a spot that came under direct light when the sun wheeled to the west in the early afternoon and probed into the corner. It gave Nealon a full view of the room in front of him, the broad shoulders and the bent heads of the other inmates. It also put him within arm's reach of an unbroken ten-year subscription of *National Geographic* that dated from the establishment of the prison itself and which was the repository of a narrative that would become a powerful enchantment for Nealon.

At first his engagement with it was fairly aimless – it was little more than a convenient way of passing the time. Cloudscapes, arid deserts, teeming coral shelves; page after page, he scanned them all, at first in a mood of passive wonderment – his eye drawn to aerial photographs of crowds and gatherings, herds of wildebeest migrating across the Serengeti, shoals of sardines photographed overhead in blue water. Then the scale of things scoping down to intimate close-ups of seal pups on pristine ice floes or a solitary compass jellyfish drifting in refracted sunlight. And then the scale of the whole thing narrowing further down to the granular world of the insect kingdom, ants and termites about their busy work. All this natural abundance a preamble to the lunatic intervention of the man-made – those sprawling urban centres under neon skies contrasted with the husks of ancient cities clutching the edges of mountain escarpments, now overrun by forest; oil tankers being dismantled by teeming metalworkers, and cleaning crews mopping up massive oil spills.

Nealon gorged on these images. Something beyond his eye for colour and composition snagged on them.

At first sight the continuous parade of images came off as a hymn to the world's plenitude, a song of praise which was careful to acknowledge both the heroism and haplessness of human intervention. How long did he spend looking at an aerial photograph of a massive Californian reservoir whose surface was covered entirely with black plastic balls to prevent it from evaporating into the noonday sky?

And then a curious segue, something he could not have anticipated. The passing days with their tight routine hardened in him like a lens. By night, in his cell, the images he had consumed during the day sifted down inside him to become a compacted layer of appreciation, a broadened and deepened sense of the world. Those shoals and swarms, those pristine snowdrifts and sand dunes, those cities and temples overrun with jungle vegetation – this is where we have our being and this is what we believe in. That was how it presented itself to Nealon at first, a surge of cheap cosmic sentiment, an expansive gratitude. But there was also, to Nealon's mind, a clear sense of things falling away from what was pristine and whole into filth and fragment. Those oil spills and poisoned lakes, those great gyres of plastic waste spiralling in the southern Atlantic. There were things coming apart, falling away from their proper being.

And in the long hours after lockdown, this idea turned in Nealon ceaselessly, drawing him down to unsettled sleep.

Another ten miles of narrow road before turning onto the motorway. There is a change to the light, a definite thinning of the darkness.

This motorway was newly opened while he was away, a straight incision through space and time. It gives Nealon a clear sense of speed and he settles deeper into the lulling rhythms of the journey. The car gathers around him, pointed into its own headlong surge, and Nealon holds a steady speed, around sixty-five mph. He is glad of the real peace it offers him.

The lights of a service station come up in the distance and he slows down to pull into the pumps. There is already a van ahead of him and a 4x4 parked near the grass margin with a man in the passenger seat eating something out of a serviette. What has these men up so early, Nealon wonders. What work has drawn them from their beds at this hour?

He puts thirty euros' worth of unleaded in the tank and walks into the brightly lit interior. Behind the counter is a young blonde woman in her late teens. According to the tag on her blouse her name is Anja. Despite the hard light and the dozy smile, Nealon sees that she will turn out to be a real beauty. Those features will chisel out with age to their proper definition and when she learns to carry herself at her proper height, she will turn heads which is a short step from breaking hearts. She has all that ahead of her and Nealon is happy to see it as clearly as if it were unfolding before his eyes. Right now, however, she is anxious to please. Nealon can feel the warm nimbus of heat coming off her across the counter. He has not expected such haptic feedback so early in the morning, and the thought comes to him that in some other world it would be a good and right thing to reach out and touch her face.

For one moment the idea swims in the light like a real possibility.

The heat and the smell of breakfast things from the deli are having an effect on him: Anja is saying something to him now, asking him if that is all. Is that all?

He snaps to with a start, 'Yes, that's all, thirty euros of petrol. Oh, and plus a twenty euro top-up for the phone.'

He fumbles in his jacket for his wallet. The simple transaction is becoming a hopelessly complex affair. After a moment he is glad to find his wallet and hand over the cash. The whole kerfuffle is worth it for the smile.

'Thank you,' she says, 'have a good day.'

A good day.

The idea startles him so much that he is still thinking about it when he is back in the car and swinging out of the forecourt. He very nearly pulls out in front of a van he hasn't spotted in the inside lane which goes blaring by in a white blur. He catches sight of an enraged face behind the steering wheel, passed by in a flash before he can summon a response.

The incident rattles him and he drives in the slow lane for the next half-hour.

The next news bulletin adds little by way of hard information.

Reports that a complete wing of the Mater Hospital has been requisitioned as a quarantine unit are as yet unconfirmed. In the context of a terrorist attack the measure seems reasonable and proportionate but Nealon's whole sense of what's happening is still out of kilter, everything drifting out of focus.

He is still turning the possibilities over in his mind when the first checkpoint looms up ahead of him. A cop in a high-visibility vest flags him down with a torch and guides him into the checkpoint fifty yards farther on, to where two more Guards are flanked by a pair of soldiers in full battledress and communications headsets. Nealon coasts towards them and pulls up. One of the cops sweeps his torch across the front of his car, taking in the make and number plate before switching the beam to Nealon's face, letting it linger there for a long moment. Then a quick sweep of the car's interior before he steps back and turns his mouth onto his shoulder to speak a few words. He then waves Nealon through between the soldiers who have moved off to opposite sides of the road.

Nealon pushes on, watching the checkpoint disappear behind him. It feels like he has come through some sort of portal, some fissure in the world through which time and circumstances are inexplicably altered.

The Guards and soldiers have faded completely from sight when the phone goes off on the seat beside him, the backlit screen casting a blue halo around it.

'You're going to meet two more of those,' the voice says. 'They'll be no problem, just keep driving nice and steady.'

'What do you make of this threat thing, how real is it?'

'I wouldn't know,' the voice answers without apparent interest.

'Or who's behind it?'

'I wouldn't know that either.'

'Your hand is nowhere in any of this?'

'This is not my sort of thing, just drive carefully.' And with that the phone goes dead.

Nealon does not wonder any more at the abruptness of these interventions. His own ready compliance with them is something to dwell on another time.

The city appears shortly before sunrise, spreading across the horizon like a chain of coals. A sodium glow rises above it like some vast corrosive. The skyline has enough sense of itself to offer up spires and clock towers through this vertical tide. The first drops of rain fall on the windscreen.

On the western approach, the traffic is heavy and his speed slows to less than twenty miles an hour. It slows further and Nealon settles to a long crawl through a succession of roundabouts that eventually take him along the river towards the quays. Beyond the city's central bridge, he spots the neon sign of a multistorey car park. The digital counter over the entrance tells him that there are sixty-three vacant places in the two levels above the ground floor. Taking his ticket at the entrance barrier he drives up the spiral driveway and finds a spot in the middle of the second floor.

The whole structure smells of wet concrete, oil and salt blown in from the sea below. It wraps around him in a damp swathe. The concrete floors and pillars echo with the sound of car doors slamming followed by the chirp of electronic locks being activated. Enamelled light sifts in from the sea. Nealon takes the holdall from the back seat and walks towards the exit, deciding at the last moment to take the staircase which is deserted all the way to the ground.

He exits the car park onto the docks. The seafront spreads out before him like an expanse of hammered sheet metal. Nealon has the unwelcome feeling that he has been pressed from the car park into the cold light of this small city.

The morning sky is swollen with clouds now driving rain through the grey light in a steady fall; this day is down for good. Some people are already abroad, a harassed breed with their eyes fixed on the ground, dispirited before the day has drawn breath. They have about them the resentful look of men and women who wish they were elsewhere, anywhere. Standing under the concrete lip of the entrance Nealon watches a Securicor van and a Garda escort make their way along the street and turn left onto the bridge from which he has come.

Part of this city's creation myth speaks of how this whole frontage was reclaimed from the sea, the land extended stone by stone to raise this dockland area above the high-water mark. Ships from Britain and Spain would dock and unload cargoes of wine and salt in exchange for fleece and marble from the outlying area. The sea pressing its old claim on the land is especially vivid this morning as the water swells against the docks.

Nealon's own history comes back to him also.

Some years ago he had walked this same street towards the bus station at the bottom of the hill. He was leaving at last and happy to do so. Happy to be putting behind him several years of menial work which had carried him through his twenties, years pissed away smoking dope and skulling pints and sweet talking biddable young women with all the work he would do when his season of drink and dope had run its course. He had worked, off and on, as a set carpenter and painter for a theatre company, knocking together gazebos and domestic interiors out of sheets of plywood and MDF. The work had been steady in an off-and-on sort of way, enough to keep him in rent and drink, which was as far as his ambition stretched at the time. But somewhere in the days and nights of ceaseless talk he had the suspicion there was something out there which occasionally revealed itself to him as a vague but beckoning promise that he would be rewarded if only he would take the chance. And Nealon surprised himself by paying heed and finding that he was well open to the idea of change. So, he took that promise in good faith and packed a bag, pulled the door of his bedsit in the Latin Quarter closed, leaving behind him two months' unpaid rent and an electricity bill pushing near four figures.

Four hours later, he stepped off a bus on the other side of the country and into that first morning of what he would call the Iron Age.

And now, years later, standing in that same grey light out of which ghosts and other wraiths assert themselves, Nealon would not be surprised to catch a glimpse of his former self walking towards him in a long coat and with the knees out in his jeans, the uniform at the time of the down-at-heel genius. And what words would he trade with this younger man? At this moment he does not feel up to it; too many questions hum around him, too many unsettled things.

He heads into the rain, pulling his collar up around his ears. The street turns along the quays and leads towards the city bridge where the hotel is directly ahead of him, cornered into the morning light like a liner that has just docked. It has a sullen presence; Nealon can feel the light and air it has disturbed to take up its place in the world. He feels its weight on the earth under his feet, how it has compressed the water table beneath.

Inside, he steps into the chaos of a crowded foyer where three uniformed receptionists are tending to a slew of guests who are milling around with bags and cases at their feet and coats thrown across their arms. There is a dense anxiety in the air. People are checking various documents and maps and hassling a couple of visibly stressed travel reps who are standing in the middle of the throng, making vacant, placatory gestures with open hands. It's a coach party of some sort and it's clear that news of the security alert has found its way to them.

Nealon moves off to one side. He'll give this a minute, wait for it to clear. He stands with his back to a large canvas. It is an unframed piece, flared with daubs of pink paint which surge diagonally from a dense centre point in the bottom left-hand corner only to give way at its outer edges to a spreading white nimbus. It is suggestive of some explosive moment or energy losing its purpose and vitality the longer it expends itself. If the piece has a title Nealon cannot see it anywhere. A seething annoyance blooms in him. What aspect of this piece persuaded the buyer that it would lend tone to any public space? And why, on this day and at this hour, would he himself rise to a provocation like this? Or more accurately, why would he provoke himself like this?

The crowd of tourists is thinning out, the reps and guides shepherding them to various halls and suites of the hotel. At the check-in desk, Nealon is faced with a determinedly cheerful young woman with her hair pulled back over a shiny brow. She checks through her register and tells him, yes, Mr Nealon, you are booked in, a single room on the third floor overlooking the quays, but that the room will not be ready till midday. He could if he wishes leave his bag here and have some breakfast in the main dining room which will be open for another two hours; the expense would be added to his room.

Nealon nods and hands over the holdall gratefully. If there is anything he hates, it's lugging baggage of any sort.

Travel light no matter how far the distance, nothing but his own four bones if he can manage it. He is glad to leave the bag aside; it enables him to feel closer to himself, more compact, as if he is finally commanding his own space as he should.

In the dining room the tables are arranged in a lowered central arena, square tables with white tablecloths fully set out with cups and cutlery. There is one free table to the left where someone has just left a rubble of breakfast things. Nealon claims the place by throwing his jacket over the chair. A waitress moves immediately to clear the table while Nealon moves off to the buffet which is set out on a raised dais against the wall, a long table lain with silver covers and bowls of fruit.

Nealon has no interest in food. He never had and often, in a pious mood, thinks it is one of the most useless and self-caressing passions of his generation. Nevertheless, he now has the country lad's desire for something warm in his belly – as if he has already done a day's work. He scoops up scrambled eggs, rashers and tomatoes with a couple of pieces of toast and, feeling slightly embarrassed at the pile of food on the plate, he makes his way back to the table which is cleared and perfectly set with a pot of coffee in its centre.

It is now five minutes to eight, so he reaches into his jacket and pulls out the headphones for his mobile phone, plugs them in and switches on the radio. By the time the news comes on he is well into his breakfast. The newsreader's tone has not altered from the earlier bulletins. The same note of cautious incredulity still underscores her frustration at being unable to add much to what is already known. Clear information goes no further than confirmation from the Department of Defence that security forces are on maximum alert and that several unspecified parts of the National Emergency Plan have been mobilised. A spokesman will not confirm the exact nature of the threat, implying that revealing its precise nature may jeopardise whatever plans are in operation to neutralise it. The bulletin continues with other stories of the wider world, all with the wan aura of footnotes about them. For the moment there is no wider world; this threat is the only world there is.

Nealon switches off the phone and places it face down on the table. Why face down, he wonders. Is there some reason why he should want to have the back facing up?

He'd found the radio to be a great boon during those months in detention when he had spent his time sharing a cell with a rotating cast of those awaiting trial or those already sentenced. All were better sleepers than himself, big and small men with their backs humped and their faces turned to the wall as they sawed and snored through the night in the bunk beneath him. Overhead, in the dark hours Nealon plugged himself into the radio and spent his time scoping through a slew of preset stations. Time and again he found himself returning to the local station with its varied playlist of country-and-western songs and show-band hits, old favourites interspaced with curious local announcements and messages. Names and places called to him in the dark. Places he knew of but had never been to, their names brightening the night. From the top bunk his imagination spread out to these towns and villages with announcements like

Maire Heane in Killasser, Jimmy needs to contact you, will you please turn on your mobile?

Or something like

There are two bullocks on the road at the speed-limit sign outside of Crossmolina, drivers need to be careful.

Or most memorable of all on a particularly stormy night he had listened to the presenter warn motorists that

Outside Bohola there's a galvanised roof on a shed that gabled onto the road and it's in danger of being whipped off in sudden gusts. Anyone driving that way needs to be careful.

In his cell Nealon marvelled at the connectedness implicit in these messages, the confident nexus of shared concerns and dangers which held these communities together. He himself seemed to have been born to the margins of things, prowling around the edges, looking in from the darkness.

The food feels good in his belly.

It's warm and solid but it brings with it also a wave of fatigue which he is glad to succumb to. He picks up the phone and his jacket and makes his way back to reception where he persuades the anxious receptionist with some glib banter that he will take any available room as soon as possible rather than wait for his one to be made up. The receptionist grimaces at the request but he gives her his widest smile which seems to assure her that the task is well within her ability. Sure enough, after a few phone calls and various computer cross-checks she moves him from the third floor to a vacant single on the fourth. He allows her one last smile as he takes the key card and bag before crossing the foyer to the lift.

Four floors up he steps into a vacant corridor which is lit along its length by a series of triangular uplighters, an art-deco spin on the medieval sconce. The alternating rhythm of lights and doors along the length of the hall gives Nealon the impression that he is trapped in the spinal column of a giant vertebrate.

His room is down towards the end, past the house-keeping trolley stacked with bedclothes and towels. After closing the door behind him, Nealon has no memory of doing anything other than lying face down on the bed and falling asleep.

This Plague of Souls

The world returns to him in drifts of light and rhythm. This is sleep and something beyond sleep. And as long as he keeps his eyes closed he is borne up in a swaying motion where the world is complete in itself.

As long as he keeps his eyes closed.

He wakes fully clothed on the bed.

The watch on his wrist tells him there is now less than an hour before the meeting. A shower seems like a good idea; a clean start, so to speak. He goes into the bathroom and stands under the pulsing spray of hot water, running it cold towards the end and for as long as he can bear it on his bald head. Then a few practised sweeps of the razor before changing into jeans and a fresh shirt.

He feels good.

The food in his belly is fully digested and with sleep behind him he might never be in better shape to face whoever it is he's going to meet. Ten minutes now before the appointed time. He picks up his phone and has a last scan through it for any missed calls or messages.

There are no calls, no messages, nothing.

That was a mistake. A sliver of confidence leaks from him, he can feel it in his legs. He curses and draws a hard breath to steady himself. Time to go.

Out in the hall the door closes heavily behind him under its own weight. He steps into an empty lift and presses down.

The foyer is nearly deserted now, the early morning chaos having been sorted for the moment; there is a single receptionist on the desk.

Now that the area is cleared Nealon is surprised at the lighted air of the place. A vaulted ceiling over an open stretch of polished floor runs towards the reception desk and seating along the walls. Has the whole place expanded in his sleep, he wonders. His gaze is drawn upwards into the curve of the ceiling with its ribbed plasterwork. For a sharp moment he is back in the hayshed with his father sheltering from a passing shower, the same press of light over his head. But there is something else here too, something expectant. This broadening sense of space, the way sound travels here . . . this has the feel of a train station, a place where journeys intersect. Nealon would not be surprised to see platform numbers, or a destination board appear high up on a wall, the air suddenly jarred with tannoy announcements.

That idea cuts through the years, returning him in an instant to his first visit to the Hauptbahnhof in Berlin. This was during his time in the wilderness, his years of wandering. New to the world then and with clear eyes, he was not yet above gazing around him in wonder. Looking up at the giant destination board with all its alphabetically tiered names he had the irreducible certainty that he was at the centre of the world. Trains to all points: Madrid, Moscow and Mannheim. As far away as Vienna and Vladivostok, Zagreb. The known world, he said to himself. And up at the top – you couldn't make it up – Archangel, a city he may have invented himself or heard about on the margins of his consciousness. At that moment he envisioned it as a penal colony of some sort or a cluster of oil derricks within the Arctic Circle, a black smear across some pristine landscape, settled by a community of convicts, riggers and prostitutes. Nealon saw himself visiting it someday. He would settle well in a place like that.

Nealon checks the run of his thoughts. Hold your concentration, he tells himself. Now is not the time for riffing on like that.

A pair of leather chairs by the window have a clear view of the street outside and the dock basin beyond with boats and ships anchored within. Traffic pours steadily through the rain. In high summer it's easy to see how this whole area would fill with light, the sun ringing off the oil tanks standing at one end of the docks. Today however, it feels that if you took too many steps in this grey light it would sift the colour from your skin, shear every atom of its proper light and shade, all gone elsewhere.

On the opposite wall a large TV screen is locked on to RTÉ News with the sound turned down. It's covering sports news – soccer, horseracing and boxing. For a baffled moment Nealon wonders how, on a day like this, the world can find time for such foolishness. After a few moments his mood drifts towards some understanding. Yes of course, what else would the world be doing? Fun and games are as good a way to spend this day as any other.

Nealon sees that there is some movement in the football market, some last-minute switching and selling before the transfer window closes. The bulletin is using a clip montage to illustrate the talents of a gifted mid-table striker who has just been bought by a club with title ambitions. Goals rain in. Left foot, right foot, headers, penalties, free kicks, the full array of this young striker's gifts on show. He looks handy right enough, Nealon concedes. He could well be the difference between being champions or the runners-up spot at the end of May. With support from midfield, he could tip the balance in a tough end of season run-in.

'He might be the answer, surely,' a voice beside him says quietly, lifting the thought clean out of his head. 'But can he make the step up, that's the question. Mid-table to top four, it's a big ask.'

Nealon tamps down the impulse to react immediately or make any sudden movements. For three beats measured by the hammering in his chest he waits before turning to the voice beside him.

The man presents himself in profile, his hands deep in his pockets with his chin raised as if striking some resolute pose for a painter or photographer somewhere on the other side of the foyer. He stands perfectly still, staring at the television screen, content apparently to give Nealon whatever time he needs.

He is squarely built, blocky in a grey suit that is gathered around his ankles. There may have been a time when he could have worn such a suit, but that time is well in the past. He has the pallor of a man in early old age who is carrying considerable weight on his frame. There is however a real density of muscle about him, hard across the shoulders and through the chest. The profile reminds Nealon of all those big men from his childhood whom he met at marts and fairs buying livestock, men bulked up in topcoats and wellingtons, carrying lengths of ash plant or Wavin piping, men leaning on the bars of pens and crushes to cast their eyes over calves and weanlings. Now this man rocks forward on the balls of his feet, in no hurry apparently, full of patience. The distance between them is about eighteen inches, a span finely gauged to be just inside Nealon's personal space.

The man turns and puts his hand out. Nealon takes it without hesitation. It feels as it should, thick and muscled, the hand of a tradesman – a bricklayer or plasterer. Like my father's hand, Nealon says to himself, the same blunt heft that comes from a life of physical labour. He recalls the pressured inclination towards the clenched grip in which the handles of spades and shovels rested. It has been a long time since Nealon has shaken such a hand.

'We'll sit down,' the man says, motioning to the leather seats near the window.

The man takes the seat with its back to the wall and pushes his feet out in front of him, scanning the whole foyer. Nealon notes that he has already gathered himself and looks comfortable. He's evidently settled down for a long session of whatever it is that's going to unfold between them. And there's no hurry apparently; this man has all the time in the world.

'I didn't spot you there for a minute,' the man says.

'I was standing in plain sight.'

'The hair threw me, it's very severe.'

'It was time for a change.'

The limpness of his response irks Nealon. He is convinced that he has lost this opening flurry. But the man seems uninterested, and his gaze has turned to the television where RTÉ News has come full circle to the story of the security alert. A reporter is standing in front of Government Buildings, doing a piece to camera. Soldiers in full battledress man the entrance behind him.

'What do you make of this ruckus,' the man asks, 'this whole terror alert thing?'

'It looks serious.'

'It does surely.'

'I passed through those checkpoints,' Nealon says, 'but that's all I know. Has anything else happened?'

'Not that I've heard, the whole thing is short on specifics. I've made a few calls but am none the wiser. I'm told there will be a government statement at midday.'

Nealon looks at his watch. 'That's a long time to keep us in the dark. I thought they would have moved quicker to clarify and give information.'

'No doubt they are choosing their moment. And trading has been suspended on the stock exchange also.'

There is no difficulty now in squaring this man to the voice on the phone. The voice is filled out in the body, both coming together in a powerful statement of presence. And he has always been fat, Nealon sees that now. This is not a man who has been overwhelmed by this surfeit of flesh in the doldrums of middle age. He is too comfortable with his bulk, too heedless of his own corpulence. There is nothing of the rue he has noticed so often in men his age who have succumbed to flesh. This man has lived comfortably in himself his whole life.

'Is there any word on what it is exactly?' Nealon asks. 'Is it a bomb or biological or chemical or what . . .?' The words sound unlikely in his mouth, strange and without history, belonging to other jurisdictions.

'There's no word so far. I'd be surprised if it was a close-quarter attack. My bet is that it's something targeted at our telecom infrastructure.'

'Any word from the security forces?'

'None at all,' says the man with waning interest. 'I know as much as you do.'

'Strange days,' Nealon ventures.

'Strange days indeed,' the man concurs. And then, in a sudden swerve, 'But it was bound to be our time sooner or later, the way the world is at the moment. The only question now is what exactly it is and how big.'

The man speaks with such bland indifference that Nealon has difficulty sifting his words for any sign that he is withholding some knowledge of what's really going on. He notes how easily they have moved from the thrust and parry of their phone calls into something more equable and collusive. They might be two men with some business other than what is to hand right now.

A clutch of tourists exits the lift, five or six men and women dragging wheelie cases behind them. Rain gear in various dayglo colours is worn or draped across forearms. A uniformed rep crosses the floor and starts immediately to soothe and orient them with broad hand gestures and an anxious expression. The man shakes his head.

'What in the name of god would tourists want in this part of the world at this time of year?'

'Their timing isn't great, surely.'

'I could never understand it, driving around this country in the pissing rain, looking at things. Jesus, if you have that much money burning a hole in your pocket, I can show you something better to do with it.'

'It wouldn't be my choice either,' Nealon admits. 'Each to their own though.'

'I suppose.'

Nealon notes how easily he has fallen into league with the man, how they are buddies now, sharing this bafflement at the world's callowness. Nealon marvels that the man can find so much worthy of his attention. It could be a ploy, he admits, a tactic to wind down the clock with trivia and distraction before he moves in for the kill. You need your wits about you here, he tells himself.

None of this answers the fundamental questions though. What does this man want and what, in exchange, does he have to offer? Before he can mull the questions a moment longer the man speaks suddenly across his thoughts.

'So, this freedom thing,' he says, 'how is it going for you?'

'It would go a lot better if I was left in peace.'

'I'd believe that. You wouldn't swap it for the other thing though.'

'No, I would not.'

The man nods. 'The longest remand prisoner in the history of the state. Remind me again, how long was it?'

'You know all that yourself, we have already discussed it.'

'It was a long stretch all right, it would give a man plenty of time to think.'

'Yes.'

'If thinking was what you wanted to do.'

'Let's cut the shit,' Nealon says softly. 'Why are we here, what do you want from me?'

The man studies him so evenly that Nealon has a parched feeling he has erred, that he has revealed an unwise readiness to come to the point.

'We're here to talk,' the man says softly, settling farther into the depths of the chair. 'Just a chat.'

Nealon shakes his head. 'I understood it to be more involved than a chat. An exchange of information, clarification, that there were things you did not know but that I could throw light on. So what are these things you need to know and how can I clarify them?'

The man considers, his gaze drifting towards the reception desk. When he eventually speaks his tone is hoarse, coming from some dry place within him. It's the voice of a man who has smoked too much in his time, a voice rising out of parts that are well cured from the incessant transit of blue smog through them.

'There are things we know we know,' he says, 'and things we know we don't know, the known knowns and the known unknowns. But there are other things which present very real problems, and these are the unknown unknowns, all the things we don't know we don't know. That's what we're going to discuss here today.'

'I know the quote,' Nealon replies, 'from the man who wanted a war on the cheap and who was shown the door when it ended in chaos. It will be written on his headstone.'

'Be that as it may, it's as clear a statement of these troubled times as you could wish for. Only a fool would dismiss it.'

'There's never been a shortage of fools,' Nealon ventures sagely, 'and who is to guess which is which sitting here?'

The man guffaws shortly. 'No, no, two wise men, that's all we have here.' And then, without dropping a beat, he adds, 'I'd love a cup of tea. Will you have a cup yourself?'

Nealon is taken by surprise. 'I'll have a coffee,' he blurts.

'Nothing stronger?'

'No.'

'I could never drink coffee myself, never got a taste for it.'

'It's not for everyone.'

'That's for sure.' He raises a hand and a waitress from the other side of the foyer comes across. 'Tea and a coffee please.'

The waitress moves off, drawing a silence with her that bridges the long moment to the next consideration. Nealon takes up the cue.

'I don't have all day.'

The man considers for a short moment. 'I'll paint you a picture to begin with. Just so we're both clear where this is all coming from.'

'You didn't come here with any doubts about me.'

'True.'

'So, let's move on.'

'As a gesture of good faith, I can guarantee that nothing said here will go beyond these walls.'

'How about your name as a gesture of good faith, that would be a better start.'

The man shakes his head. 'My name won't make you one bit wiser. It is the least valuable and interesting thing about me. I have much more to tell than my name.'

'And I'm supposed to take your word for all that?'

'You can take what you want, but at the moment it's all I've got. I suggest that you neither confirm nor deny anything I say. You can draw attention to any inconsistencies in my story. How about that?'

Nealon spreads his hands in a gesture of disavowal. Now that they are coming to the real work of this meeting the man has his whole attention. His concentration narrows down to the precise sound of the man's words, every part of him straining to sift and gather in the consequences of whatever he is about to say.

'I come from the south-east,' he begins, 'not a part of the world you'd be familiar with. Flatter and more hospitable than this. But my background is something like your own – a small farm, a few head of cattle. Like many a young man of my generation I joined the Guards after school and after my training I was posted here and there. That was the seventies and eighties, a wild and extravagant time in this country, kidnappings and robberies and para-militaries. A lot of questionable things were done and some of it was well outside the rules but that was the game at the time and I played it like everyone else. In the late nineties, post ceasefire, I was taken up with organised crime around Dublin, all the drugs and that new gener-ation of thugs who rose up in the wake of the General – I became familiar with that whole gangland community. I had my quota of convictions and my share of cases thrown out of court for one reason or another as well. You win some, you lose some, that's how it goes. Along the way I picked up a postgraduate qualification in conflict resolution and on the strength of it I went on secondment with NATO in the former Yugoslavia, securing the peace and overseeing elections. That was a bit of an eye-opener all right, trying to keep neighbours from killing each other. So, after two years of that I came home and spent a further couple of years on administrative duty, racking up my pension before I retired for good. And that's about it, that's what brings me to this moment here.' The man's expres-sion is an open question to Nealon.

'That's as dry a telling as you could make of a life.'

'It was a life all right, thirty years and more. I don't know what it says about it that I can scope through it so quickly.'

'It might be a pack of lies for all I know, beginning, middle and end.'

'You can believe it or not but all I'll say is that I have better things for doing with my time than sitting here codding you.'

'So now it's my turn.'

'This is all about exchange.'

'My past is public knowledge,' Nealon says. 'There's no shortage of stuff on me out there. I'd hoped there would be more, then it would have been easier to establish that I should not have been standing trial.'

'Let me tell you what I know, my read on you and your situation.'

'You have the bit between your teeth.'

'Bear with me,' the man urges softly, 'a couple of broad strokes and if you say nothing, we'll take it that I am on the right track.'

Nealon does not move. He is aware that his face is set in a rictus of concentration but not at all sure that he could move now even if he had the wish to. His spine and hips are cross-locked into each other.

The waitress arrives with a tray.

'But tea first,' the man says brightly, leaning back to let the waitress place her tray on the table. He then sets to work briskly pouring and spooning. Nealon waves the milk aside.

'You drink it black?'

'Yes, something you learn in prison – the milk is watered down till it's blue.'

'I'd be awake all night if I drank coffee,' the man said, pushing himself back in the seat with the cup and saucer on his lap. 'The mind racing and going nowhere.'

The cup of tea clearly pleases him. 'Nothing like it,' he says contentedly, 'nothing at all.' He lays the cup down.

'So, let us begin,' he says. 'Your name is John Francis Nealon, the only child of John and Edna Nealon, solid country folk of forty acres and a small herd of dry cattle. Better off than most though because your father had seasonal work as a forester with Coillte in those early years. According to the law of the time your mother gave up her job as a clerk in the motor-tax office when she married your father in the spring of seventy-three. A year later, when she was eight months pregnant, they took a trip to Dublin and arrived there just in time to take the full brunt of an explosion square in the broad of her back outside on Talbot Street. You were born out of that shambles, a miracle of tenacity and obstetric promptness. You spent four weeks in an incubator, registration number 0101570s, in the National Maternity Hospital being fed through the nostril until you were adjudged strong enough to be released into the care of your father who had come to Dublin with a pregnant wife but whom political circumstances and history replaced with a son. I don't how he felt about this trade-off, but we do know that he never remarried and that he gave up his job as a forester to care for you full time. The two of you lived together in that house with

124

no woman ever crossing the threshold until one night when you were eighteen years old, he came home with a few pints on him – he had been to a funeral – and went to bed with the paper and that was where you found him the following morning, dead of a brain tumour; he was in his early fifties. This was four months before your Leaving Cert. Eight weeks after his funeral, a cattle truck backed into the yard and you sold off the entire herd and rented the land out to Shevlin, your neighbour, before steadying yourself and settling to studying for your Leaving Cert which you passed with flying colours, an A in art being the high point. You spent the next few years studying painting and drawing in Galway RTC, where in a series of national competitions you distinguished yourself as the most gifted draughtsman of your generation. A unique instinct for line and shade expressed itself in an ambitious series of charcoal drawings and ink miniatures of Galway's industrial landscape, its docklands, breaker's yards, the outlying dumps and quarries. Drawn from the gothic drama of waste and deterioration, it was a young man's work of a certain type, even if it was all rendered on an intimately delicate scale. In your final year you discovered the work of Gerhard Richter and your whole practice took on a sociopolitical shading, a new theme with no previous fore-shadowing in your work. Your graduate exhibition was a startling series of ten portraits of the 1981 hunger strikers which were worked up from newspaper cuttings and docu-mentary footage. Any qualms your tutors and examiners had about your right or ability to tackle such a theme were swept aside by the technical skill and brute emotivism of your execution. You graduated with distinction and were awarded a travel scholarship which you took up immediately and promptly drank away in four months travelling in Eastern Europe; any notion of further study was put on the long finger for the time being. You returned to the city and spent the next couple of years working as a set carpenter for a theatre company and a film studio that made B-movie thrillers for the South American market, while living the full bohemian life, drinking and smoking dope and wooing young women. Three years you spent at this, knocking together stage sets from sheets of plywood and four-by-twos, the finest talent of his generation pissing himself away in dope and drink and soft chat. Your next move – this is something we can talk about, I have my own ideas on it but I'd be interested to hear how they square with your version – was to fill a rucksack, pull the door on your bedsit and take a bus across the country to our fair capital where you roomed with a loose community of artists and writers in Temple Bar. This is the period of your life that is of great interest to me. These are the years when we have to piece you together from bits and pieces of indirect evidence, from effect rather than cause. We know you did more work on independent movie productions, set design and stage building again. This went on for two to three years, no great change from what you'd been doing in the west. But gradually you drifted away from all of that and fell off the radar altogether. Around the same time an insurance scam came to the attention of the police, people falling into public-works potholes and excavations, turning up at hospitals with injuries and making large claims from the city. The whole thing was traced to a man who had leased a couple of garages across Dublin. He had no previous convictions but was felt to be behind the staging of these accidents and crashes. This is a giddy period of your life, a bit obscure and not so detailed as I would like – we can come back to it because I have questions. The next thing then is that you show up back in the home place with a woman – the fair Olwyn – and some intention apparently of making a new life for yourself. The role of the good husband and the loving father suited you for a while. That period lasted for about six years during which time you had a child and seemed to settle into a quiet life of domestic bliss. You left down your paints and brushes and got work as a first-fix carpenter, roofs and floors, making good money during the building boom. There is no evidence from this time that you did much painting or artistic work. Whatever you were doing came to an abrupt halt when you were arrested at your home in the middle of the night and charged with multiple cases of identity theft that had left several bank accounts drained of their funds. The government laboured to put a charge against you and the trial collapsed within days. The prosecution's case was a shambles. All of a sudden you were released, a free man who returned home to your own house which you found cold and empty with no sign of wife or child anywhere and which has stayed that way to this day which is why we are both here as we are now.'

And so he finishes. He spreads his hands to indicate that this is the honest truth, he has laid all his cards on the table. 'So, can we agree that I am talking to the right man?'

Nealon holds a steady gaze, his facial muscles calcified. Outside the window a steady pour of traffic moves along the quays. Beyond the traffic there is a pile of lobster pots stacked at the water's edge. Pink buoys and black pots held together with blue rope – an unlikely reminder, so near the city's centre, of its origins as a small fishing village, the invigorating roughness that lies beneath its commercial gloss and cultural pretension.

The man nods. 'Sound,' he says, 'a nod is as good as a wink.'

Nealon is shook. He has not foreseen any version of this meeting in which he would be sitting in a hotel foyer listening to a man unspooling his whole life in a way that made more sense coming from him than anything he himself had experienced. Such an unbroken telling of it makes him wonder how he has remained so fragmented and disordered to himself. How has he failed to see such continuance? This whole thing falls outside any idea of the life he knows as his own.

Nealon drifted there for a moment. When he comes to, the man is looking at him and nodding his head by way of assuring him.

'That's your story.'

'So you tell me.'

'OK, now that we have our introductions out of the way let's get on with the business at hand.'

'I'd welcome that.'

'I'll tell you what I see.'

Nealon holds up a hand in a stalling gesture. 'No, I don't give a shit what you see or think you see.'

'You might think different in a few minutes.'

'If my time is being wasted, I'm out of here.'

'Suppose I tell you that I know where your wife and child are at this moment?'

Nealon is too surprised to do an effective job of hiding the fright that sparks the length of him. It is already too late to hide it and the look on the man's face tells him he knows he has landed a telling blow.

'I have your attention now.'

'For the moment.'

'Good.'

'You can tell me where they are?'

'Yes.'

'At this moment?'

'At this moment.'

The man leans forward to pour himself another cup of tea, milk first and then two sugars, stirring with a tidy turn of the spoon. The gesture may be deliberate, a bid for dramatic pause, but Nealon prefers to believe he is ordering his thoughts.

'There is a lot to be said for boredom,' he begins, 'boredom and the vacant mind. You never know what might take root in it. Two months after retiring, I found time weighing heavy in my hands and that I was at a loss. There is only so much golf you can play and so many box sets you can watch. And the novelty was wearing off the grandkids as well; you can only put up with so much squealing and shouting through the house. Also, I was getting under the wife's feet, cramping her space and her time. I was getting in my own way as well, if the truth be told. Couldn't settle on anything, and the few projects I had set up – security consultancy – were slow in getting off the ground. Reading the paper and going for walks, whiling away the days into the evening, hours after hours. Christ, it's true what they say about men, we do a bad job of retirement, we don't have the wit or imagination to cope with all that free time. We don't know how to spend it or fill it out to a proper shape. Anyway, with all this loose time my mind began to play out over a couple of things I had come across in my working life. You know the way it is, thinking about things and mulling things over. That's what I would do towards the end of each day, a glass of that good retirement whiskey in the sitting room, my eyes closed and letting my mind range over a lot of the stuff I had known and seen on the job. Sort of blue-sky thinking . . . And that's how it came to me in the beginning. Just the faintest flickering, a few sparks and fragments scattered all over the place, winking out of the darkness at me. Nothing at first to snag the attention but glints and shards across borders and time zones, the tiniest pieces echoing to each other within my own boredom.'

Nealon shakes his head in disbelief. 'Boredom as a mystical state, a way of seeing to the heart of things. You're not going to convince me.'

'Bear with me. A few angled glimpses in the begin-ning, things sparking off each other at a distance, that's how it was for a long time. But the longer I looked the more I thought I recognised a kind of pattern, a kind of deep grammar ingrained across the whole thing that hinted at a source. To tell the truth I could hardly believe it at first. I thought it was all in my own head and that what I was looking at was the workings of my own mind and not something out there in the world itself, so to speak.'

Nealon leans forward. 'Keep talking in riddles like this and I will be out of here in two minutes.'

'OK, I'm coming to the details now. The more I looked the more I gradually became convinced that there really was something out there, something more than glitter and chance. And for a time, I contented myself with that explanation, the world was plenty big enough to throw up such structured alignments of its own accord, such things could happen. But the longer I kept looking at this thing with all its incidents and emerging patterns the more I suspected a guiding hand behind it. And it wasn't the design and structure which led me to that belief, but the evident will and desire that was clear in every line of it – those were the elements which sang highest and most clearly. Not what it was but what it aspired to be. And then, just when it appeared that the whole thing was becoming clearer it showed me something else entirely. In the deepest grammar of itself, in all its tides and rhythms I saw not so much a pattern as a signature. And it was blurred at first and it took me a long time to read it, but in the end there was no mistaking it.'

The man pulls up, obviously sensing the moment for dramatic pause. Nealon turns aside to gaze out the window at the passing traffic, his attempt at studied indifference.

'You're wasting my time,' Nealon says eventually,

placing both hands on the arms of his chair to push himself to his feet.

'Two years ago,' the man continues abruptly, 'I tracked a chartered plane coming out of Luanda. After seven hours it touched down in Lisbon and eighty-seven refugees — men, women and children with various injuries and medical conditions — were herded into a Red Cross field hospital. Does that mean anything to you?'

'Why would it mean anything to me?'

'Of course. Around the same time,' he continued, 'I followed the development of a breastfeeding programme in Lahore. I saw all the facilities and logistical backup that was put in place, the salaried nurses who were sent out into the communities to latch neonates to the breast. Does that mean anything?'

Nealon's laughter is genuine. He throws his head back, his mouth open to the ceiling. The man nods and continues.

'More details? OK, one last one. On the outskirts of Kokrobite in Ghana there is a small desalination plant owned by a local co-operative and running on German technology. It provides water to a town of about four thousand people, mostly fishermen. I watched the official opening online, the local big man raising a glass of distilled water into the light, the midday sun shining clear through it before he downed it in one to illustrate its purity. Does any of that ring a bell?'

Nealon shook his head and the man nodded.

'There's a lot more where that came from.' The man lets the silence swell out the moment. Nealon shakes his head.

'So, these projects spread all over the world, all these good works, what do they have to do with me?'

'That's what I'd like to know.'

'You think I have something to do with all these things?'

'Yes, I'm sure of it.'

'That's crazy.'

The man nods as if in agreement. 'You can sit there denying it till the cows come home but that is not going to get us very far.'

'It's difficult to plead guilty to things I have no hand, act or part in.'

'No one said anything about guilt – I was thinking in terms of stepping forward and taking a bow, taking credit.' The man leans forward on his elbows, joining his hands together in an attitude of prayer. If he closes his eyes now it will complete the picture of the father confessor, the role he has surely come here to play today, Nealon thinks. But before the thought completes itself the man continues.

'OK, have it like that. I'll tell you what we'll do. I'll give you one more and you don't have to say yes or no to it. But if you want to remain silent on this last one then I will take it that we are still in business, so to speak. How about that? Remember that silence is no admission of guilt.'

Nealon says nothing, his face set in a complete lack of expression.

'Sound so,' says the man, 'we'll continue. Less than an hour's drive away from here one hundred acres of mixed agricultural land was bought by an online bidder at a public auction over a year ago. A lot of it is good quality grazing land but some of it also is scrub and forest. The sloping topography gives it access to water supply and plenty of frontage. Initial rumours that it was going to be some sort of tourist parkland were disappointed when public notice was posted that the whole parcel would be the focus of the largest rewilding project in this part of the country. One hundred acres stripped of residual nitrates and invasive species and returned to native flora and fauna. How about that, does that ring any bell with you?'

Nealon remains rigid-faced and expressionless.

The man shakes his head in an elaborate show of fatigue. 'That's all well and good but if you keep on denying everything then we are not going to get any work done today.'

'What do you want me to do? I can't admit knowledge of something I know nothing about, that helps neither of us.'

'Let's try something else, let's go right back to the beginning and see what we know.'

'Anything would be clearer than this.'

'A couple of years ago three BMWs were stolen across the country and disappeared without trace. A year later they were found burned out along the hard shoulder of the M1. It was hardly a coincidence that they all surfaced together in the same burned-out state. But what came to light also was that a flash drive had gone missing from one of the cars, a fact that had been kept quiet from the beginning. This flash drive belonged to a Health Service Executive financial officer, and it contained the files of over two hundred and fifty patients across all sectors of the health service – can you see where this is going?'

'The HSE has been losing and misplacing medical files all over the place for the last decade.'

'True enough, theft and losses of laptops and hard drives.'

'A whole cache of files in a bog in west Galway.'

'Yes, a community warden made his reputation opening those rubbish bags.'

'OK, so all these files went missing on the HSE, where does the story go from there?'

'It goes somewhere unexpected. For the longest time no one knew that flash drive had gone missing. There were sensitive issues of professional embarrassment around the loss, enough to keep it out of the public realm. Keeping a lid on the whole thing and staying silent was thought to be the best way of dealing with it. But of course, sticking your head in the sand will only work for so long. Gradually it came to light that the insurance policies of a number of these patients listed on the flash drive had been hacked. Basically, and there is a complex series of moves behind this, they had been cashed in and the realised funds had been rerouted elsewhere. This only came to light when people tried to settle up for various medical procedures of their own, and all of a sudden they found that their policies had been bled dry.'

Nealon shakes his head. 'Medical insurance policies cannot be hacked like bank accounts, that's nonsense.'

'I know it's not that simple.'

'It's not like some digital heist, policies cannot be bled dry, as you put it.'

'You don't have to tell me, I know all the documentation – the clinical records, the invoices and receipts, the medical histories and treatment regimens that have to be falsified, the timelines that have to be synched, signatures and stamps. Whole identities have to be established, it's seriously complex. It's been an education going through this stuff, you don't have to tell me anything about it.' The man regards Nealon, spreading his hands by way of invitation. 'Do you want to take up the story yourself?'

'It doesn't take a genius to see where it's going.'

'You're right, these people now find their policies underwriting goodwill projects all over the world.'

'You could spot that ending a mile off.'

'There's no prize for that. But it's not just their policies – the names and identities, that's the crucial part.'

'Yes.'

'So far, we have tracked down twelve of them with their names and money sponsoring projects in seven different jurisdictions. It remains to be seen if that's the end of the whole thing or if more will be uncovered. There's a task force sifting through the files and sorting out how many have been hacked. Who knows what the following weeks will uncover?'

Nealon closes his eyes and pushes his head back. On any other occasion he would enjoy sitting in this chair. In fact, it is one of those chairs he has always coveted for himself, the sort with armrests and support, the type from which one might make judgements on how to put the world to rights. But that's not on his mind now; the world can wait. This discussion has gone on long enough already and the man shows no sign of addressing the topic he has come to talk about.

The thought has hardly completed itself in his mind when the man speaks again. 'How long has it been since you've seen Olwyn and the little lad?'

'Two months.'

The answer blurts from Nealon before he has a chance to pull across it. There it is: two months. As a length of time it is meaningless on this strange day. But for Nealon it is an accurate gauge of pure loss, a measure of true loneliness. And the longer this meeting goes on, the less certain he is that anything he learns here will alleviate that loneliness. He is growing convinced that there is something useless about this day. It has that ashen stain to it even in these morning hours.

This inverse light draws his mind towards Olwyn. The time of day, the unknown distance.

Where is she, what is she doing now?

If things are right in her world and running to their proper schedule Olwyn will be sitting down to a mid-morning snack somewhere. And she is most likely sitting alone. She has always preferred to eat alone; silence added something to food, she claimed. Given the choice she would seldom eat with Nealon himself, preferring to take her bowl or plate into the next room where she would eat gazing out the window with such an expression of vacant satisfaction on her face that Nealon, when he first encountered it, marvelled that someone so intuitively smart as

Olwyn could erase so completely every trace of intelligence from her face. How was such self-annulment possible? How could you slip from your own attention so completely? What links to the self were undone in such moments?

Two military transits roll by outside the window, spray flying in their wake, their diesel-engine roar vibrating heavily.

'And, of course *this* was bound to happen,' the man says.

'That's the second time you've said that.'

The man nods without taking his eye from the street. 'It is and I'll say it again if anyone wants to listen.' He turns to Nealon. 'This terrorist thing was as predictable as night following day. Any clown could see it coming.'

'No one here seems to have seen it.'

'It has happened before.'

'Not here it hasn't.'

'No, not here right enough. But it seems to have passed people by – not so long ago, Russia hit Estonia with a massive denial-of-service attack that took down their travel infrastructure and telecom network. Just a friendly reminder that they were keeping an eye on them and a not-so-friendly hint that they should make more of an accommodation with their ethnic Russian population.'

'This seems more than a jerk on the leash.'

'Maybe, but anyone not seeing it coming can only be wilfully blind.'

'You're saying we drew it on ourselves?'

'Of course we did. The way we have manoeuvred ourselves into a corner . . . there was an article in the *Guardian* a while back.'

'There's always an article in the *Guardian*.'

'A long article about the Shannon stopover and prisoners.'

'Yes, I read it, it was a ball of smoke, beginning middle and end.'

'You think so?'

'Of course it was, craw-thumping and sermonising, every line of it.'

'It had the ring of truth for me, I have to say.'

'There wasn't a shred of evidence in it.'

'And you need evidence?'

'It's a serious charge, that the country is complicit in the rendition and torture of prisoners, that's about as serious as it gets. The least that writer could have offered was some verification. And his indictment runs deeper than that. He claims the whole house is rotten from the ground up and that a part of our economy rests on the broken bodies of those detainees who are being shipped through our airports to unmarked sites for enhanced interrogation. Apparently we've turned a blind eye and traded our souls for a mess of biotech and IT components. But he produces no documents, no recorded conversations, no legal instrument he can point to.'

'And unless you see you will not believe.'

'I need more than a two-thousand-word screed in the *Guardian*.'

'And what would convince you?'

'Evidence, I said. Testimony, interviews, pictures. It's not too much to ask.'

'Not if you want to look foolish.'

'When did evidence make us look foolish, when did we stop looking for that sort of verification?'

'You're forgetting who wrote that article,' the man said.

'No, I'm not forgetting who wrote the article. I know his work, I know his name and reputation.'

'If you know his name, you know it's evidence enough.'

'No one has that kind of saintly clout.'

The man shakes his head with something next to pity. 'This is the man who was right about Blair in Iraq, he was right about Snowden and he was right on David Kelly. What more do you want? And as for sermonising, you're forgetting that he did six months in an al-Qaeda prison in Mali. So, this isn't from the pulpit, this is from the Cross. And did I mention that his first trade was as a constitutional lawyer?'

'So, his word is gospel?'

'He doesn't need anything more than his own signature.'

'That's the way the world's gone?'

'You can turn that question into a statement and that will bring you abreast of things.'

I didn't know I was that old, Nealon thinks. I come from a different age.

The man gives a tired smile. 'And he assures us that it's going to get worse. The next dump of documents will have all the evidence you're looking for. It will back up everything he has said in that article.'

Nealon suffers an intense rush of vertigo, his whole being surging upwards and leaving some shell of himself in the chair. He did not expect this encounter to swell out into the great stories of the age. Blair, Iraq, Snowden, al-Qaeda – these names belong to a different order of consequence, a sharper climate altogether. Someplace higher and wider, where the air is thinner and serious things come unmoored. There is nothing hospitable in that realm for Olwyn, Cuan and himself. Nealon wants something simpler from this moment – to put his own world in order, everything and everyone where they should be, and not have to heed the great stories arcing through the blue light over his head.

His disbelief has got the better of him now. It sweeps through him in a buoyant surge, as if the world were instantly stripped of some essential ballast. This is one of those moments when he could do with laying his hand on Cuan's head, just to steady himself.

Unless he could feel he would not believe.

'It's odd to hear you putting forward such a staunch defence of this country, you of all people.'

'I'm full of surprises.'

'I would have thought that you would see such a charge as entirely likely if not probable.'

'I would have thought that my experience makes the case for the supremacy of evidence. What brings you here?' Nealon counters suddenly. 'What is it about you that enables you to see these things so clearly?'

'I've come here in good faith,' the man says. 'I have no interest in coming here to sneer or taunt.'

'Boredom – the mind's restful play – did not pull all this together, there is something clawing at you.' For the first time Nealon has the slight impression that he might be prising open some of this man's defences. 'No boredom

I have ever heard of constructs something like this. What were you looking for?'

'There is a terrible lack of imagination out there,' the man says. 'A whole world reacting to circumstance and stimulus. But no new ideas, no new initiatives. And that's why I came here, to see for myself. Was I going to see a true visionary or some crude ideologue?'

'And how's that search going for you?'

'I believe I'm on the right track. Your name is writ deep into this, even if for the moment I cannot say why. And do you want to know something else? Even if you are guilty, even if you are responsible for the theft of all those insurance policies and the misery it caused those people, I would still think it a good thing to have you walking the earth. It is a more dangerous place with you in it, that's for sure, but it is also a more complete one.'

'It sounds like you are willing to pay a high price for having someone like that doing the rounds.'

The man gestures towards the news on the TV. 'Who knows how this threat will go down. They might be glad to reach for your template when they have to put things back together.'

'You give me too much credit, put too much faith in me.' There is a note of levity in Nealon's voice now. Part of him is enjoying the back and forth of it all.

'I don't think so, I'm not a man who loses the run of himself so easily.'

'So I saw all this?' Nealon gestures to the broad day with all its menace. 'My burning bush revealed this whole day with all the soldiers in the streets and checkpoints along every road. That was my vision and apparently I have constructed some world against this same day. Is that what you are telling me?' Nealon pulls up. He senses himself about to tip into a needling sarcasm and he does not want that.

'We can sit around picking holes in this for as long as you like; that's easy but there's no prizes for that. Admiration is the proper response. The breadth and the scope of it, how its ambition will heal and seal those flaws. That's what we should be doing. We shouldn't be small and mean in the face of it.'

A family has entered the foyer. They look disoriented, baffled. Eventually, after some dithering, they take up the seats along the wall opposite. Young parents with two children, a toddler girl and a boy who is around the same age as Nealon's.

'What's your lad's name? Conan?'

'Cuan.'

'Cuan, I beg your pardon.'

'What do you want to know for?' If I don't get a grasp of this right now, this whole encounter will run away from me, Nealon thinks. Too much blather and bonhomie, now it is time he gave me something. 'I'm still waiting,' Nealon says. 'I've come here in good faith, but so far all I'm getting is some tinfoil-hat global conspiracy. Either I hear something right now or I walk.'

I should have kept my mouth shut, Nealon berates himself. That whining note in my voice.

The man nods. 'You're right, we shouldn't forget the real reason we're here. It must have been tough returning

143

to that house with no wife or child anywhere, that can't have been easy. And then hanging around a full week, wandering from room to room, picking up the phone and putting it down, scrolling through it for messages you might have missed and so on. Tough days. Driving here then with the phone beside you on the passenger seat but no peep out of it, not a blink or a chirp. That couldn't have been easy either.'

'Whether I found it easy or not is beside the point. I want to know where my wife and child are. So, for the last time, if you do not want me walking out of this room right now, I suggest that you start talking . . .'

The man leans back in the seat as if suddenly conscious of how precise he needs to be. There are finical margins here, losses and gains within a hair's breadth of each other. For the first time Nealon sees that he is slightly hesitant, a single, faltering beat behind where he should be. This worries him. This is not how he needs him to be. He should be confident, sure of himself and what he has come here to say. This hesitation adds nothing solid to the exchange.

'Don't go all shy on me now,' Nealon urges, 'tell me you have more than some bullshit story about a worldwide conspiracy.'

'It would be less mysterious if it were a conspiracy.'

'My wife and child are all I care about.' The completeness of that statement takes Nealon by surprise. Apparently, some deep part of him was not aware that he had made such a commitment.

The man nods. 'Fair enough, my guess is that you

thought Olwyn and Cuan stayed on in the house after you were detained, am I right?'

'That was our home.'

'It was, and in your own mind you were going to return to it, and they would meet you at the door. You were going to gather them into your arms and pick up where you left off. Am I right?'

'It's more complex than that, but yes, I did expect them to be there.'

The man remains silent and something in Nealon shies away from the moment. 'You're telling me that they moved somewhere else.'

'Yes, that's exactly what I am telling you. They moved out of that house within a month of your detention. You didn't know?'

Nealon does not reply. For the moment there is nothing he can say across the fissure that has opened in his belly. The certainty that his wife and child were safe at home was one of the things that steadied him during those long nights in prison. It was the solid place to which his mind travelled after lockdown, his mind playing out across those miles of darkness to the house where, after Cuan went to bed, Olwyn was surely doing those evening chores to set up the next day. There was something devotional about the way he envisioned her laying out Cuan's school clothes for the morning, making his lunch and setting the breakfast things on the kitchen table. But now, to have that assurance destroyed is a shock he has no protection against.

'So where has she been, where has she been taken to?'

'No one took her anywhere, that's not how it worked.'

'So, I repeat, where is she?'

'People reached out,' the man said. 'She was lonely and afraid in the house after you were put away, the middle of winter with no one around, those long nights.'

'She would have told me, she never mentioned anything about being afraid.'

'I'm telling you now.'

'Who reached out?'

'They are both safe and happy.'

'That's not what I asked and if . . .'

The foyer is filled with a sudden thumping pressure. Nealon realises that he has been aware of it building for the last couple of moments. It's coming from outside the building, a tremendous buffeting force hammering off the windows. The whole space throbs with concussive noise. A helicopter lowers itself down over the dock basin, flattening the surface of the water, pushing down on it. It hangs in the grey light, so weighty and improbable at this distance that it consumes all astonishment in the room. With all its military decals and camouflage, it looks like something lowered from a nightmare. The whole room watches it hold for a long moment in the slanting rain before it eventually rises and banks off into the grey light, disappearing eventually into its own distance, the foyer left in throbbing silence.

The man raises his hand towards the grey light. 'They're a sign of the times, those yokes. Would you believe that not so long ago this country owned more helicopters per head of population than any other nation on earth? Can you believe that, helicopters?'

What is he talking about, Nealon wonders. How can his mind take such sudden swerves?

'Of course you missed some of that,' the man concedes, 'being inside and all. But that's what it was like when we all had money, second homes and the sky overhead black with helicopters.'

'We lost the run of ourselves all right.'

'What did we think we were doing, who did we think we were? Did we think we were now so finely evolved as a people that we could defy gravity also and ascend en masse into heaven, a nation of intoxicated angels? Of course, we thought we were looking at the end of history also – full employment, emigration reversed and a ceasefire in Northern Ireland – it was hard not to see all that as history raising a white flag, bowing out.'

The man has such a ready way with languid sermonising that he has no need of any response. Nevertheless, Nealon cannot let it go. 'I couldn't say what it was all about, some things defy all reasoning.'

'You can sing that; some things are a law unto themselves. They have nothing to do with the normal run of things, no matter how outlandish the normal run of things might be.'

There is certainly nothing normal about this day, Nealon thinks. It feels like a cessation of all that passes for normal. And what's passing here in this foyer is not time itself but that which time leaves in its wake when it departs.

Nealon feels something in him leaning towards the man. For the first time he is aware of just how oppressive his bulk is, the episcopal spread of it and how in some indefinable way it has now become Nealon's burden also. Another of his gifts, this transference of load which lightens him with each passing moment while Nealon sinks deeper into his chair under the sheer weight.

'Anyway, as I was saying. It was your signature I recognised at the centre of the whole thing, the very same MO working towards an admittedly different end. But recognisable all the same, the same stamp to the same moves.'

'So we're back to that again?'

'Only for a moment. But what I can't see was you in it. It was your signature all right, that was clear enough, but the sense I got from it wasn't of you but someone else.'

'I don't follow.'

The man nods, fully involved in the story again. He steeples his hands in front of him. 'So, I understand the architecture of the whole thing, the grandeur and ambition of the entire construct. But not the motive behind it. What is it all about? What does it hope to achieve? Is it some noble enterprise – as I hope it is – or something else entirely? Something squalid and rotten to the core.'

I'm lost here, Nealon admits. It takes him a moment to realise that he has not spoken out loud.

'All these projects spread all over the world – breastfeeding clinics, literacy programmes, a rewilding project, even a small bank – what do they all mean, how do they come together in any meaningful way?'

Nealon is tempted to own up to his own mystification, but he cannot properly do that now. There is power in the man's conviction, a faith he will not let go of.

Nealon's attention wanders and he is now looking at the TV once more. In the length of time they have been sitting and talking, the news cycle has come a full three-sixty and is back again at the footballer scoring those goals. This second time around, Nealon has a clearer appreciation of his ability. The same shower of goals once more but not as a spliced montage of different games and competitions. Now they come in a fluent cascade of skill and vision, a unified expression of something like greed. He is a genuine talent, Nealon concedes, he might indeed be the one.

'We could go back to the starting point to begin with, right back to the beginning, that might give us a handle on it.'

'We're long past that,' Nealon sighs, 'we're not going to learn anything new from a couple of burnt-out cars on the side of a motorway.'

'No, not that far, that's all staging. The proper beginning lies in insurance.'

'You're ahead of me there,' Nealon says.

'The way I see it, the whole thing begins with the insurance policies or, more accurately, the idea of insurance. Somewhere along the way you saw those policies, you saw those lives and the value they put on them set down on paper and it did something to you. There it was in pounds, shillings and pence, the price these people had put on themselves and their lives, their hedge against the world and all it brings with it – misfortune, accident and illness, life itself, the whole lot. And that's what you could not stomach, you took offence in some way or other that I cannot fathom. And the longer you looked at it the more you thought, "This sickens me, these little lives with their stunted souls, their caution and anxiety, their lack of courage and imagination." And that was the moment you seized on their names and IDs – the instruments of possession – and loosed those ghosts all over the world.'

Nealon shakes his head. 'There's an extraordinarily complex series of manoeuvres between that idea and making it work in the real world. Who has access to that kind of expertise and privileged knowledge?'

'Let's not cod ourselves, we know you have both reach and influence, we can go into your history if you want, those years in Dublin.'

'If I had that kind of reach, I would do something else with it other than what you're telling me. I don't see the point of it all.'

The man nods. 'It took me a while to see it as well and I am still not sure I have a proper grasp of it either.'

The man comes to an unexpected halt and Nealon sees something like confusion cross his face. Nealon is intrigued.

'Give it your best shot,' he urges quietly. 'All this thinking and joining dots, show me where it leads.' Nealon has his own questions, but he is not so sure that they will be answered here. Nevertheless, he will probe this moment. He is certain that there is nothing for him outside of this encounter. Anything the world has to offer him today is here in this space.

'The bit I can't make out . . .' the man begins before faltering and switching a lingering gaze to the middle distance. 'You,' he says suddenly. 'The bit I can't make out is you.' In a sudden push of confidence, he surges on. 'I see you everywhere in this, every line and corner of it, every shadow it throws is yours, your light and hand in every part of it. It all points to you and yet why? Why you?'

'I've said it's not me, I thought we had moved on from that.'

The man shakes his head. 'Let's ignore that for a moment and keep going.'

'I don't see how that helps, but if it does, fine, keep going.'

'What's behind it all? I can understand a man wanting to build something. But most men settle for a family or business or suchlike – their own little world with wife and kids, home and hearth. But this is a much bigger project, its ambition is spread a lot wider. This is the whole world we're talking about, and I want to know why.'

Nealon does not react; there is no need, this is going nowhere.

'Your mother's death, is that what's behind the whole thing?'

Nealon clenches his whole being. He would not want any vulnerable part of him to take hold of this moment or cross the space between them.

'Is that's what's behind all this,' the man persists, 'the mother you never knew and the way she died? Her last moments in this world steeped in rage and violence. Is that where this wrath comes from?'

Nealon senses that the man is now going for the jugular. 'Why wrath?' he says. 'I thought this was all about good works, all these sainted projects.'

'Yes, good works, there's no denying that. But there's something else at the bottom of it, the tone of the whole thing, like an indictment, or malice . . .' He completes the thought in silence before speaking again suddenly. 'Of course, you never knew your mother.'

'That's common knowledge.'

'Dead before you were born?'

'Not quite, but near as.'

'It's like the world broke faith with you before you drew breath.'

'It didn't smile on me, if that's what you mean.'

'A mother is not too much to ask for.'

'I wouldn't have thought it was an extravagant dream. Not in any reasonable world.'

'It must be hard to be at home anywhere after that.'

'I never gave it much thought.'

'So, is that what this whole thing is – one big act of revenge?'

'Revenge on what?'

The man thinks for a moment before speaking carefully. 'Nothing,' he says, 'nothing at all.'

'More riddles.'

'No, a world so wretched it can only be redeemed by an act of revenge.'

'I have no answer to that,' Nealon says. He spreads his hands in pure bafflement.

The moment may have passed and even if he is not wholly sure to whose advantage it has gone, he chances a full breath.

The man seems content to move on.

'Even if that is the case – even if it is just some act of revenge – there is still a lot to admire. It took me a while to draw all the pieces together but once the outline came into focus, I saw it as a thing of beauty. My favourite is the breastfeeding clinic.'

'You liked that?'

'I did, there was real imagination there, real wit also. The way you had the whole thing up and running before anyone twigged. All those babies latched on to their mothers' breasts with all the financing signed and sealed before anyone realised. Staff contracted and an outreach programme in place, supplies laid in, the whole lot. Jesus, it would be hard trying to pull the funding from that, all those babies looking up at you with their big eyes. There was some sort of literacy programme attached to it as well, if I remember.'

'If you say so.'

'I do say so. And of course, there is something miraculous about the whole thing also, the way it transmutes all those policies hedging against illness and injury into good works.'

'I hope it's of some comfort to those who have paid for it.'

'I wonder. How much comfort would you get if you were now in stage four cancer with your sixth bout of chemo and you knew that your name had authorised that plane and the transportation of those refugees. Would it bring you any comfort? Or the woman who sponsored the desalination project – what sort of consolation will it bring her? Will it fill the hole in her being where her womb used to be, will she think it a fair exchange? Because that's what we're talking about here, the real suffering at the bottom of this.'

Nealon does not reply. He allows his own stone face to hold for a long moment and anyone watching him from a distance would find it difficult to believe that he is scrabbling frantically behind it.

The man continues. 'That was probably the finest aspect of the whole thing – all the elements it brought together. From cradle to grave. It was easy to follow from that prompt – how those babies, once they'd had enough of mother's milk, would go to the next stage of picking up their books and pens, learning to read and write. It's easy to write the next chapter.'

'A narrative arc, you're saying.'

'It's not as smooth as that.'

'No?'

'The two mercenaries ransomed from the basement outside Baghdad, I'm still not sure how they fit into it. I followed their plane and watched them touch down in Büchel Air Base with their copy of the *Herald Tribune* held up in front of them, like they were in a Hollywood movie, grinning away like two asses. One of them is from Monaghan, I believe, an ex-legionnaire?'

'He could well be.'

'He's still in the National Rehabilitation Hospital. I don't know how they're going to put the soles back on his feet. They'll probably have to graft skin from his arse.'

'I'm sure he's happier there than in that basement.'

'The scope of it and the attention to detail – that's

what appeals to me. There is something there for everyone – weeping mothers and macho heroes and bleeding hearts, eco-mystics and breastfeeding fascists. Catholic in the broadest sense, everyone has a place in it.'

'So you say.'

'Everyone but the victims, that is.'

Nealon senses the provocation, another deliberate thrust on the man's part to prod a response out of him. He will have to do better than that.

'And that's the mistake you made,' the man continues, his voice tailing away in disappointment. He leans forward and Nealon is surprised to see for the first time something like real anger creasing his face. He holds his thumb and forefinger apart a fraction.

'You were that close,' he says, 'that close.'

'That close to what?'

'That fucking close! The great work of art that would have been the envy of anyone with spirit and imagination – it was within touching distance. Even those who were caught up and used by it would have forgiven you – I'm sure of that! Given time they would have reconciled themselves to their own part in it and contribution. It would have been their proud boast. But . . .' And his voice tails away on a note of regret that startles Nealon.

'I've let the world down,' Nealon says.

'That failure of imagination at the end! The tone of the whole thing as it now stands. You couldn't let it speak for itself. Instead, you fell to cheap sermonising and craw-thumping. And mark my words, in the final analysis that is what people will object to – you failed the work itself and their suffering. This is what will piss them off and turn them against you. They will have had high hopes for you and themselves in this work. All their avatars are out there in some adjacent world and existence, in some metaphysical realm they would have eventually assented to but which you contaminated with self-righteous guff. However smart it all looks – all those prisoners ransomed and those refugees delivered – they will see it as the work of a creeping Jesus, not a true redeemer. You see, that's the flaw, the whole thing is too easily interpreted as vindictive ridicule.'

'What can I say? I'm sorry everyone is so disappointed.'

The man is shaken by his own passion. There was such clumsy rawness to his outburst that it is clear he has seldom lost the run of himself like this. He now leans towards Nealon with thumb and forefinger touching each other, his face avid. 'That close,' he repeats ardently, 'that fucking close.'

'It sounds to me like there's no pleasing you. You want it but you didn't want it.'

'Yes, a tough audience, I'll give you that. But remember, they have paid dearly, there is real suffering at the bottom of this.'

A long moment now stretches between them, some bitter sediment has entered the meeting. In Nealon's peripheral vision a clutch of businessmen and women have drifted in from an adjoining space and are having some sort of stand-up meeting in the middle of the floor. In their suits and shirts, they have about them the sheen of miracle workers, men and women who juggle values and probability, the kind of work that puts them within a hair's breadth of divinity. Six or seven of them now, gathered in circle formation, each apparently taking their turn to speak.

What could be so important on a day like this when everything is beside the point? What could be so pressing?

'But at least, those unmoored souls are out there doing something to better the world while the rest of us are sitting around on our arses. Your plague of souls unleashed on the world, skimming over borders and time zones to plant their pale flags on these new territories. Their new template coming to being in a new Eden, a new sovereignty prior to politics . . .' The man spreads his hands as if further elaboration is pointless.

Nealon has heard enough for the moment. He pushes himself to his feet with both hands. 'I'll be back in a minute,' he says, heading across the floor. 'I'm going to see a man about a dog.'

There is piped music in the bathroom, all murmur and trailing chimes. Single notes sift down from the suspended ceiling through a distant drone, blending with the pine scent of the place. He recognises *Music for Airports* after a moment. Someone has given this some thought, the bathroom as a dedicated place of respite. All this determined tranquillity is offset by the fluorescent light ringing off the tiled floor and ceiling.

Nealon's reflection in the mirror convinces him that he's made a fundamental error. It is as clear to him now as a kink running through the looping progress of this whole morning: he has neglected a crucial question; it has fled his mind so subtly that he has missed it. Put simply, the first law of negotiations – keep your eye on what the other fella wants. Or to put it another way – what exactly does he possess that makes him have such a lure for the man in the foyer? It has to be something of real worth, something of consequence to have drawn this man into the light.

But what exactly is it? Is it as simple as an admission from Nealon that he is the source of that crazed, salvific construct? Would that satisfy him? Would that get him to state clearly where Olwyn and Cuan are?

He throws cold water on his face and flinches in the cold rush of nerves and synapses leaping alive. Electricity cascades down his shoulders. The shock of it returns him to Olwyn again, so he takes his phone out to check if there have been any calls or messages.

He pauses for a moment before switching on his mobile – this might not be wise.

It is not.

There haven't been any messages, as he knew there would not be. Those radial lines across his cheekbones deepen the expression of cluelessness his face sometimes relaxes to. It takes a long moment gazing at his own reflection in this merciless mirror to bury his disappointment.

When he returns to the foyer the man is scrolling through his own phone. 'I'm surprised the network is still going. I would have thought a major terrorist threat would target communications.' He stows the phone inside his jacket. 'The whole country gone dark, not even smoke signals, that's how I thought these things were done.' He gestures towards the television. 'It just came up, the first casualties being taken to hospital. Some sort of respiratory thing, parents with three children in intensive care in the Midlands. There's also a report that two communities on the east coast have been evacuated to elevated sites along main roads. They are waiting for more details.'

'That's more than disruption, it's not a denial-of-service attack.'

'It's a lot more direct — something airborne, they're speculating.'

On the TV screen, civilians are being helped into the backs of army trucks and buses by masked soldiers. The camera dwells on the older people and young mothers who are vainly trying to prevent their own panic from spreading to those children in their arms or being led by the hand. Driving wind and rain adds an extra scourge to the whole scene.

The man's mood has lifted somewhat. These latest developments, with their sense of something coherent happening at last, have brought a brightness to him now that is almost apologetic.

'It's a pity it has to be like this,' he says keenly, 'the two of us meeting this way. It would have been better under different circumstances. We could have had some craic the two of us.' He motions to the television with a fat hand. 'Do you follow the football?'

'Not soccer,' Nealon says, 'the other game.'

'I remember, you had county trials, I believe?'

'Yes.'

'Good, but not good enough, as they say.'

'Something like that.'

'It will be hard to call the championship this year. Your own crowd will be there or thereabouts?'

'Probably, we have a habit of faltering at the last.'

The man smiles and draws his hand across his forehead. 'Ye're martyrs for it all right, everyone of ye marked with the sign of faith. But no doubt you'll be there again come September with yere straw hats and red faces, chasing nurses and national schoolteachers in Coppers.'

'You follow it yourself?'

He purses his lips in mock distaste. 'No, it's all small ball where I come from. We'd have no truck with that other burlesque. Cork will be the team to watch this year, they might do the double.'

'It will be hard to listen to them if they do.'

'No harder than usual,' he counters drily. 'Incidentally, you very nearly ended up there yourself?'

'Ended up where?'

'In Cork Prison. The first warrant served for your arrest was in Cork and you were very lucky you were not put on remand there. Cork Prison would put horns on you, that's for sure. You were better off in Castlerea. How did you find it?'

Nealon shrugged and looked out the window. 'I read several volumes of *National Geographic* and I put on two stone.'

'So I see. You'll never get back to your proper fighting weight now – too far gone, too long in the tooth.'

The man grows pensive. Nealon is struck again by the ease with which he shifts mood. One moment all jovial bonhomie, the next, deep consideration with no discernible switch between.

'I often think,' the man mused, 'that there is not one among us who wouldn't benefit from a dose of it.'

'A dose of what?'

'A dose of prison, a prison sentence. In other countries people do national service or community work but my own belief is that everyone should do a year's solitary in a single cell with a barred window, no distractions and each man forced to look into his own soul . . . I'm convinced I'd thrive on it myself.'

'That's a poor picture of humanity, some would say.'

'They can say what they like. I've lived long enough and seen enough to have no illusions on that score. But of course, the paradox is that it is transgressors like yourself who shape the world with great sins and bring the law into being. The world owes you a debt, Nealon – without the likes of you, right and wrong would not be so immediately obvious.'

The man sits back then as if his point is conclusive and moreover that Nealon should be grateful for having it pointed out to him.

'I doubt that many feel so indebted,' Nealon says.

'No one is likely to come up to you and thank you for your efforts so there's no point in waiting around for that kind of applause. If you are waiting, you'd better make sure you have a good soft cushion under your arse because you will be there a while. They owe you, make no mistake about that, but not in any way you might be glad of.'

The statement begs a question, but Nealon stays silent. He is fully taken up with the rhythm and cadences of the man's speech. This man could talk for Ireland, no theme is foreign to him. His smile now broadens to a lurid grin. Finally, Nealon cracks. He spreads his hands.

'OK, how do they owe me?'

'Of course they owe you. Arrest and prolonged detention and then a botched investigation that collapsed a trial. You couldn't make it up.'

'It's all in the past.'

'And now this new gamble.'

'So I'm a gambler now?'

'That's how it looks. Ripping off insurance companies – which of us has not wanted to be that man? It's pure Jesse James. And that's your gamble – that the world will see it that way too and, once it gets over its shock, it will assent to it and come out clapping its hands.'

'It's asking a lot.'

'Yes, that's the risk. It's not enough that you're stripping these people of their identities and financial peace of mind but that you do so in a way that pours scorn on everything they've worked for and believe in. It's like a Redemptorist missionary's sermon with an added note of contempt.' He holds his hands up in a claim to innocence. 'Don't get me wrong, I'm not saying that's what you did – I believe your motives are a lot higher – but I'm saying that could be their read on it.' He leans back in the seat then, leaving the floor to Nealon. When he does not respond the man continues. 'But why would you go to such lengths? That's the question I want answered, that's the real prize.'

'You still want me to say something that will put my neck in a noose.'

'Let's say I want you to theorise, that's what you are good at.'

'I always saw myself as having a practical turn of mind.'

'That's not how history tells it. We both know you made your name as a theoretician in a world where certain things got done by hook or by crook. You saw consequences before they properly revealed themselves – that was your reputation, that was what made you valuable. The ideas man who looked to the future.'

'There's no use trying to flatter me or appeal to my vanity. I'm well beyond that now.'

'Of course. But there was always more to you than the pale theoretician, you were a more complex proposition than that. People still talk about the night you dropped Corcoran with the cattle prod.'

Nealon shakes his head slowly. The man throws his hands up in a dramatic show of mock horror. 'Don't tell me it's not true, don't take the good out of it.'

'You're talking riddles again.'

'You're too modest. The night you came down the stairs with Olwyn slung over your shoulder, wrapped in a duvet. And the cattle prod taped to your wrist. How many did you drop at the bottom of the stairs? I know Froglight went down – he denied it afterwards but there was no mistaking the limp he had for a few weeks after that. And Corcoran as well – he admits it now, but it took him years to do so. He was only a local capo at the time but now that he has his own jurisdiction, he likes telling the story against himself – look how far I've come, so to speak, how much I've learned. It's always good for a laugh. But he was a worried man for a while, he couldn't get it up for a full week after. Besides, the two women who were there that night saw it all and spread the word so there was no use denying it. And you threw her into the back of a Honda Civic and took off across the country in the middle of the night, never to be seen again. That impressed a whole lot of people – what you did and how you did it. The feeling was that if you had the balls enough to attempt that kind of thing, if you wanted it that bad, then you should be left to it. Anyway, the whole thing made your name. Did you know there was a handful of post office robberies shortly after that – young lads using pimped cattle prods?'

'This is all news to me.'

'Oh, you inspired a generation. It was quite a party trick there for a while, lads dropping each other with cattle prods just to see how much voltage they could take. But more importantly, it says something about the man you were then that a story like that could stick, true or false. When was the last time you saw Cranly?'

Nealon shakes his head.

'Your old mentor, I met him about a year ago. I was in St James's and he spotted me coming down the corridor. He put the hand out, the big shake hands, you'd swear to god we were old butties the two of us. He was in to see one of his grandchildren who was laid up with tonsillitis. He told me he was after getting a heart attack and he had pulled back on a lot of things. But he was full of advice – did I carry an aspirin with me? He swore by it – he opened up his wallet and showed me the piece of silver foil down in the corner of it. You'd have enjoyed the whole thing if you were there.'

'It sounds like fun all right.'

'You know he was our source for years?'

'I can't say I knew that.'

'I took the call that day he got shot coming out of the garage. It came over the radio and luckily I was only five minutes away. I swung the squad car around and there he was on the kerb, sitting with his jacket pulled around him, clutching his ribs. He shouted towards me, "Sit down here and look like a cop." I am a cop, I said. "Well then look more like one." Do you want me to take a look at that? "Why, are you a doctor?" No. "Well then why would you want to look at it?" He took a few shallow breaths. I could see what was on his mind. "I'm fed up of this, I can tell you . . . this is the third fucking time." And sure enough the boys scoped around again in the Primera to take a look but thought better about having a second go at him when they saw me. We watched them drive off.

'He was under our protection from then on and our best source of intelligence in that whole community. He showed me the plans for the Athy robbery a year before it was pulled off. All your work, he said, the schematics, the timelines, all the tools and hardware, the disposal and laundering – the whole lot laid out on four sheets of drawing paper. He was very proud of that – you'd swear to god he was showing me his child's homework. It looks good on paper, I said, but will it work in the real world? He rolled up the sheets with a big grin on his face and said he was sure it would, but not in the way you might think. He was halfway to the door when I said, And why should I turn a blind eye to it? He waved the roll of paper at me, This is me lending a helping hand. You can thank me later. Then, instead of working the plans himself he sold them across the city to Lawlor's crowd for an upfront fee and then sat back and watched them get torn apart by the Provisionals when they came looking for a cut of the proceeds. That was all your idea, he said proudly, your counsel, as he put it. You showed him how to do it and then showed him why he shouldn't do it. There was a bigger prize, you said, all you needed was patience. And that's how you made your reputation. You had an eye for the bigger prize.'

'Jesus, no shortage of stories.'

'I've a million of them, don't go short.'

It takes a moment of focused will on Nealon's part for him to wipe all this from his mind. His attention is drawn to the two soldiers who have taken up position at opposite corners of the street outside. One stands beneath the neon sign of the hotel and the other on the corner opposite with a clear view down the two converging streets away from the docks. They are watchful, arms at port. This is the patrol formation perfected by the British Army through those long years of moving through Belfast streets.

166

'The boys are out, they're taking this serious,' he observes.

'A maximum-security alert. Apparently, there are gradations of terror.'

'I would have thought it came in only one shade.'

'The Yanks have a better take on this kind of thing,' the man continues, gesturing towards the soldiers. 'They do these things better. I was over there a few years ago and I was amazed to see that their terror comes colour-coded – yellow to red – an idiot's guide, so to speak. It's up there on billboards at train stations and airports and so on. You know immediately how to respond, what your responsibilities are. Of course, that's the great thing about the Yanks: their paranoia, the faith of their fathers. Childish enough as faiths go, but sharp enough to keep you on your toes. I often think we could learn something from them. Maybe we're not paranoid enough, we take things too much for granted, that's what's wrong with us.'

'Speaking of faith, a Redemptorist mission, you said, that's a pre-decimal reference if ever there was one.'

'Something you wouldn't be familiar with.'

Nealon shakes his head. 'No,' he said, 'you're forgetting I was an altar boy; I remember them well. They would arrive in our village towards the end of autumn when the turf and hay was saved and tell us of the delights of hell. Hell was very close to their hearts.'

The man waved his hand dismissively. 'That was the Vatican II stuff, the milk-and-water version. You're too young to have got the full fire-and-brimstone treatment.'

But Nealon's memory is clear on this. Those weeks

after Samhain when the clocks went back and the nights began to tighten down to full winter darkness. The whole parish would make its way to the church outside the village in which men sat on the left and women to the right listening to those passionate preachers. And this was a different age, a time when men wore suits and topcoats and the older among them at the back of the church would spread their handkerchiefs on the floor for fear of scuffing the knees of their trousers on the cold stone.

Nealon remembers well the authority with which these missionaries took to the altar, sure of their message and their audience. Some of them would ignore the pulpit altogether and mic-in-hand command the space like cabaret artistes. He remembers also the night a young priest raised the monstrance from the altar as one would heft a large trophy bone, and held it aloft over his head before feigning suddenly to throw it in a lunging arc over the heads of the congregation to the back of the church. And like every other soul in attendance Nealon's head turned involuntarily to where surely the sacred totem had crashed through the glass partition, shattering the sanded image of the Holy Ghost as radiant dove. When he'd turned back, the young priest was calmly replacing the monstrance back on the altar, soaking up the shock throughout the congregation with a fine sense of drama. He went on then to clarify his point about how much more sacred the person sitting beside them was compared to the sacred instrument he had feigned to throw. And how scandalous would it have been if he had thrown it? Surely it would make headlines. *Priest Hurls Sacred Vessel in Church; Vatican Inquiry.* But how much more offensive to God if we sought injury to one or other of our neighbours? Were not those to the left and right of us more valuable in the sight of God than any chalice or monstrance? Did He not dwell in our neighbour and was not an injury to him an injury also to God?'

Nealon is surprised at how clearly the whole thing comes back to him now. He remembers being impressed at the time by the analogy. Yes, God was present in our neighbour, he affirmed that night; we are all brothers and sisters in Christ; the world is one. His father was not so easily convinced. Pulling out of the car park an hour later he commented drily

'Those lads know damn all, but you have to listen to thunder.'

'What will it profit a man if he gains the world but loses his soul?' the man now says. 'That was one of their favourite themes. It was finely chosen, no doubt about it, especially in my part of the world where people hadn't a pot to piss in. It was no hard job to turn your eyes to heaven when there was so little of this world you could call your own.'

Before Nealon can answer, the man's gaze is drawn to the plasma screen on the wall. It's pushing on to midday, RTÉ News is about to come on. The receptionist behind her desk reaches out with the remote to turn up the sound.

How come the TV signal has not been jammed, Nealon wonders. Wouldn't that be the first thing you'd do if you were taking over the world? Shut the whole lot down – all satellites, transmitters and telecom masts, all the ways a country has of talking to itself, the country going dark across all spectrums, nothing but a black smudge on the sea when seen from the air. Why hasn't that happened? Is it so difficult?

The man is taking a great interest in the screen, leaning forward with his elbows on his knees. Looking at the broad shoulders and the rigid set of his jaw, Nealon has an idea that all the men in his life have gathered to this foyer and coalesced into this single being before him. He sees his father – that focused concentration and heedlessness to all around him. And there's Shevlin also – that constant angling for an edge. And all those bulky cattle jobbers who made their way into his yard. Blunt men who were not born to money but who by way of work and native guile are not short of it now. And many others besides, all caught up and overlaid in this one flesh-and-blood man before him.

And with that idea comes a second one – that with no mother ever in his life he himself has no existence unto himself except what he owes these men, all their accrued habits and impulses, all their characters. He is the hybrid offspring of all the men who have crossed his life in one way or another since his motherless childhood: small farmers, foresters, cattle jobbers, these sons of the soil without pretence. It is not a comfortable thought. It is not one that gives him a better hold on this moment, nor warms him to the man who sits so comfortably opposite him, and who seems to have so little regard for what may happen to this day.

Nealon is conscious of his own fear now, it has begun to claw him from within. This day is most certainly cast

170

in whatever baleful shape or fate it will eventually take. He is not hopeful.

He finds it difficult to concentrate on the news bulletin. The newscaster's face fills the screen. She is a beautiful blonde woman in late middle age. Nealon recalls that her life over the past year has been made hell by a stalker whose targeted attention has led to her needing twenty-four-hour Garda protection. Right now, she is cueing up the government statement at midday. The man gestures at the screen.

'I wonder what he'll say, what sort of shapes he'll throw.'

'Our minister?'

'Yes.'

'An appeal for calm and a few words of assurance — something like that, I'd imagine.'

'He'll want to be equal to the moment, a crisis leader. But he needs to be careful as well. The last time a minister for defence did an interview like this he frightened the bejesus out of the whole country.'

'I remember that, it was after 9/11. Iodine tablets arrived in the post to each household a few days after.'

'Yes, for all the good they were.'

Three ambulances speed along the docks in convoy, trailing a smear of blue and green light through the rain. A wailing scarf of noise follows. This blatant urgency of speed and colour has a sudden effect on Nealon. It shifts the threat focus from the political to the personal and for the first time he recognises the situation as something with a capacity for real, personal pain.

This will bring all sorts of grief, he says to himself.

It takes him a moment to realise his mistake; right from the beginning he has interpreted this as a political disturbance, a security matter, without ever having made the imaginative leap to flesh-and-blood casualties in his life or in the life of others. And how sluggish is this realisation? Always lagging behind himself, late as ever to real insight. Now his wife and child are out there, and for the first time he has a real sense of their vulnerability.

On the couch to his left a couple sit staring into the middle distance. They already have the settled look of people who are used to waiting, they have picked up the sullen pulse of it. So too with the others all around, the same dull patience has taken hold. Directly opposite, a young man with a laptop looks up from the screen with a baffled expression on his face. Evidently, something in his calculations does not add up, and he sees that whatever is on the screen might not square with the facts of this moment or the facts as they will be in about fifteen minutes time. Nealon feels sorry for him, he can sympathise with his betrayal.

For a moment Nealon has the impression that the whole world is arrested in mid pulse, noises frozen at their peak, the world stalled on the off-beat. Through the large window he sees that the traffic along the docks has congealed into a gelid flow, as if the entire scene has emerged in the wake of a single brushstroke trailing a chroma close to the grey end of white.

And all around him a submerged panic building in pressure.

Nealon has a developed sense of occasion, an instinct honed to gauge the specific gravity of any given situation. And he senses now that all sorts of difficult convergences give these hours an intensity that will resonate long after this day is closed.

And this is also a moment of pledges and resolutions.

He looks around him. How many in this foyer have already resolved that if they remain unscathed by whatever's coming towards them, they will meet their new lives with a firm purpose of amendment, turn over new leaves, make clean starts?

And there will be a rush of conceptions in this anxiety, Nealon thinks. People will give of themselves one last time, they will not spare themselves. A pale and anxious brood will spawn in these hours. Nine months from now, there will be a spike in the nation's birth rate, a twitchy generation of pale infants with an innate awareness of their own anxious origins.

But how exacting will any pledges and resolutions be if made under these conditions? Will these children be binding, children brought into being as their parents cross their fingers behind their backs? Surely pledges made under such extraordinary conditions will be easily appealed, easily rescinded. Nealon is impressed that a moment like this allows itself to reach such speculative themes.

Nealon is conscious of this. All the weighing in the balance which is taking place around him, all the self-evaluation as the whole country tightens down in a stress whine.

If the man opposite has any such worries, he is

doing a clean job of keeping them hidden. For the moment he seems to have subsided completely into the bulk of himself, slumped in the seat now with his neck disappeared into a puddle of flesh over the collar of his shirt. Nealon permits himself an inward smile. In this at least he has the upper hand; there is no beating the clock. Without opening his eyes, the man now brings up the tips of his fingers and begins to massage the left side of his head. Seeing his closed eyes, Nealon has the irrational thought that the whole world is cast in darkness because of them. But if it is dark, at least Nealon feels light in himself; he is coming through strong in this final stretch with a surplus of energy and mental acuteness.

He feels OK.

Better than OK; he has done well, not conceded anything, not given anything away. He feels assured that anything he has spilled about himself is nothing more than a few harmless details. He has betrayed nothing of himself, neither affirmed nor denied anything so nothing had been lost. If he has not won an outright victory, he can at least congratulate himself on having held his own. Call it a draw, something he would have settled for at any point during the past few hours.

The man looks up. 'So, tell me how it ends?' he says. 'How does it play out in your head?'

'This terror thing?'

'No, fuck that, it's of no interest. The insurance scam.'

'You know more about that than I do.'

'I'm not sure. But I believe you see something like a

new world rising out of the stem cells, the broad strokes you have laid down.'

'A new Big Bang?'

'Something like that. Some blinding episode of light and sound before the smoke clears on a sunlit upland which is populated by a drift of ragged refugees. The wretched of the earth, the halt and the lame, finally come to claim their birthright. All swelled with mother's milk and clutching their primers and pencils. A world rethought; a world made whole once more.'

'It sounds to me like more of the same.'

'No, no, no,' the man says ardently, 'that's where you're wrong, this is that pristine moment before the whole thing fractures into borders and ideologies.'

'Teed up with the same flaws, for the same fall.'

'I don't think so. This world of yours has different origins altogether, there's real suffering at the bottom of it. Cancers and heart attacks, war wounds and car-crash injuries, every insult the body is prone to, every pathology that would waylay it. It will recognise its own virtue in these things and rise up into the better version of itself.'

'You have a lot of faith in all this pain.'

'I don't know why I am telling you any of this, you know all of it.'

'So you keep telling me.'

To the west a lone tower crane breaks the horizon over the city. Even at this distance and in such failing light the cross-hatched structure of the jib is visible. The graceful upholding of itself against the sky is something to wonder at. Nealon remembers hearing the phrase *self-erecting cranes*. How were such things possible? From what still point do they evolve? There is something lonely about this one standing in free-slew mode, a weathervane over the city. Engineers and tradesmen are always glad to see cranes dismantled and leaving building sites – it marks the moment when things return to a human scale and become more manageable. And apparently there is a shortage of such cranes in the Western hemisphere. They have all migrated east, whole forests of them raised over cities in India and China. This one stands as a lonely sentinel against a neutral sky.

On the TV screen a reporter is standing in some municipal building gesturing towards a vacant podium behind her. This, evidently, is the place from where the government will address the nation. The podium is framed in the centre of an arched opening, Doric columns to the left and right while in the background a broad staircase rises and sweeps up out of sight. The staging is clearly designed to lend antique depth and fortitude to whatever this message will be.

The nation will take its cue from this visual prompt. Minutes from now it will turn as one towards this spot. Already there is a sense of things being put on hold; Nealon can feel the creeping stasis all around him. All over the country, talks, meetings and negotiations are being rescheduled till after this whole thing clarifies; there will be no deals or agreements struck till then. Those men with their percolation tests and the woman with her loyalty points will, for the moment, forget all about those things. And the woman who received such hopeful news about her fertility issues will have her happiness shadowed by a world that can give itself to such recklessness. All travel documentation that has expired during the last couple of days will stay that way for the foreseeable future while the idea that time itself might need adjustment when this whole thing is over will keep the woman chasing the dive watch pondering.

'I'll toss you for it,' the man says, starting upright in the chair as if he has been suddenly summoned.

'Toss for what?' Nealon replies. All his faculties clench to focus within him, his mental vectors hardening to a narrow lens.

'The announcement,' the fat man says heavily. 'True or false, heads or tails.'

Nealon cannot help it. He feels his face crumble, bafflement surfacing in every line of his brow as if he is seeing something appalling at a great distance. The man is no less amazed.

'Nealon, Nealon,' he implores softly, 'don't tell me you haven't thought this through, don't tell me you're going to stumble at the last.'

Nealon is silent.

The man shakes his head. 'I'm disappointed, very disappointed. You of all people. Games and constructs, this is what you do. Don't tell me you didn't consider this fully.'

Nealon withers in his gaze. Everything about the blanched look on this man's face tells him all he needs to know about a sudden loss of faith. A spasm of pain passes through him, warping the features of his face. Anyone seeing him across the foyer must wonder how he has sustained such a debilitating injury sitting in an open armchair in broad daylight.

'A simulation,' the fat man says, 'a war game. It's been on the cards for ages, a full-scale security exercise to gauge how the various parts of the military and civil defence system align against a threat like this. To assess our readiness for the real thing. *Homo ludens*, Nealon, this is what we do.'

There is no disguising Nealon's failure. Even so, the nature of his defeat is obscure. There is something deeper than intellectual pride at issue – there are real stakes here. The fact that he could not, for all his gifts, suspect the difference between the fake and the real thing leaves him exposed in a way he has not anticipated. And it is clear now to Nealon that the man had foreseen this from the opening moment and has factored it into all the questions and responses of the last two hours. And now those hours are gone and the chances of being able to rethink his position or what he has said are gone too. There is no going back now, nowhere to go back to. Impossible to say also what, if anything, of himself he has betrayed or to what disadvantage he has put himself. And he is too tired now to go toe to toe with the fat man any longer, too far off his peak.

True or false.

Real or fake.

One or zero.

Nealon feels the sudden age of himself, all his years crowding in on him once and for all. Not only is his youth behind him but several hard thresholds and markers are fading into the distance also. Things he will never do again no matter how much energy or commitment he might summon to them.

The thought of Olwyn and Cuan out there in the threat of this day harrows him. They are lost to him now, lost and plotting against him. He checks his watch. Cuan is at school and Olwyn is sitting at a table somewhere with divorce papers spread out before her, drawing up a list of charges against him. He is certain of that. He reaches for his phone.

'Forget about it,' the man says.

'What?'

'She's not going to call; I can assure you of that.'

'If I could talk to her . . .' That pleading note in his voice again.

'What would you want her to say, "Guess where I am?" It is too late for that.'

Nealon says nothing.

'Don't cod yourself with that old sentiment. If she does not want to be found, she will not be found. Stop holding your breath, she's gone.'

'People don't just evaporate.'

'No, but they can't be conjured out of thin air either.'

He will never see them again, his wife and child. The truth of that strikes through Nealon's whole frame. They are lost to him completely and this is him letting them go, relinquishing them. And this realisation is not sudden. It is backdated to the moment he crossed the threshold of the house and stepped into a void that had a lot more to do with himself than any empty house. That was when he knew. And every moment and step since then, through every room and corridor, has opened the distance between them that little bit more.

And this is how it should be, he sees that now. They should not be within any psychic distance of him for fear such virulent unworthiness would shrivel and waste them. He feels it coursing in his limbs, this malignance which all his lives and errors have crossbred in him.

And something more than time and space is opening up between them. It is not that they have left and moved on or elsewhere, it's that he has evolved to a higher solitude that is almost divine in its refinement.

There is no one or nothing left to him now.

Wife and child gone, both parents dead, his talent renounced, his own land rented to another name. He is unloved and unspoken for. And there is clarity here, a loneliness so pure that only someone truly native to it could live in its corrosive glare. Olwyn and Cuan are out of reach, somewhere they cannot hear his voice. His hold on their world is loosening by the moment and it is clear that what is happening today is just the wider context within which something more intimate and crushing will come to pass.

This moment is the test of him, the measure and mettle of all he has become. He is conscious of the need to meet this sudden trial with all the poise he can manage. But what reserves does he draw on now, what measure of grace has he laid by?

Nealon gets up from his chair. He wants to be standing

for whatever happens in the next few minutes, he wants to face it standing up. He plants his feet under him and rises into such a rush of blood to the head that there is a sudden shift of everything around him. Sheets of light fold through each other and the whole moment becomes a layered nexus at which all his pasts and present come together. All his confusions and contradictions converge in a morph of space and time across the whole foyer which now sifts through every lighted space he has ever known – all the bedrooms and kitchens, prison cells, train stations and hotel foyers, all the hallways and corridors he has ever walked. And finally, the hayshed he stood in as a child with his father to shelter from the same swathes of rain that now cross the foyer in tumbling greyscale beneath the humming sound of it falling on the galvanised roof.

But now that sacred memory comes with a difference. As always, the two of them side by side, staring at the hills in the far distance. That is as it ever was. But it is no trick of the light that has raised his father's hand and placed it on his head. There it is. He feels the weight of it down the years, heavy on his spine, pressing something of him into the ground.

Is this what he sees now? The attentive cruelty of this moment, where a memory he would hold against all he has lost is shown to be a flaw bred in the marrow, handed down from father to son. And how far back does it go? Does it place him at the end of a long line of inherited faithlessness that reaches back into the first instant when the world itself was birthed out of a pure loneliness? How does he plumb the depths of this moment?

And never an end to it, his father had said.

Rain thickens in these final moments, rain from an older time hollowing out the distance across the foyer in the depths of which the television glows.

Nealon hears the angelus bell tolling over the city.

The man turns to him. 'Are you saying your prayers?'

Nealon has nothing to say. Rain is teeming down now.

'I'll give you a start: *The Angel of the Lord declared . . .*'

Everyone is standing to face the screen, rain pouring across their faces.

The signature tune for the news bulletin calls out. A brass fanfare over an electronic jitter snags beneath the peal of the angelus bell. On the screen, a revolving satellite image of the world and its borders clears to show the newsreader sorting some pages on her desk.

The man reaches towards him with an open hand; in it is a single coin.

'Heads or tails,' he says.

The newsreader lifts her face to speak.

'Call,' the man says, 'call.'

THE

CHICKPEA

COOKBOOK

10 9 8 7 6 5 4 3 2 1

Ebury Press, an imprint of Ebury Publishing,
20 Vauxhall Bridge Road,
London SW1V 2SA

Ebury Press is part of the Penguin Random House group of companies
whose addresses can be found at global.penguinrandomhouse.com

Penguin
Random House
UK

Text copyright © Ebury Publishing 2017

Design copyright © Ebury Publishing 2017

Heather Thomas has asserted her right to be identified as the author of this
Work in accordance with the Copyright, Designs and Patents Act 1988

First published by Ebury Publishing in 2017

www.eburypublishing.co.uk

A CIP catalogue record for this book is available from the British Library

ISBN 9781785036545

Printed and bound in China by C&C Offset Printing Co., Ltd.

Penguin Random House is committed to a sustainable future for our
business, our readers and our planet. This book is made from Forest
Stewardship Council® certified paper.

Design: Louise Evans
Photography: Joff Lee
Food stylist: Mari Williams
Editor: Lydia Good

THE

CHICKPEA

COOKBOOK

EBURY
PRESS

CONTENTS

DINNERS

BAKING, BREAKFASTS
& DESSERTS

INTRODUCTION

There's a lot more to chickpeas than just hummus. These small legumes are so versatile that they can be eaten whole, mashed, puréed, sprouted or ground into flour. In many parts of the world, they are a staple food; in many others, they play an important role in street food culture – whether it's roti in Trinidad, falafels in the Middle East, or puri in India. They also make great snacks – simply roasted and spiced, wrapped in a Mexican tortilla or encased in a paper cornet, Sri Lankan-style.

ORIGINS AND HISTORY

The botanical name for these little dried pulses is *Cicer arietinum* – *arietinum* refers to their shape, which is similar to the skull of a ram (*aries*). From the other part of its name, *Cicer*, comes the Italian name for this pulse, *ceci*, the French *chiche* and our own chickpea. In Spain and Mexico chickpeas are known as *garbanzos*, and in India they are called *gram* or *chana*.

Chickpeas are one of the world's oldest foods. These legumes have been cultivated in India and southwest Asia since ancient times and have been eaten throughout the Levant and Mediterranean regions for centuries.

AROUND THE WORLD

In Mexico and the United States, chickpeas are used in salads and as a filling for quesadillas, burritos and tacos. The flour is used to make gluten-free wraps, tortillas and nachos. In the Caribbean, chickpeas form the basis of some traditional fiery curries, as well as a spicy filling to be encased in roti.

In Greece, Turkey and the Levantine, chickpeas are mashed or puréed and made into hummus (the Arab name for these pulses) or a thick lemony soup, or are baked with aubergine (eggplant), tomatoes and peppers, or folded into a bowl of chilled sour yoghurt flecked with chopped dill and mint.

In Egypt and North Africa, chickpeas are a staple food and are synonymous with the countries' cuisine. These pulses have been cultivated in the region since at least 2500BC and feature in many snacks, appetizers, salads, stews and tagines. As well as the ubiquitous falafels, ground chickpeas, along with sesame seeds and spices, are used to make *dukkah*, a spice blend which is sprinkled over food or used to coat fried vegetables and fish.

In India, chickpeas are added to curries, mashed in dhal or ground into gram flour to make bhaji, pakoras and batters for frying meat and vegetables.

In Western Europe, chickpeas have long been popular in the Iberian Peninsula. They are often served as tapas or added to salads and grilled vegetables, stewed with spicy chorizo or mixed into rice. In Italy they pop up in flatbreads and street food, such as *panelle* – chickpea fritters. Chickpea soup is the traditional dish served on Palm Sunday in Provence, while chickpea crêpes and pizza bases (*socca*) are a speciality of Nice.

PREPARING, COOKING AND FLAVOURING

Dried chickpeas must be soaked overnight or, preferably, for 24 hours before you cook them in a pan of simmering water (see page 12). However, for speed and convenience you can simply use canned ones; they are so good that it's almost impossible to taste the difference. Be sure to keep a few cans in your store cupboard so that you never run out.

Their pleasant nutty taste is enhanced by a wide range of flavourings: tahini, chilli and warm spices; tart lemons and limes; olive and sesame oils; coconut milk, tamarind and fresh herbs.

A HEALTHY FOOD TREND

Chickpeas have been identified as one of the healthiest foods we can eat and have been embraced enthusiastically by a new generation of chefs and home cooks due to their nutritional benefits and versatility.

They are also a great snack food – roasted, spiced, made into crispy chips, blended into a smooth dip or a grainy hummus. Their crunchy texture, nutty flavour and ability to make you feel full without all the fat, sugar and calories of most snacks make them a 'win-win' ingredient, both nutritionally and taste-wise. It's no wonder they are becoming one of the most popular global foods, and definitely worthy of a cookbook dedicated exclusively to them.

BASIC
RECIPES

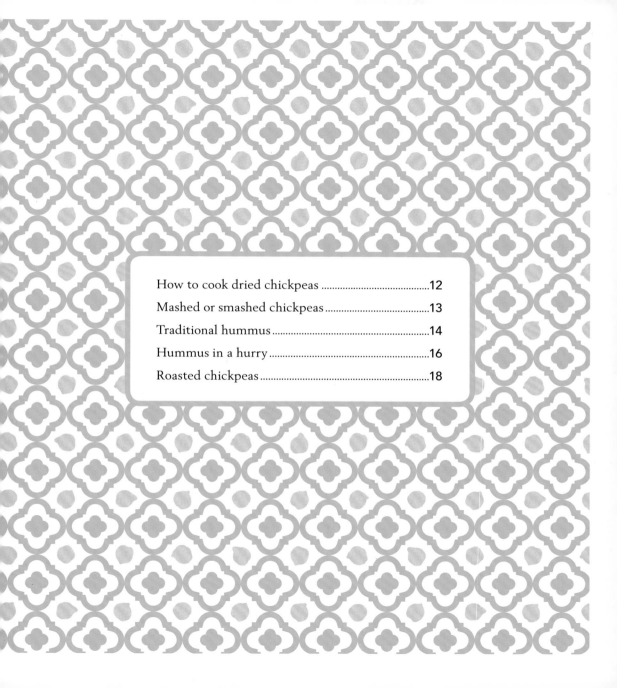

HOW TO COOK DRIED CHICKPEAS

PREP: 24–48 HOURS | **COOK:** 1–4 HOURS

Dried chickpeas must be soaked before cooking and, depending on the recipe, will also need cooking before you use them, so make sure you build enough time into your planning for this. If you are cooking at the last minute, you should use canned chickpeas so that you can skip both steps.

1 Put the chickpeas into a bowl and cover with cold water, then leave to soak for at least 24 hours – you can leave them for up to 48 hours, if you like. The rule of thumb is that they've had long enough when they have doubled in size and weight. Some cooks add bicarbonate of soda (baking soda) to the soaking liquid to soften the chickpeas and give them a fluffy texture when cooked.

2 Drain and rinse the chickpeas in a colander or sieve. Put them into a saucepan and cover them with plenty of fresh cold water. If you like you can add a cut onion, some sprigs of herbs (thyme, oregano, rosemary), a bay leaf or a garlic clove to enhance the flavour.

3 As soon as the water is boiling, reduce the heat until barely simmering and cook gently until the chickpeas are really tender but not mushy. Depending on those you are using, this can take anything from 1–4 hours, so be patient and keep checking them on a regular basis.

4 When cooked, remove the pan from the heat and drain the chickpeas in a colander. They are now ready to eat. Alternatively, leave to cool and then store in a sealed container in the refrigerator for up to 3–4 days for making hummus and falafel, adding to salads, soups and stews, or using as a garnish.

MASHED OR SMASHED CHICKPEAS

PREP: 5–10 MINUTES

You can eat mashed or smashed chickpeas as a vegetable or side dish with a main course, such as a stew, casserole, roast or griddled chicken or meat. Or serve them as a topping for bruschetta and pizza, or use as a filling for pitta pockets and tortilla wraps. Prepared this way they are also delicious on the side of a brunch dish – crushed chickpeas, avocado slices and poached eggs go together perfectly.

To prepare the chickpeas, use either canned or dried and cooked chickpeas; use a potato masher to smash them coarsely, then slacken the mix a little with a glug or two of olive oil and a squeeze of lemon juice. Season with salt and pepper to taste and flavour with spices, garlic or crushed seeds (cumin is very good).

In Italy, they sometimes stir grated Parmesan cheese and finely chopped parsley into mashed chickpeas; in Mexico, the preferred added flavourings are a handful of chopped coriander (cilantro) and some finely diced chilli. In many Middle Eastern countries, onions that have been cooked slowly in olive oil to a melting, caramelized consistency are stirred into the mashed chickpeas, then the whole dish is dusted with paprika or dotted with fiery harissa and served with roast lamb. Or you can simply mash cooked chickpeas with some crushed garlic and Greek yoghurt then stir in some chopped dill, grated lemon zest and seasoning.

TRADITIONAL HUMMUS

SERVES: 4 | **PREP:** 15 MINUTES | **SOAK:** 24 HOURS | **COOK:** 1–4 HOURS

250g/9oz (1¼ cups) dried
    chickpeas
1 tsp bicarbonate of soda
    (baking soda)
100g/3½oz (scant ¾ cup)
    tahini
3–4 garlic cloves, crushed
juice of 1 large lemon, plus
    extra for drizzling
fine sea salt crystals, to taste
olive oil, for drizzling
finely chopped parsley, for
    sprinkling
za'atar, paprika or sumac,
    for dusting (optional)

Made in the traditional way with dried chickpeas, hummus can be served as a dip but also as a topping for bread or toast, as a filling for pitta and wraps, or even as a base for topping with roasted vegetables, spicy lamb or grilled chicken. Most people enjoy hummus cold as a snack but in the Levant it's often eaten warm for lunch or even breakfast.

1 Put the chickpeas and bicarbonate of soda into a large bowl and cover with plenty of cold water. Give them a stir and set aside to soak for 24 hours.

2 The following day, drain the chickpeas and rinse thoroughly. Transfer them to a large saucepan, cover with cold water and bring to the boil. Reduce the heat to a simmer and cook gently until tender – this may take up to 4 hours.

3 Remove from the heat and leave to cool before draining the chickpeas – reserve the cooking liquid; don't throw it away.

4 In a bowl, stir together the tahini, garlic and lemon juice to make a thick paste. Add a little of the reserved cooking liquid to loosen it.

5 Transfer to a food processor and add the cooked chickpeas – reserving a few whole chickpeas for the garnish. Blitz to a rough purée, then add some more of the reserved cooking liquid until you get the desired consistency. It should be quite soft (but not runny) and a little grainy – not too smooth. Season to taste with salt.

6 Spoon into a serving bowl and drizzle with olive oil and lemon juice. Top with the reserved whole chickpeas, then sprinkle with parsley and za'atar, paprika or sumac (if liked). It is best eaten warm with triangles of pitta bread.

– Give the hummus a subtle hint of spiciness by adding a good pinch
of ground cumin before blitzing everything together. Alternatively,
sprinkle some crushed cumin seeds on top.
– Try sprinkling with some finely chopped raw red onion, some
caramelized onions or toasted pine nuts.
– For a creamier texture, thin the hummus by stirring in some 0%-fat
Greek yoghurt in place of some of the reserved cooking liquid.
– For a really colourful hummus, sprinkle with fresh pomegranate
seeds – perfect for Christmas!

FLAVOURINGS
Try one of the following:

SMOKY: Blitz with roasted or grilled red (bell) peppers for a lovely
colour and slightly smoky flavour.

MEDITERRANEAN: Try drained sun-dried or sunblush tomatoes. Just
add to the food processor with the chickpeas, tahini, garlic, lemon and oil.

GREEN: Coriander (cilantro), flat-leaf parsley or basil will add
attractive green flecks and a fresh, distinctive taste.

HOT: A pinch of dried chilli flakes will add a touch of heat, as will
a dusting of cayenne pepper or a drizzle of harissa.

ROOT VEG: Mix in some puréed roasted sweet root vegetables.
Experiment with beetroot (beets), carrots or parsnips. Perfect for
comfort eating during colder months!

INDIAN: For an Indian-style variation, add some garam masala,
toasted sesame and black mustard seeds. Top with a spoonful of
spicy chutney or pickle and serve with naan bread or poppadoms.

CRUNCHY: A sprinkle of dukkah or some toasted seeds, such
as sunflower, pumpkin, cumin, fennel or crushed coriander seeds,
will add crunch.

MEXICAN: Use lime juice instead of lemon and blitz with some
avocado, coriander (cilantro) and diced fresh chilli.

SUPERFOOD: Use half chickpeas and half edamame beans.
Instead of tahini, blitz with 2 tbsp white miso, plus olive oil and garlic.
Drizzle with dark sesame oil and sprinkle with edamame beans and
toasted sesame seeds before serving.

HUMMUS IN A HURRY

SERVES: 4 | **PREP:** 10 MINUTES

If you're rushing and don't have time to cook – or forgot to soak the chickpeas overnight – use canned instead. They're so quick and easy and, what's more, their flavour and texture aren't discernably different from dried ones cooked from scratch.

1 Just drain the canned chickpeas well, reserving the liquid, then rinse them in a sieve under running cold water.

2 Pat dry with kitchen paper (towels) and blitz in a blender or food processor with some tahini (you will need 2 tbsp for each 400g/14oz can chickpeas), crushed garlic, olive oil and lemon juice to taste, or use measurements on page 14.

3 Add some of the reserved chickpea liquid (aquafaba) or extra oil or lemon juice until you end up with the consistency you want. Season and/or flavour to taste (see the suggestions on page 15). Serve in a bowl drizzled with oil and more lemon juice, if desired, plus a sprinkling of paprika or za'atar.

LOW-FAT VERSION

If you're on a diet or watching your waistline, you can try this low-fat version – it's only 150 calories per serving. Eat it with crispbreads, rice cakes or fresh vegetable dippers, including sliced (bell) peppers, carrot or cucumber, celery sticks, broccoli or cauliflower florets, cherry tomatoes or chicory (Belgian endive) and radicchio leaves.

1 x 400g/14oz can chickpeas, drained and rinsed (reserve the liquid)
2–3 garlic cloves, crushed
1 tbsp tahini
juice and grated zest of ½ lemon
½ tsp ground cumin
2 tbsp 0%-fat Greek yoghurt
salt and freshly ground black pepper
paprika, for dusting

1 Blitz the chickpeas, garlic, tahini, lemon juice and zest and cumin to a thick paste in a food processor or blender. Use a little of the reserved chickpea liquid to thin the mixture to the consistency you want.

2 Spoon into a bowl and stir in the yoghurt. Season with salt and pepper, and lightly dust with paprika before serving.

ROASTED CHICKPEAS

MAKES: 500G/1LB 2OZ (3 CUPS) | **PREP:** 10 MINUTES | **COOK:** 25–35 MINUTES

2 x 400g/14oz cans
  chickpeas, drained
  and rinsed
2 tbsp olive oil
½ tsp fine sea salt
flavourings (see below)

Roasted chickpeas are great to munch on and make a crunchy, nutritious snack. You can use canned pulses to make this or cook dried ones from scratch. As well as being healthy, these roasted chickpeas are also versatile; not only do they lend themselves to a wide range of flavourings but they also stay fresh and crisp for a few days.

1 Preheat the oven to 200°C, 400°F, gas mark 6.

2 Put the chickpeas into a bowl with the olive oil, sea salt and the flavourings of your choice (see below), then lightly toss everything together until the chickpeas are all evenly coated.

3 Spread out the chickpeas in a single layer on a baking tray (cookie sheet) with a raised edge. Roast in the oven for 25–35 minutes, turning once or twice, until crisp and golden brown. Watch them carefully towards the end to make sure they don't catch and burn.

4 Remove from the oven and leave to cool on the tray before eating, or storing in a sealed container or plastic bag at room temperature.

FLAVOURINGS

Choose from one of the
following:

SPICY
1 tsp chilli powder
1 tsp ground cumin
1 tsp smoked paprika
good pinch of cayenne pepper

GREEK HERBS & LEMON
1 tsp ground coriander seeds
1 tsp ground fennel seeds
½ tsp ground cumin seeds
1 tsp garlic powder
juice of ½ small lemon

THAI
1 dried kaffir lime leaf,
  processed to a powder
pinch of crushed dried chilli
  flakes
½ tsp Thai curry paste
½ tsp turmeric
1 tbsp soy sauce
1 tbsp coconut oil (instead
  of olive oil in recipe above)

MOROCCAN

1 tsp ground cumin seeds
½ tsp ground coriander
    seeds
½ tsp ground cinnamon
½ tsp paprika
¼ tsp ground ginger
¼ tsp light brown sugar
pinch of ground cloves
pinch of cayenne pepper
pinch of allspice

INDIAN

1 tsp garam masala
1 tsp ground cumin
½ tsp ground coriander
pinch of ground cinnamon
pinch of cayenne pepper
1 tsp muscovado sugar

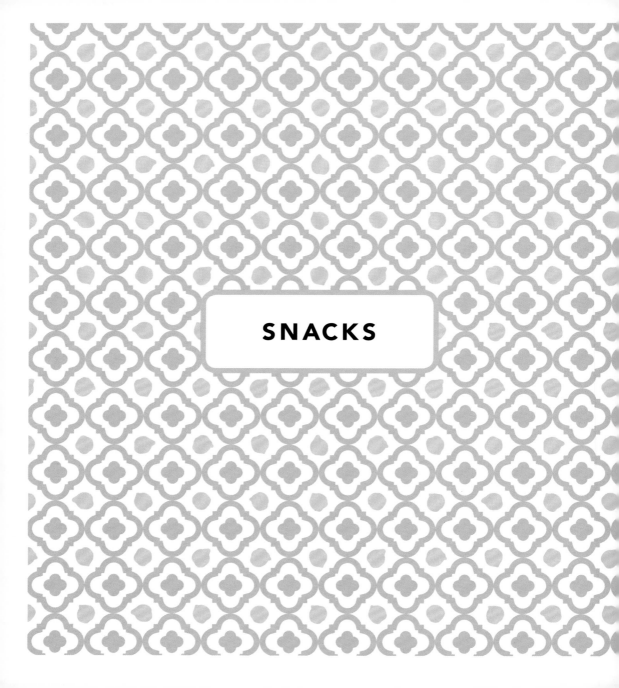

SNACKS

BAKED SWEET POTATOES WITH CHICKPEAS & TZATZIKI

SERVES: 4 | **PREP:** 15 MINUTES + 30 MINUTES DRAINING | **COOK:** 45 MINUTES

4 medium sweet potatoes
125g/4oz (½ cup) cubed
   pancetta (optional)
1 tbsp olive oil
1 red onion, diced
2 garlic cloves, crushed
1 x 400g/14oz can chickpeas,
   rinsed and drained
100g/3½oz (3 cups) baby
   spinach leaves
squeeze of lemon juice
salt and freshly ground
   black pepper
2 tbsp toasted pine nuts

For the tzatziki:
½ cucumber, coarsely grated
2 garlic cloves, crushed
1 tbsp olive oil
250g/9oz (generous 1 cup)
   Greek yoghurt
juice of ½ small lemon
1 small bunch of mint,
   finely chopped
salt and freshly ground
   black pepper

You can make the tzatziki in this recipe a day in advance; simply cover and leave in the refrigerator overnight. Silky, sharp yet cooling, it perfectly complements the rustic earthiness of the sweet potatoes and chickpeas.

1 Make the tzatziki: put the cucumber in a sieve over a bowl and sprinkle with a little salt. Stir lightly and set aside for 30 minutes to draw out the water. Gently squeeze out any remaining water and transfer the cucumber to a clean bowl with the garlic, oil, yoghurt and lemon juice. Stir in the mint and season to taste with salt and pepper.

2 Preheat the oven to 200°C, 400°F, gas mark 6.

3 Bake the sweet potatoes in the oven for about 45 minutes or until softened. Meanwhile, heat a large frying pan (skillet) and cook the pancetta, if using, over a medium–high heat for 3–5 minutes, tossing and turning them, until golden brown. Remove from the pan.

4 Add the olive oil, red onion and garlic to the pan and cook over a medium heat for 6–8 minutes, stirring occasionally, until tender. Reduce the heat and stir in the chickpeas. Cook gently for 2 minutes, then add the spinach. Leave it to heat through for about a minute, just long enough for it to wilt. Add the lemon juice and seasoning to taste.

5 Cut a cross in the top of each baked sweet potato and push to open it up. Top with the chickpea mixture, sprinkle with toasted pine nuts and serve with the tzatziki.

OR YOU CAN TRY THIS...
– Instead of tzatziki, serve with hummus (see page 14).
– Vegetarians can replace the pancetta with chopped plum tomatoes.
– Make the tzatziki chunkier by stirring in sliced spring onions (scallions).
– For a slightly bitter flavour, use wild rocket (arugula) instead of spinach. Or use dill instead of mint for a delicate flavour.

MASHED CHICKPEAS & CHICKEN SHAWARMA WRAPS

SERVES: 4 | **PREP:** 20 MINUTES | **MARINATE:** 30 MINUTES | **COOK:** 8–10 MINUTES

675g/1½lb boneless skinless chicken breasts
1 x 400g/14oz can chickpeas, rinsed and drained
1–2 garlic cloves, crushed
1 tbsp fruity olive oil
good squeeze of lemon juice
1 tsp cumin seeds, crushed
4 large wraps or flatbreads
harissa, to serve (optional)

Spicy chicken and chickpeas make a great combo in this easy-to-eat wrap. If you have time, marinate the chicken overnight in the refrigerator to enhance the flavours to the maximum, but if you are in a hurry, set it aside at room temperature for 30 minutes while you prepare the chickpeas and salad.

1 Make the marinade: dry-fry all the spices in a small frying pan (skillet) for 1–2 minutes until they release their aroma. Tip them into a large bowl and stir in the lemon juice, olive oil, garlic, ginger and coriander. Season generously with salt and pepper and add the chicken. Turn the chicken breasts in the marinade until evenly coated, cover, then leave to marinate at room temperature for at least 30 minutes, or overnight in the refrigerator.

2 While the chicken is marinating, coarsely mash the chickpeas with the garlic, olive oil, lemon juice and crushed cumin seeds. Season to taste.

3 Next, make the tomato and parsley salad: Mix all the ingredients together in a bowl and set aside.

4 When you're ready to cook the chicken, heat a large heavy-based frying pan (skillet) or ridged griddle pan over a medium–high heat. When the pan is hot, add the chicken and cook for 8–10 minutes, turning occasionally, until golden brown on the outside and cooked and tender inside. If the chicken is quite thick, cook for longer. Remove from the pan and rest for a few minutes before slicing.

5 Heat the wraps or flatbreads in a large frying pan over a low heat or in a low oven according to the packet instructions. Spread with the mashed chickpeas and top with the tomato and parsley salad and the chicken. Roll up or fold over and serve dotted with harissa, if using.

For the marinade:
1 tsp sumac
½ tsp ground cumin
½ tsp smoked paprika
½ tsp ras el hanout
½ tsp ground turmeric
pinch each of ground
    cinnamon and cardamom
juice of ½ lemon
2 tbsp olive oil
2 garlic cloves, crushed
2.5cm/1in piece fresh root
    ginger, peeled and grated
handful of coriander
    (cilantro), chopped
salt and freshly ground
    black pepper

*For the tomato and
    parsley salad:*
85g/3oz baby plum or
    cherry tomatoes, diced
½ red onion, diced
1 large bunch of flat-leaf
    parsley, finely chopped
1 tbsp olive oil
1 tbsp lemon juice
salt and freshly ground
    black pepper

OR YOU CAN TRY THIS...

– Use chicken thighs or even diced lamb fillet instead of chicken breasts.
– Vary the spices in the marinade according to personal preferences or
    what you have in the store cupboard: ground coriander, nutmeg and
    allspice are all suitable.
– Substitute fresh coriander (cilantro) for the parsley in the salad.
– If you're in a hurry, instead of preparing the mashed chickpeas,
    use ready-made hummus and spread over the wraps.
– Pitta breads are a good stand-in for flatbreads or wraps if you don't
    have any. Keep a couple of packets handy in the freezer and lightly
    toast before filling.

SPICED PAKORAS WITH COCONUT RAITA

SERVES: 4 | **PREP:** 30 MINUTES | **STAND:** 15 MINUTES | **CHILL:** 1 HOUR (FOR BEST RESULTS)
COOK: 20–30 MINUTES

For the pakoras:
300g/10oz (4 cups) gram
    flour (chickpea flour),
    sifted
1 tsp garam masala
1 tsp ground turmeric
1 tsp black mustard seeds
1 tbsp lemon juice
1 tbsp sunflower oil, plus
    extra for deep-frying
300g/10oz potatoes, diced
300g/10oz red onions, diced
handful of spinach leaves,
    trimmed and chopped
1 small red chilli, shredded
1 small bunch of coriander
    (cilantro), chopped
1 tsp fine sea salt
spicy mango chutney, to serve
1 lime, cut into wedges,
    to serve

For the coconut raita:
100g/3½oz (scant ½ cup)
    thick Greek yoghurt
2 tbsp coconut milk
½ tsp ground cumin
¼ cucumber, halved,
    deseeded and finely diced
1 small bunch of mint,
    finely chopped
salt and freshly ground
    black pepper

In India, chickpeas are ground into warm, earthy-flavoured flour and used for making these little spicy, deep-fried savoury bites. Not only is the flour gluten-free but it is high in protein and minerals, too. These days, most large supermarkets and health food stores sell chickpea flour – it's also known as besan flour, garbanzo bean flour and chana or dal flour.

1 Make the coconut raita: mix together the yoghurt, coconut milk and cumin in a bowl. Stir in the cucumber and mint, then season to taste with salt and pepper. Cover and chill in the refrigerator for at least 1 hour, or overnight if wished.

2 To make the pakoras, mix together the flour and spices in a large bowl. Stir in the lemon juice and sunflower oil, then add enough tepid water in a thin stream, stirring all the time, to make a smooth, thick batter that will coat the back of a spoon. Leave to rest for 15 minutes.

3 Stir the vegetables, chilli, coriander and sea salt into the batter, distributing them evenly throughout, until everything is well coated.

4 Heat the oil for deep-frying in a deep fryer or wide heavy-based saucepan or deep frying pan (skillet) until it reaches 160°C/325°F. If you don't have a sugar thermometer to measure this, just drop a small piece of bread into the hot oil – it's ready when the bread sizzles and turns golden brown.

5 Add tablespoonfuls of the vegetable pakora batter to the pan, in batches of a few at a time, and fry for about 5 minutes until the vegetables are cooked and the batter is really crisp and golden. Remove with a slotted spoon, drain on kitchen paper (towels) and keep warm while you cook the remaining pakoras.

6 Serve immediately with the coconut raita, mango chutney and lime wedges.

OR YOU CAN TRY THIS...

- Vary the spices in the batter: experiment with chilli powder, ground cumin, grated fresh ginger and garlic.
- Instead of the red onion, mix in a bunch of chopped spring onions (scallions).
- You could use a packet of ready-diced frozen vegetables from the supermarket – peas are traditional and very good.

SPICY CHICKPEA & AVOCADO TACOS WITH FIERY SALSA

SERVES: 4 | **PREP:** 15 MINUTES | **COOK:** 15–20 MINUTES

1 tbsp olive oil
½ red onion, diced
1 garlic clove, crushed
1 tsp chilli powder
½ tsp ground cumin
½ tsp smoked paprika
1 x 400g/14oz can
    chickpeas, rinsed and
    drained, OR 1½ cups,
    dried chickpeas, cooked
handful of coriander
    (cilantro), chopped
juice of ½ lime
1 ripe avocado, peeled and
    stoned (pitted)
4 hard taco shells
salad leaves
salt and freshly ground
    black pepper

Serve these delicious tacos the Mexican way – in a basket lined with a brightly coloured cloth. Almost anything goes when it comes to fillings, you could stir the chickpea mix into some chilli con carne, or just mix the pulses with some cold chicken or refried beans for a veggie option.

1 Make the salsa: set a heavy-based frying pan (skillet) over a medium–high heat and when it's really hot add the tomatoes and the chilli to the pan – don't add any oil. Cook for about 5 minutes or so, turning occasionally, until squashy and the skins are starting to blacken. Peel and discard the chilli skin and put it into a large pestle and mortar with the garlic and cooked tomatoes. Pound together and break up the tomatoes so you end up with a loose paste. Stir in the onion, coriander and lime juice and season to taste with salt.

2 Heat the olive oil in a frying pan (skillet) over a medium heat. Cook the red onion and garlic for about 5 minutes, stirring occasionally, until the onion is tender. Stir in the spices and then add the chickpeas. Reduce the heat and warm through gently for 2–3 minutes. Stir in the coriander and lime juice and remove from the heat. Allow to cool a little.

3 Lightly mash the avocado in a bowl and gently stir in the chickpea mixture. Season to taste with salt and pepper.

4 Line the taco shells (heated according to packet instructions) with the salad leaves and then divide the chickpea mixture among them. Top with a spoonful of salsa and serve immediately.

For the fiery salsa:
200g/7oz baby plum or
  cherry tomatoes
1 jalapeño chilli
2 garlic cloves, crushed
1 small red onion, diced
1 small bunch of coriander
  (cilantro), chopped
juice of 1 small lime
sea salt crystals

OR YOU CAN TRY THIS...

– Top the tacos with any salsa – mild, fruity or hot.
– A spoonful of sour cream or thick natural yoghurt will take
  some of the heat out of the salsa.
– Use medium-sized tortillas instead of taco shells; heat them until
  slightly charred then fold or roll them around the chickpea filling.

ONION BHAJIS WITH SEEDY MANGO CHUTNEY

SERVES: 4 | **PREP:** 20 MINUTES | **COOK:** 10–15 MINUTES

2 onions
100g/3½ oz (scant 1 cup) gram flour (chickpea flour)
1 tbsp melted ghee or butter
2 tbsp natural yoghurt
2 garlic cloves, crushed
2 tsp grated fresh root ginger
1 tsp cumin seeds
¼ tsp ground turmeric
½ tsp hot chilli powder
4 fresh curry leaves, chopped
large handful of coriander (cilantro) leaves, finely chopped
sunflower oil, for deep-frying
yoghurt or raita, to serve

Hot, crisp onion bhajis are a real treat. Serve them as a snack or party food, or even with boiled rice and some Indian salad or vegetables as a main course. This is a fresh chutney (not a cooked one), so it will be at its best for only a few hours.

1 Make the chutney: dry roast the mustard seeds in a small pan set over a medium–high heat until they start to pop and release their aroma. Remove from the pan immediately and mix with the other ingredients. Set aside.

2 Cut the onions in half and thinly slice each half – they shouldn't be too thick as you want them to cook and become tender very quickly.

3 Put the gram flour into a large bowl and stir in the melted ghee or butter and yoghurt plus enough cold water to create a thick batter.

4 Stir in the garlic, ginger, spices, curry leaves and coriander, then fold in the onions to distribute them throughout and coat them in the batter.

5 Heat the oil for deep-frying in a deep-fat fryer or a deep heavy-based saucepan. Use a sugar thermometer to check when it reaches 180°C, 350°F. Or you can drop a tiny piece of batter into the hot oil and if it sizzles and floats immediately the oil has reached the required temperature.

6 Start adding tablespoons of the mixture to the hot oil, a few at a time. Cook quickly until crisp and golden all over and remove with a slotted spoon. Drain on kitchen paper (towels).

7 Eat hot with the seedy mango chutney or some cooling yoghurt or raita.

For the seedy mango chutney:
1 tsp black mustard seeds
1 ripe mango, peeled, stoned
 (pitted) and diced
1 small red chilli, deseeded
 and diced
2.5cm/1in piece fresh root
 ginger, peeled and finely
 chopped
good pinch of ground
 cinnamon
pinch of caster (superfine)
 sugar
1 tbsp lime juice
few sprigs of coriander
 (cilantro), finely chopped

OR YOU CAN TRY THIS...

– Add a diced fresh chilli to the bhaji batter instead of chilli
 powder. If you like hot and spicy food, use both.

– Experiment with spices and seeds in the bhajis – try fennel,
 nigella or sesame seeds, or garam masala or ground coriander.

– For sweeter results, use red onions instead of white or yellow.

SPICY CARROT FALAFELS WITH CORIANDER (CILANTRO) PESTO

MAKES: 12 SMALL FALAFELS | **PREP:** 20 MINUTES | **COOK:** 5 MINUTES

50g/2oz finely grated carrot
1 x 400g/14oz can chickpeas, rinsed and drained
1 small green chilli, deseeded and diced
1 garlic clove, crushed
grated zest of 1 lemon
1 small bunch of flat-leaf parsley, finely chopped
2 tsp plain (all-purpose) flour
½ tsp baking powder
1 tsp cumin seeds
1 tsp coriander seeds
salt and freshly ground black pepper
sunflower oil, for shallow frying

For the coriander pesto:
50g/2oz (scant ½ cup) walnuts or pecans
large bunch of coriander (cilantro)
50g/2oz (½ cup) grated Parmesan
2 garlic cloves
pinch of coarse sea salt crystals
150ml/5fl oz (generous ½ cup) olive oil

This recipe makes enough falafels to feed 4 people as a snack. If you're serving them as a light lunch, double the quantities below. Falafels make a delicious filling for panini, pitta bread and wraps: add some tomatoes and salad and a drizzle of tahini or a light spreading of hummus.

1 Make the coriander pesto: place the nuts in a blender with the coriander (stalks and leaves), Parmesan, garlic, salt and a little of the oil. Blitz to a sludge and then add the remaining oil in a thin stream through the feed tube, blitzing until smooth.

2 To make the falafels, squeeze any excess moisture out of the carrot and pat dry with kitchen paper (towels). Put in a food processor with the chickpeas, chilli, garlic, lemon zest, parsley, flour, baking powder and salt and pepper to taste.

3 Dry-fry the cumin and coriander seeds in a small pan over a medium heat for about 1 minute until they release their aroma. Take care not to let them burn. Remove immediately and add to the other falafel ingredients. Blitz in the food processor until everything is well combined. Divide the mixture into 12 equal-sized portions and shape each one into a small ball.

4 Heat the oil in a large frying pan (skillet) and when it's hot, add the falafels. Cook for about 2 minutes and then turn them over and cook the other side. They should be golden brown. Remove from the pan and drain on kitchen paper (towels).

5 Serve the hot falafels immediately, drizzled with the coriander pesto.

OR YOU CAN TRY THIS...
– Make a creamier pesto by stirring in a spoonful of Greek yoghurt.
– For a more substantial snack, eat these falafels with warm pitta or flatbreads.

BRUSCHETTA WITH SMASHED CHICKPEAS & TOMATOES

SERVES: 4 | **PREP:** 5 MINUTES | **COOK:** 10 MINUTES

2 tbsp fruity olive oil
1 red onion, thinly sliced
3 garlic cloves
2 sprigs of rosemary,
    leaves picked
few sprigs of flat-leaf
    parsley, chopped
1 x 400g/14oz can chickpeas,
    rinsed and drained
4 small sprigs of cherry
    tomatoes on the vine
4 thick slices ciabatta
salt and freshly ground
    black pepper

This Italian snack is really delicious and so simple to make. You can eat it when you're feeling peckish or even as a light lunch or supper. Known as *ceci* in Italy, chickpeas are often dressed with olive oil and flavoured with herbs, made into hearty winter soups or ground into flour to make flatbreads and pancakes.

1 Heat 1 tablespoon of the olive oil in a small frying pan (skillet) set over a low heat. Cook the red onion for about 5 minutes until starting to soften.

2 Meanwhile, crush 2 of the garlic cloves and mix with the rosemary leaves, the chopped parsley and the remaining olive oil. Blitz in a blender or crush in a pestle and mortar. Stir into the red onion and cook for 1 minute.

3 Add the chickpeas and cook gently for 2–3 minutes until heated through. Lightly mash some of them with a fork – not too much – leaving some whole. Season to taste with salt and pepper.

4 Meanwhile, cook the cherry tomatoes for a few minutes on an oiled griddle pan or pop them under a hot grill (broiler) until they are slightly charred and starting to soften.

5 Lightly toast the ciabatta. Cut the remaining garlic clove in half and rub over the toasted bread. Top with the smashed chickpea mixture and griddled tomatoes. Serve immediately.

OR YOU CAN TRY THIS...
– Use any bread for the bruschetta, including seedy, whole-grain, sourdough or country bread, or even a baguette sliced in half.
– Instead of rosemary try fresh basil leaves or oregano.
– Grilled (broiled) sweet (bell) peppers make a great topping for the smashed chickpeas, or even a spoonful of caponata.

MEXICAN CHILLI CHICKPEA DIP

SERVES: 6–8 | **PREP:** 10 MINUTES

2 x 400g/14oz cans
   chickpeas, drained
   (reserve the liquid)
1 tsp ground cumin
½ red onion, diced
6 thin spring onions
   (scallions), sliced
1 garlic clove, crushed
2 green chillies, diced
1 small bunch of coriander
   (cilantro), chopped
2–3 tbsp fruity olive oil
grated zest and juice of
   1 lime
salt and freshly ground
   black pepper
chilli powder, for dusting
tortilla chips, to serve

This dip is a Mexican version of hummus, flavoured with chillies, coriander (cilantro) and lime. It's really quick and easy to make and goes well with pre-dinner drinks if you're entertaining family and friends.

1 Put the chickpeas, cumin, red onion, spring onions, garlic, chillies, most of the coriander (reserve a little for sprinkling over the finished dip), olive oil and lime zest and juice into a food processor.

2 Blitz to a thick, coarsely textured purée and season to taste with salt and pepper. If the dip is too thick, you can thin it to the desired consistency with some of the reserved liquid from the canned chickpeas.

3 Spoon the mixture into a serving bowl and sprinkle with the reserved coriander and a dusting of chilli powder. Serve with tortilla chips.

OR YOU CAN TRY THIS...
– Serve this dip with warm flatbreads or pitta, or even crudités.
– Add diced tomato or use lemon zest and juice instead of lime.
– If you're not a fan of spicy food, take some of the heat out of this dip by using just one mild chilli.
– Use as a filling for quesadillas or stuff it with some salad leaves and sliced tomatoes into split pitta breads or wraps.

HUMMUS WITH PARMESAN & STICKY SHALLOTS

SERVES: 4 | **PREP:** 20 MINUTES | **COOK:** 30 MINUTES

225g/8oz small shallots
   (or pickling onions),
   peeled
2 tbsp olive oil
1 tbsp balsamic vinegar
25g/1oz (¼ cup) pine nuts
handful of flat-leaf parsley,
   chopped
bunch of chives, snipped
leaves stripped from 1 sprig
   of rosemary
1 garlic clove, crushed
grated zest and juice of
   ½ lemon
2 tbsp tahini
2 x 400g/14oz cans
   chickpeas, rinsed and
   drained (reserve the
   liquid)
60g/2oz Parmesan cheese
honey, for drizzling
flatbreads or pitta, to serve
sea salt crystals and freshly
   ground black pepper

This way of serving and flavouring a simple hummus makes it more substantial and elevates it into something really luxurious. Serve it as a dip or on separate plates as a pretty appetizer.

1 Preheat the oven to 180°C, 350°F, gas mark 4. Place the shallots on a baking tray (cookie sheet) and drizzle with the olive oil and balsamic vinegar, turning them until coated all over. Cook in the oven for 20–25 minutes until tender, sticky and golden brown.

2 Meanwhile, dry roast the pine nuts in a small frying pan (skillet) set over a medium–high heat for 1–2 minutes, tossing them until golden brown. Watch them carefully to make sure they don't burn.

3 In a food processor, blitz the pine nuts, herbs, garlic, lemon zest and juice, tahini and 1 can of drained chickpeas to a coarse paste. Grate half the Parmesan and add to the mixture. Thin to the desired consistency with water or the reserved liquid from the canned chickpeas.

4 Gently warm the remaining chickpeas in their reserved liquid. Drain and stir into the hummus. Season to taste with salt and pepper and transfer to a shallow dish.

5 Top with the sticky shallots and drizzle with honey. Shave the remaining Parmesan and scatter over the top. Serve immediately with warmed flatbreads or pitta.

OR YOU CAN TRY THIS...
– Instead of serving with bread, roast some sweet potato or butternut squash wedges to dip into the hummus.
– Sprinkle with roasted seeds or dukkah or finely chopped herbs.
– Pecorino or Grano Padano can be substituted for Parmesan.
– Instead of pine nuts, toast or dry-roast some cashews, hazelnuts or walnuts.

ISRAELI MASABACHA

SERVES: 4 | **PREP:** 15 MINUTES | **SOAK:** OVERNIGHT | **COOK:** 1–4 HOURS

250g/9oz (1¼ cups) dried
　　chickpeas
4 garlic cloves, unpeeled
60ml/2fl oz (¼ cup) fruity
　　olive oil
60g/2oz (generous ¼ cup)
　　tahini
½ tsp ground cumin
juice of 1 large lemon
paprika, for dusting
¼ red onion, diced, to garnish
fine sea salt and freshly
　　ground black pepper
pitta bread, to serve

For the lemon sauce:
60ml/2fl oz (¼ cup) fruity
　　olive oil
2 tbsp tahini
generous handful of parsley,
　　finely chopped
1 small red chilli, shredded
3 tbsp lemon juice
fine sea salt

For the best results you need to cook dried chickpeas from scratch after soaking them overnight with bicarbonate of soda (baking soda) – follow the basic recipe for this on page 12. You could make this classic dish with canned chickpeas but the texture and flavour will not be as good.

1　Soak and cook the chickpeas as per the basic recipe on page 12, adding the unpeeled garlic cloves to the pan of cooking water. Simmer until the chickpeas are tender, then drain, reserving some of the cooking liquid and 4 tablespoons of chickpeas.

2　Peel the cooked garlic and place in a food processor with the hot chickpeas, olive oil, tahini, cumin and lemon juice. Blitz to a creamy purée. If it's a bit too coarse, add some of the reserved chickpea liquid to get the desired consistency. Season to taste with salt and pepper.

3　Make the lemon sauce: stir all the ingredients together in a bowl until smooth and well mixed, or blitz in a blender or food processor. It should be a smooth pouring consistency and not too thick. Thin it with some cooking liquid if necessary.

4　Spoon into a serving bowl, swirling it around and making a slight hollow in the middle. Dust with paprika and scatter with the reserved whole chickpeas and diced red onion. Pour the lemon sauce over the top and serve warm with pitta bread.

OR YOU CAN TRY THIS...

– In Israel, this is sometimes served with hard-boiled eggs for breakfast.
– Scatter with toasted pine nuts or seeds of your choice.

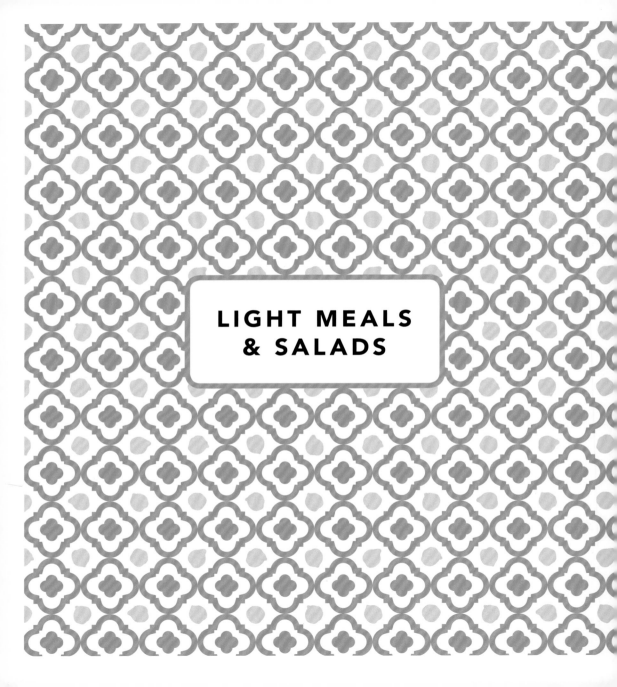

LIGHT MEALS
& SALADS

CHICKPEA, FETA & BEETROOT COUSCOUS SALAD

SERVES: 4 | **PREP:** 10 MINUTES | **COOK:** 25–30 MINUTES

3 red or yellow beetroots (beets)
250g/9oz giant couscous
300ml/½ pint (1¼ cups) vegetable stock
2 tbsp olive oil
grated zest and juice of 1 lemon
25g/1oz (¼ cup) pine nuts
1 x 400g/14oz can chickpeas, rinsed and drained
handful of flat-leaf parsley, chopped
handful of mint, chopped
pinch of ground allspice or paprika
125g/4oz (1 cup) crumbled feta cheese
salt and freshly ground black pepper

Giant couscous is now available in most supermarkets and delis. It is more filling and has a different texture from the smaller regular grains.

1 Preheat the oven to 180°C, 350°F, gas mark 4.

2 Wrap the beetroots in a sheet of kitchen foil and place on a baking tray (cookie sheet). Roast in the oven for 25–30 minutes until cooked and tender.

3 Meanwhile, cook the couscous, according to the instructions on the packet, in the vegetable stock. Fluff it up with a fork and stir in the olive oil, lemon zest and juice. Season to taste and transfer to a serving bowl.

4 Heat a small heavy-based frying pan (skillet) over a medium–high heat and toast the pine nuts, tossing them occasionally, for 2 minutes until golden brown. Don't let them burn.

5 Peel the beetroots and cut them into large cubes or small wedges. Stir into the couscous with the chickpeas, chopped herbs and ground spice. Crumble the feta over the top and sprinkle with the toasted pine nuts. Serve warm.

OR YOU CAN TRY THIS...

– Use roasted vegetables instead of beetroot: red onion and fennel wedges, chunks of (bell) peppers, butternut squash and aubergine (eggplant) or baby carrots all work well.
– Mix in roasted baby plum tomatoes or drained sunblush or dried tomatoes with torn basil leaves.
– Chopped preserved lemon and juicy raisins will add a Moroccan flavour.
– Omit the feta and top with griddled sliced halloumi or grilled (broiled) harissa chicken for a more substantial dish.
– Stir in cubed chorizo and diced chilli to add heat and spice.

MOROCCAN ROASTED CARROT & CHICKPEA SALAD

SERVES: 4 | **PREP:** 10 MINUTES | **COOK:** 30–40 MINUTES

600g/1lb 5oz baby carrots, trimmed
1 red onion, cut into thin wedges
1 tsp smoked paprika
1 tsp ground cinnamon
2 tsp cumin seeds
grated zest and juice of ½ orange
2–3 tbsp olive oil
1 x 400g/14oz can chickpeas, rinsed and drained
75g/3oz (generous ¼ cup) stoned (pitted) dates, cut into thin slivers
small bunch of mint, finely chopped
drizzle of pomegranate molasses
120ml/4fl oz (½ cup) Greek yoghurt
pinch of dried chilli flakes
sea salt and freshly ground black pepper
pitta or flatbreads, to serve

You can use large woody carrots and cut them into matchsticks but the sweet baby or Chantenay carrots look prettier, cook quicker and are more tender.

1 Preheat the oven to 180°C, 350°F, gas mark 4.

2 Put the carrots, onion, ground spices, cumin seeds, orange zest and olive oil into a bowl and stir until everything is coated and glistening in the spicy oil.

3 Transfer to a roasting pan and cook in the oven for 30–40 minutes until the carrots and onion are tender. Stir in the chickpeas and return to the oven for 5 minutes.

4 Transfer the warm roasted carrot mixture to a serving bowl and stir in the dates, mint and orange juice. Season to taste with salt and pepper.

5 Swirl the pomegranate molasses into the yoghurt, sprinkle with chilli flakes and serve with the warm carrot and chickpea salad and some toasted pitta or flatbreads.

OR YOU CAN TRY THIS...

– For less sweetness, use lemon zest and juice instead of orange. If you have a sweet tooth, drizzle a little honey over the spicy raw carrots before roasting.
– Sprinkle the warm salad with crumbled feta or goat's cheese.
– Scattered with pomegranate seeds, this makes a colourful winter dish.

LEBANESE FATTOUSH & CHICKPEA SALAD

SERVES: 4 | **PREP:** 15 MINUTES | **COOK:** 3–4 MINUTES

1 x 400g/14oz can chickpeas,
    rinsed and drained
350g/12oz baby plum
    tomatoes, chopped
8 spring onions (scallions),
    finely sliced
½ cucumber, diced
bunch of radishes, trimmed
    and thinly sliced
2 baby gem lettuces,
    shredded
1 bunch of mint, chopped
1 bunch of flat-leaf parsley,
    chopped
4 pittas or flatbreads, toasted
seeds of ½ pomegranate

For the lemon sumac dressing:
grated zest and juice of
    1 lemon
5 tbsp fruity olive oil
1 garlic clove, crushed
1 tbsp sumac
salt and freshly ground
    black pepper

Fattoush is a popular and colourful salad throughout the Levant. Everything in it should be chopped, sliced or shredded and should have plenty of crunch. It's a great way to use up some leftover stale pitta bread or flatbreads.

1 Put the chickpeas, tomatoes, spring onions, cucumber, radishes and lettuce into a large serving bowl and mix together with the chopped herbs.

2 Make the lemon sumac dressing: whisk all the ingredients together in a bowl or shake vigorously in a screw-top jar until well combined.

3 Toast the pitta or flatbreads or heat them in a lightly oiled griddle pan until warm and just starting to crisp. Break them into small bite-sized pieces and add them to the salad at the last minute just before serving so they don't lose their crispness.

4 Sprinkle the dressing over the top and lightly toss until everything is glistening. Check the seasoning, adding more salt and pepper if necessary, and scatter with the pomegranate seeds. Serve immediately.

OR YOU CAN TRY THIS...
– Sprinkle with 1 teaspoon toasted cumin or fennel seeds.
– Add grilled (broiled), raw or bottled green, red or yellow (bell) pepper strips.
– Instead of spring onions, add a finely chopped red onion.
– Vary the herbs – torn basil or chopped coriander (cilantro) will give a distinctive aromatic flavour.
– Use halved cherry tomatoes in place of baby plum ones, or vary the colours. You can buy packs of mixed red, yellow, orange and purple mini tomatoes.
– Make the dressing spicier with a teaspoon of za'atar; or sweet and sour with a squeeze of pomegranate molasses.

ROASTED SPICY AUBERGINE (EGGPLANT) & CHICKPEA SALAD

SERVES: 4 | **PREP:** 15 MINUTES | **COOK:** 20 MINUTES

2 aubergines (eggplants)
3 tbsp fruity olive oil,
    plus extra for grilling
    (broiling)
2 tsp harissa
1 radicchio, trimmed and
    separated into leaves
balsamic vinegar, for
    drizzling
1 x 400g/14oz can chickpeas,
    rinsed and drained
1 small red onion, diced
75g/3oz wild rocket
    (arugula) or watercress
handful of parsley or
    coriander (cilantro),
    finely chopped

For the yoghurt and tahini
*   dressing:*
240ml/8fl oz (1 cup)
    natural yoghurt
2 tbsp tahini
1 garlic clove, crushed
2 tbsp olive oil
grated zest and juice of
    1 lemon
sea salt and freshly ground
    black pepper

This warm salad is surprisingly filling and makes a good lunch or light supper dish. If wished, you can add the chickpeas to the aubergine (eggplant) for the last 5 minutes of roasting time to warm them through and coat them in the spicy oil.

1 Preheat the oven to 190°C, 375°F, gas mark 5.

2 Make the yoghurt and tahini dressing: put all the ingredients into a bowl and mix together well, seasoning to taste with salt and pepper.

3 Cut the aubergines into thin slices lengthwise. Mix together the olive oil and harissa and brush over both sides of the aubergine slices. Arrange the aubergine on a baking tray (cookie sheet) and cook in the oven for about 20 minutes until golden brown and tender.

4 Meanwhile, lightly oil a griddle pan and place over a high heat. Add the radicchio to the hot pan and cook for 2–3 minutes until slightly charred on both sides. Remove from the pan and drizzle with a little balsamic vinegar.

5 Put the roasted aubergines into a large bowl with the warm radicchio, chickpeas, red onion, rocket or watercress and herbs. Lightly toss everything together and drizzle the yoghurt and tahini dressing over the top. Serve immediately while still warm.

OR YOU CAN TRY THIS...

– For some crunch, sprinkle with toasted seeds or nuts before serving. Or top with ruby red pomegranate seeds.
– If you can't find radicchio, use red or white chicory (Belgian endive).
– Use a lemony vinaigrette or a balsamic dressing instead of yoghurt.
– Make the salad more substantial by adding crumbled feta cheese or grilled (broiled) halloumi.

QUINOA, CHICKPEA & ROAST VEGETABLE SALAD

SERVES: 4 | **PREP:** 15 MINUTES | **COOK:** 30 MINUTES

1 red (bell) pepper, deseeded and cut into chunks

1 yellow (bell) pepper, deseeded and cut into chunks

1 large red onion, cut into wedges

1 sweet potato, cut into chunks

4 garlic cloves, unpeeled

olive oil, for drizzling

200g/7oz (scant 1¼ cups) quinoa (dry weight)

480ml/16fl oz (2 cups) vegetable stock

1 x 400g/14oz can chickpeas, rinsed and drained

1 small bunch of parsley, finely chopped

For the lemony dressing:
3 tbsp olive oil

juice of 1 lemon

1 tbsp sumac

pinch of sugar

salt and freshly ground black pepper

Quinoa deserves its 'superfood' status. It's packed with protein, is high in fibre and is gluten-free.

1 Preheat the oven to 200°C, 400°F, gas mark 6.

2 Arrange the peppers, red onion and sweet potato in a large roasting pan. Tuck the garlic cloves in between the vegetables and drizzle everything with olive oil. Turn the vegetables in the oil to coat them.

3 Roast in the oven for about 30 minutes until tender. Squeeze the garlic cloves out of their skins and mix into the roasted vegetables.

4 While the vegetables are roasting, rinse the quinoa under cold running water, then drain in a sieve. Heat the stock in a saucepan until it boils, then tip in the quinoa and reduce the heat to a simmer. Cover the pan and cook for 15 minutes until the quinoa is tender and has absorbed most of the stock. When the quinoa is cooked, the sprout or 'tail' will pop out of each seed.

5 Turn off the heat and set aside for 5 minutes before straining off any excess stock. Fluff up the quinoa with a fork.

6 Mix the quinoa, roasted vegetables (reserving the oil left in the pan) and chickpeas together in a serving bowl. Stir in the parsley.

7 Blend together the dressing ingredients with the oil from the vegetables, pour into the salad and toss. Serve warm.

OR YOU CAN TRY THIS...

– Vary the roasted vegetables: try butternut squash, pumpkin, carrots, beetroot (beets), courgettes (zucchini) and cherry tomatoes.
– Instead of quinoa, use couscous or a tabbouleh made with bulgur wheat.
– Spice it up with some diced chilli, harissa or a dusting of cayenne pepper.
– Fold in some baby spinach leaves until they wilt.

SUPERFOOD & CHICKPEA SALAD

SERVES: 4 | **PREP:** 15 MINUTES | **COOK:** 10 MINUTES

400g/14oz Tenderstem broccoli, trimmed and each stalk cut in half

2 tbsp sunflower seeds

1 tbsp pumpkin seeds

1 tbsp black and/or white sesame seeds

75g/3oz (½ cup) shelled pistachio nuts

75g/3oz sunblush tomatoes in olive oil

1 x 400g/14oz can chickpeas, rinsed and drained

125g/4oz (2 cups) mixed sprouted seeds, e.g. alfalfa, broccoli, radish, amaranth

1 avocado, peeled, stoned (pitted) and thinly sliced

125g/4oz soft creamy goat's cheese, cut into small pieces

pinch of dried chilli flakes

salt and freshly ground black pepper

This salad is a beautiful way to make chickpeas even more super, combining them with nutrient- and protein-packed greens and seeds in this colourful salad for a satisfying and healthy lunch or light dinner.

1 Make the honey vinaigrette: whisk all the ingredients together in a bowl or combine and shake vigorously in a screw-top jar until thoroughly blended and smooth. Add some of the oil from the sunblush tomatoes, if wished (see step 4).

2 Steam the broccoli in a steamer or a colander placed over a saucepan of simmering water for 3–4 minutes until it is just tender but still a little crisp with some 'bite'.

3 Toast the sunflower, pumpkin and sesame seeds with the pistachios in a frying pan (skillet) set over a medium–high heat for 1–2 minutes, tossing them gently, until golden brown. Remove from the heat and leave to cool.

4 Drain the sunblush tomatoes, reserving the oil for the dressing, if wished, and cut them into small pieces. Mix with the chickpeas, sprouted seeds, warm broccoli and avocado in a large bowl. Toss gently in the honey vinaigrette and season to taste with salt and pepper.

5 Arrange on 4 serving plates and scatter with the goat's cheese. Sprinkle with the chilli flakes, toasted seeds and pistachios and serve immediately.

For the honey vinaigrette:
4 tbsp fruity olive oil
1 tbsp cider vinegar
juice of ½ lemon
1 garlic clove, finely
    chopped
1 tsp honey mustard
2 tbsp runny honey

OR YOU CAN TRY THIS...

– Instead of sunblush tomatoes, used dried or halved baby plum
  tomatoes.
– If you don't have broccoli, use crispy kale and carrot matchsticks.
– A creamy blue cheese, such as Gorgonzola, can be substituted for
  goat's cheese.
– If you can't get the thin Tenderstem broccoli, use purple sprouting
  or calabrese cut into small florets and halved.
– Sprinkle with toasted cashews or hazelnuts instead of pistachios.
– To make the salad more filling, stir in some cooked quinoa or
  buckwheat.

WARM BACON, GRIDDLED HALLOUMI & CHICKPEA SALAD

SERVES: 4 | **PREP:** 10 MINUTES | **COOK:** 15–20 MINUTES

8 extra-thin smoked streaky
    bacon rashers (slices)
2 tbsp olive oil
1 large aubergine
    (eggplant), cubed
1 garlic clove, crushed
1 x 400g/14oz can chickpeas,
    rinsed and drained
1 ripe avocado, peeled,
    stoned (pitted) and
    cubed
handful of mint,
    roughly chopped
100g/3½ oz mixed
    salad leaves
200g/7oz halloumi
    cheese, sliced
salt and freshly ground
    black pepper

For the tahini dressing:
3 tbsp fruity olive oil
grated zest and juice of
    1 small lemon
1 tbsp tahini
1 small red chilli, deseeded
    and diced (optional)

Bacon and creamy avocado are a marriage made in heaven, and the chickpeas add protein and crunch to this delicious salad.

1 Heat a large frying pan (skillet) and, when it's really hot, add the bacon and cook for 2–3 minutes each side until golden brown and crisp. You don't need to add any oil as some fat will come out of the bacon. Drain on kitchen paper (towels) and crumble into small pieces.

2 Add the olive oil to the pan and when it's hot, cook the aubergine and garlic over a medium heat for about 5 minutes until tender and golden. Remove with a slotted spoon and drain on kitchen paper (towels).

3 Mix the aubergine with the chickpeas, avocado, mint and salad leaves in a large bowl. Season lightly with salt and pepper.

4 Whisk together all the ingredients for the tahini dressing or combine and shake until well blended in a screw-top jar. Use to gently toss the salad.

5 Heat a ridged griddle pan and cook the halloumi in batches over a medium heat for 1–2 minutes each side until golden.

6 Divide the salad among 4 serving plates and top with the griddled halloumi and crumbled crispy bacon. Serve immediately.

OR YOU CAN TRY THIS...

– Use cubed pancetta instead of bacon, or even some crisp dry-fried slices of Parma ham (prosciutto).
– To make the salad more substantial, add tomatoes, spring onions (scallions), or griddled or bottled sliced (bell) peppers.
– Spice it up by sprinkling the cooked aubergine with a pinch of cayenne or drizzle the griddled halloumi with some sweet chilli sauce.

SPANISH CHORIZO & CHICKPEA HASH

SERVES: 4 | **PREP:** 10 MINUTES | **COOK:** 15–20 MINUTES

3 tbsp olive oil, plus extra
    for frying eggs
2 red onions, diced
1 red or yellow (bell) pepper,
    deseeded and diced
2 garlic cloves, crushed
175g/6oz chorizo, diced
500g/1lb 2oz boiled new
    or old potatoes, diced
1 x 400g/14oz can chickpeas,
    rinsed and drained
1 tsp paprika
4 medium eggs
handful of parsley,
    finely chopped
salt and freshly ground
    black pepper

Another great dish for breakfast or brunch, this is a delicious way to use up leftover boiled potatoes (or baked or roasted ones). The chorizo adds spice and the chickpeas give it a little crunch and an earthy flavour.

1 Heat the olive oil in a large heavy-based frying pan (skillet) over a low–medium heat. Add the red onions, pepper and garlic and cook gently, stirring occasionally, for about 5 minutes until the onions and pepper are tender.

2 Stir in the chorizo and cook, turning occasionally, for 2 minutes. Add the potatoes and continue cooking for 8–10 minutes until the potatoes are golden brown and crisping. Add the chickpeas for the last 5 minutes of the cooking time to warm through. Season to taste with salt and pepper, and dust with the paprika.

3 Meanwhile, break the eggs into a separate non-stick frying pan (skillet) sprayed with a little oil, and cook until the whites are set but the yolks are still runny. You can set the top of the whites by popping the pan under a hot overhead grill (broiler) if wished.

4 Divide the chorizo and chickpea mixture among 4 serving plates and top each one with a fried egg. Sprinkle with parsley and serve.

OR YOU CAN TRY THIS...
– Use cooked sweet potatoes instead of regular ones to add colour and sweetness.
– If you like your food hot and spicy, sprinkle with diced red or green chilli before serving.
– Add a Mexican touch by substituting parsley with coriander (cilantro).
– Stir in some chopped tomatoes with the chickpeas.

CHANA DAL

SERVES: 4 | **PREP:** 15 MINUTES | **COOK:** 35–45 MINUTES

200g/7oz (1 cup) split
   chickpeas (chana dal)
960ml/32fl oz (4 cups) water
1 bay leaf
1 tsp ground coriander
½ tsp ground turmeric
½ tsp garam masala
pinch of ground cardamom
1 tsp salt
4 tbsp chopped coriander
   (cilantro)

For the tarka garnish:
2 tbsp rapeseed or
   sunflower oil
1 small onion, thinly sliced
2 garlic cloves, thinly sliced
1 red chilli, shredded
4 whole cloves
1 tsp mustard seeds
   (black or yellow)
1 tsp cumin seeds

In India, chickpeas are often split to make a thick, spicy golden dal, which is particularly warming on cold days. It tastes good served plain with just a spicy tarka garnish or topped with some spiced roasted vegetables, griddled chicken, or prawns (shrimp).

1 Put the split chickpeas into a large pan and pour the water over them. Add the bay leaf, ground spices and salt, and bring to the boil.

2 Reduce the heat to a simmer and cook, partially covered with a lid, for 30–40 minutes until the liquid has been absorbed and the dal is tender and moist. Check it from time to time: if it's getting too dry, add a little more water; if it's still soupy, cook a little longer.

3 While the dal is cooking, make the tarka garnish. Heat the oil in a frying pan (skillet) over a medium heat and cook the onion, stirring occasionally, until tender and golden brown. Increase the heat and add the garlic, chilli, cloves, mustard and cumin seeds. Cook for about 1 minute until the mustard seeds start popping. Do not allow the garlic to brown. Remove from the heat immediately.

4 Transfer the hot dal to a large bowl and spoon the tarka garnish over the top. Sprinkle with the chopped coriander and serve.

OR YOU CAN TRY THIS...
– For the tarka, use curry leaves or a dried red chilli instead of a fresh one.
– Add grated fresh root ginger or ginger paste to the tarka.
– Using a red onion will make the tarka sweeter and more colourful.

CHILLI CHICKPEA FRITTERS

SERVES: 4 | **PREP:** 15 MINUTES | **COOK:** 20 MINUTES

125g/4oz (generous 1 cup)
    plain (all-purpose) flour
½ tsp baking powder
½ tsp fine sea salt
150ml/5fl oz (generous ½
    cup) semi-skimmed milk
1 medium egg, beaten
1 x 400g/14oz can chickpeas,
    rinsed and drained
1 small bunch of spring onions
    (scallions), thinly sliced
1 red chilli, deseeded and
    diced
grated zest of 1 lemon
1 small bunch of flat-leaf
    parsley, chopped
olive or sunflower oil for
    frying
freshly ground black pepper
sweet chilli sauce,
    for drizzling
green salad, to serve

For the seedy herb yoghurt:
1 tbsp cumin seeds
240g/8oz (1 cup) thick
    Greek yoghurt
1 small bunch of mint, finely
    chopped
1 small bunch of dill,
    finely chopped
salt and freshly ground
    black pepper
paprika, for dusting

These are great for a weekend brunch. They don't take much time to make and cook, and you can serve them drizzled with maple syrup with some crisp-fried bacon or halloumi.

1 Make the seedy herb yoghurt: toast the cumin seeds in a small dry frying pan (skillet) set over a medium–high heat for 1–2 minutes until they start to release their aroma. Watch them carefully so they don't catch and burn. Reserve a few of the seeds and grind the rest to a powder in a spice grinder or pestle and mortar.

2 Mix the yoghurt with the ground cumin seeds, mint and dill in a small serving bowl. Season to taste with salt and pepper. Dust with paprika and sprinkle with the reserved toasted seeds.

3 Make the fritters: sift the flour and baking powder into a bowl. Add the salt and gradually beat in the milk and egg until you have a smooth, thick batter. You can do this in a food processor if wished.

4 Add the chickpeas, spring onions, chilli, lemon zest and chopped parsley. Season with plenty of ground black pepper and mix well, distributing them evenly throughout.

5 Heat a little oil in a shallow non-stick frying pan over a medium–high heat. When the pan is really hot, add large spoonfuls of the chickpea mixture. Cook for 3–4 minutes until golden brown, then flip the fritters over and cook the other side. Remove from the pan and keep warm while you cook the remaining fritters in the same way.

6 Serve the hot fritters, drizzled with sweet chilli sauce, with the seedy herb yoghurt and a green salad.

OR YOU CAN TRY THIS...
– Add canned sweetcorn kernels and diced red (bell) pepper to the batter.
– Omit the chilli and add extra herbs or finely chopped capers
    or gherkins.

TUSCAN CAVOLO NERO & CHICKPEA SOUP

SERVES: 4 | **PREP:** 15 MINUTES | **COOK:** 1 HOUR

3 tbsp olive oil
1 large onion, finely
  chopped
1 leek, cleaned, trimmed
  and chopped
3 celery sticks, chopped
2 large carrots, diced
2 garlic cloves, crushed
1.2 litres/2 pints (5 cups)
  vegetable stock
450g/1lb ripe tomatoes,
  chopped (or 1 x 400g/
  14oz can)
2 large potatoes, peeled
  and cubed
stripped leaves of 2 sprigs
  of thyme
stripped and chopped leaves
  of 1 sprig of rosemary
1 x 400g/14oz can chickpeas,
  rinsed and drained
250g/9oz cavolo nero, ribs
  and stems removed and
  leaves shredded
salt and freshly ground
  black pepper
fresh green pesto, to serve
  (optional)

The Italians often add chickpeas and beans to hearty vegetable soups, not only for flavour and texture but also to make them more filling. This earthy soup is a meal in a bowl. Cavolo nero is a strongly flavoured cabbage from Tuscany with very dark, greenish-black leaves. It's available from many supermarkets, greengrocers and farmers' markets, but you can use kale or dark green cabbage instead.

1 Heat the olive oil in a large saucepan and cook the onion, leek, celery, carrots and garlic over a low heat for 8–10 minutes, stirring occasionally, until softened but not coloured.

2 Add the stock, tomatoes, potatoes and herbs and bring to the boil. Reduce the heat and simmer gently for 45 minutes until all the vegetables are cooked and tender.

3 Add the chickpeas and cavolo nero and cook for another 5 minutes until the cavolo nero has wilted but still has some bite and looks fresh. Season to taste with salt and pepper.

4 Meanwhile, make the Parmesan crisps. Preheat the oven to 180°C, 350°F, gas mark 4 and line a baking tray (cookie sheet) with baking parchment. Place 4 circular heaps of grated Parmesan on the paper, well apart, and bake for 5 minutes or until the cheese melts and spreads. Remove from the oven before they start to brown and set aside to cool and crisp up.

5 Serve the soup in shallow bowls with a spoonful of pesto (if wished) and the Parmesan crisps.

For the Parmesan crisps:
125g/4oz (2 cups) grated
  Parmesan

OR YOU CAN TRY THIS...
– Use dried chickpeas instead of canned. Soak overnight, then rinse
  and drain (see page 12) before adding to the soup with the stock.
  Simmer for at least 1½ hours until cooked and tender before stirring
  in the cavolo nero.
– Vary the vegetables – courgettes (zucchini), fennel, chard and
  spinach all add flavour.
– To make it more filling, add a handful of macaroni or vermicelli
  about 10 minutes before the end of cooking.

GRIDDLED SALT & PEPPER SQUID WITH HUMMUS

SERVES: 2 | **PREP:** 20 MINUTES | **COOK:** 2–4 MINUTES

600g/1lb 5oz squid, cleaned
3 tbsp olive oil, plus extra
   for cooking
1 tsp black peppercorns,
   crushed
1 tsp coarse sea salt flakes,
   crushed
pinch of dried chilli flakes
1 quantity hummus
   (see page 14)
juice of 1 lemon
olive oil, for drizzling
½ x 400g/14oz can
   chickpeas, rinsed
   and drained
few sprigs of coriander
   (cilantro), finely chopped
2 spring onions (scallions),
   finely sliced
sweet chilli sauce and rocket
   (arugula), to serve

Squid is very easy to prepare yourself if you're not squeamish about it, otherwise you could ask your fishmonger to do it for you. You can also buy it frozen in packets from most supermarkets if you can't find any fresh.

1 Wash each squid under running cold water and pat dry with kitchen paper (towels). Cut off the tentacles without piercing the ink sac. Discard the hard 'beak' at the base of the tentacles.

2 Cut off the 'ears' on the sides of the 'hood' and remove the skin with your fingers. Slice open the hood and lay it out flat with the inner surface facing you. Score it in a diamond pattern with a sharp knife. If it's very large, cut it into smaller pieces.

3 Brush the squid 'hoods' and tentacles with olive oil and sprinkle with the crushed peppercorns, salt and chilli flakes, pressing them into the squid.

4 Brush a griddle pan or large frying pan (skillet) with oil and set over a high heat. When the pan is really hot, add the squid and cook for 1–2 minutes until the squid is just cooked and tender. Don't overcook or it will become tough. If it's a small pan, cook the squid in batches.

5 Put a mound of hummus on each serving plate and add the squid. Drizzle with lemon juice and olive oil. Scatter with chickpeas and sprinkle with coriander and spring onions. Serve immediately, while piping hot, with sweet chilli sauce and rocket.

OR YOU CAN TRY THIS...

– Prepare the squid in the same way and mix into a light batter with the crushed pepper and salt. Deep-fry until golden brown and serve with the hummus.
– For a really hot and spicy version, use Sichuan peppercorns instead of black ones or ½ teaspoon of each.

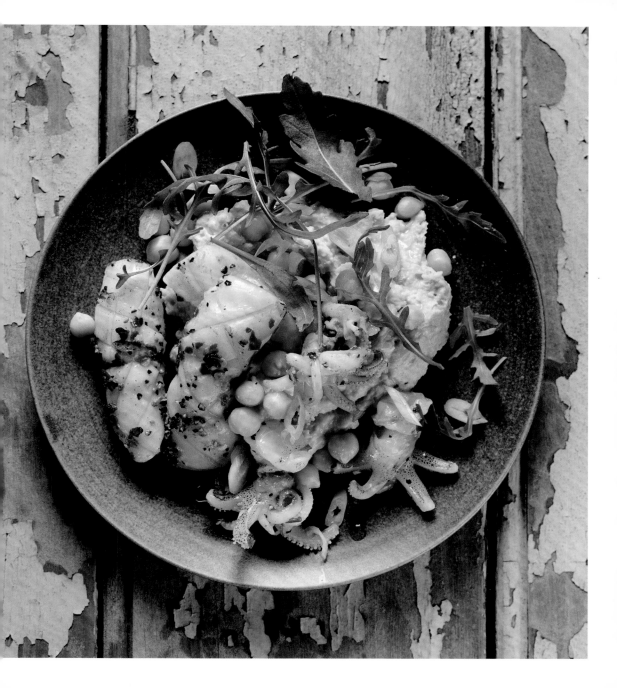

MOROCCAN CHICKPEA SOUP WITH RAS-EL-HANOUT

SERVES: 4 | **PREP:** 10 MINUTES | **COOK:** 1¼ HOURS

3 tbsp olive oil
1 large onion, finely
    chopped
3 celery stalks, chopped
3 garlic cloves, crushed
1 tsp ras el hanout
1 tsp ground cinnamon
1 tsp ground cumin
1 tsp ground coriander
pinch of freshly grated
    nutmeg
pinch of saffron strands
1 litre/1¾ pints (4¼ cups)
    vegetable stock
1 tbsp tomato purée (paste)
4 juicy tomatoes, chopped
2 x 400g/14oz cans
    chickpeas, rinsed
    and drained
1 preserved lemon,
    rind chopped
small bunch of flat-leaf
    parsley or coriander
    (cilantro), chopped
salt and freshly ground
    black pepper
lemon wedges and warm
    flatbreads, to serve

This spicy soup can be made in advance and tastes even better reheated the following day. It freezes well, too. Ras-el-hanout is a fragrant spice mix, which is widely used in Morocco and other North African countries. You can buy it in most supermarkets and delis or online.

1 Heat the olive oil in a large heavy-based saucepan and cook the onion, celery and garlic, stirring occasionally, over a low heat for 8–10 minutes until tender but not browned.

2 Stir in all the spices and saffron and cook for 1 minute before adding the vegetable stock, tomato purée and tomatoes. Turn up the heat and bring to the boil briefly, then reduce the heat to a bare simmer, add the chickpeas and cook gently for 1 hour. The liquid should reduce and you'll end up with quite a thick soup.

3 Stir in the preserved lemon and chopped herbs. Cook for a few more minutes and season to taste with salt and pepper.

4 Ladle the soup into serving bowls and serve with lemon wedges and some warm flatbreads.

OR YOU CAN TRY THIS...
– Instead of fresh tomatoes, use canned ones.
– Vary the spices: add ground ginger or even chilli, if wished.
– To increase the heat of the soup, serve with a dash of harissa paste.

ROMAN PASTA E CECI

SERVES: 4–6 | **PREP:** 15 MINUTES | **SOAK:** OVERNIGHT | **COOK:** 3–4 HOURS

250g/9oz (1¼ cups) dried
    chickpeas
4 tbsp extra-virgin olive oil,
    plus extra for drizzling
1 onion, chopped
1 garlic clove, crushed
1 carrot, diced
2 celery sticks, diced
2 tbsp tomato purée (paste)
960ml/32fl oz (4 cups)
    vegetable stock
2 sprigs of rosemary
75g/3oz (¾ cup) grated
    Parmesan, plus the rind
200g/7oz (scant 2 cups)
    small soup pasta or tubes,
    e.g. ditalini
handful of flat-leaf parsley,
    finely chopped
sea salt and freshly ground
    black pepper

This is a classic Roman dish – half soup, half stew. It's cheap and simple food at its best, and so easy to make, too. Prepare it in advance as it will keep well for several days and can be reheated for lunch or supper.

1 Soak the chickpeas overnight (see page 12) then simmer in fresh water for 2–3 hours until tender. Drain well.

2 Heat the olive oil in a large heavy-based saucepan and cook the onion, garlic, carrot and celery, stirring occasionally, for 8–10 minutes over a low–medium heat until really tender.

3 Stir in the tomato purée then add the vegetable stock, rosemary, Parmesan rind and most of the cooked chickpeas – reserve about one-quarter of them to add later. Bring to the boil, then reduce the heat and simmer gently for 25–30 minutes.

4 While the soup is cooking, cook the pasta according to the instructions on the packet.

5 Remove the rosemary and Parmesan rind from the soup and discard. Blitz the soup in a blender or food processor until smooth. Return to the pan and add the remaining chickpeas and the cooked pasta. Season to taste with salt and pepper and heat through very gently for 5 minutes.

6 Serve sprinkled with chopped parsley and grated Parmesan and drizzled with olive oil.

OR YOU CAN TRY THIS...
– Use 2 cans of chickpeas instead of dried to prepare and cook the soup in under an hour.
– Instead of discarding the Parmesan rind after cooking, chop it into small pieces and add to the soup.

TRINIDAD CHICKPEA & SWEET POTATO ROTI

SERVES: 4 | **PREP:** 30 MINUTES | **REST:** 1 HOUR | **COOK:** 45 MINUTES

225g/8oz (generous 2 cups) self-raising flour, sifted
good pinch of ground turmeric
½ tsp salt
1 tbsp sunflower oil, plus extra for brushing and frying
120ml/4fl oz (½ cup) tepid water
West Indian hot sauce or spicy mango chutney, to serve

For the chickpea and sweet potato filling:
2 tbsp olive oil
1 red onion, finely chopped
2 garlic cloves, crushed
1 large sweet potato, peeled and diced
1 tbsp curry powder
good pinch of ground allspice
1 x 400g/14oz can chickpeas, rinsed and drained
120ml/4fl oz (½ cup) vegetable stock or water
100g/3½ oz baby spinach leaves
salt and freshly ground black pepper

Roti is a popular snack and street food throughout the Caribbean. Serve it with some fried golden plantains or a healthy salad.

1 Make the roti dough. Put the flour, turmeric and salt into a bowl and drizzle the 1 tablespoon oil over the top. Start mixing in the water, a little at a time, until you have a soft dough. If the mixture is too dry, add a little more water. Knead the dough lightly for a few minutes then cover and set aside to rest for at least 30 minutes.

2 Divide into 8 equal-sized pieces and roll each one out into a thin circle. Lightly brush half of each circle with oil and fold over. Brush half of the semicircle with oil and fold again. Set aside for 30 minutes.

3 While the roti dough is resting, make the filling. Heat the oil in a heavy-based frying pan (skillet) and cook the red onion and garlic over a low–medium heat for 5 minutes, stirring occasionally. Add the sweet potato and cook for 5 minutes, then stir in the curry powder, allspice and chickpeas. Stir in the stock or water and simmer for 15–20 minutes until the vegetables are tender and the liquid has evaporated. Stir in the spinach until wilted and season to taste with salt and pepper.

4 Roll out the roti into thin circles and fry, one at a time, in a little hot oil in a frying pan (skillet) for 2–3 minutes until golden brown underneath and puffy, then turn over and cook the other side. Drain on kitchen paper (towels) and keep warm, covered with a cloth.

5 Divide the filling among the roti pancakes and fold over or roll up each one. Eat immediately with hot sauce or mango chutney.

OR YOU CAN TRY THIS...
– Use coconut milk instead of stock or water to make the filling.
– Pumpkin, butternut squash or potato can be substituted for sweet potato.
– Use any curried filling for the roti – try chicken, prawns (shrimp) or even minced (ground) beef.

ITALIAN CHICKPEA PANZANELLA SALAD

SERVES: 4 | **PREP:** 15 MINUTES | **STAND:** AT LEAST 30 MINUTES

450g/1lb ripe juicy tomatoes
2 red or yellow (bell) peppers
225g/8oz stale bread, e.g.
   country loaf or ciabatta,
   torn into pieces
2 tbsp red wine vinegar
90ml/3fl oz (generous ¼ cup)
   really fruity green olive oil
1 small red onion, roughly
   chopped
3 tbsp capers, drained
1 x 400g/14oz can chickpeas,
   rinsed and drained
1 garlic clove, crushed
pinch of dried chilli flakes
   (optional)
handful of basil leaves,
   roughly torn
8 small mozzarella di bufala
   balls (bocconcini)
balsamic vinegar, for
   drizzling
sea salt and freshly ground
   black pepper

Chickpeas add protein, extra fibre and crunch to a summery Tuscan salad. The most important thing when making this dish is to use the right bread. Never use a fresh loaf or soft white bread – a rough, coarse-textured, dry loaf that will hold its shape and not go soggy is always best.

1 Cut the tomatoes into bite-sized chunks and put them in a sieve or colander suspended over a bowl to catch the juice. Sprinkle with a little sea salt and set aside.

2 Pop the peppers under a preheated hot grill (broiler), turning them occasionally, until they start to blister and blacken all over. When they are cool enough to handle, discard the skins, ribs and seeds and cut the flesh into bite-sized pieces, not too small.

3 Put the bread into a large bowl and sprinkle with the vinegar and 1 tablespoon of the olive oil. Add the red onion, capers, chickpeas, drained tomatoes and peppers.

4 Whisk together the tomato juice, olive oil, garlic and chilli flakes (if using) until smooth. Season to taste with salt and pepper. Pour over the salad and toss gently until everything is well coated.

5 Sprinkle with the torn basil and leave to stand for at least 30 minutes to allow all the flavours to develop and mingle. Tear the mozzarella balls in half and scatter over the salad. Drizzle with balsamic vinegar and serve.

OR YOU CAN TRY THIS...
– In a classic panzanella, some anchovies in oil are mashed into the dressing.
– Add chunks of cucumber or spring onions (scallions).
– Instead of large tomatoes, use a pack of the small multi-coloured ones for a colourful red, yellow and purple salad.

MEXICAN TORTILLAS WITH CHICKPEAS & SPICY FRIED ONIONS

SERVES: 4 | **PREP:** 10 MINUTES | **COOK:** 30 MINUTES

4 tbsp olive oil

2 large onions, 1 thinly sliced and 1 diced

½ tsp chilli powder

1 red chilli, diced

2 garlic cloves, crushed

1 x 400g/14oz can (scant 2 cups) chopped tomatoes

1 x 400g/14oz can chickpeas, rinsed and drained

175g/6oz baby spinach leaves

handful of coriander (cilantro), chopped

4 large corn tortillas

1 ripe avocado, peeled, stoned (pitted) and thinly sliced

50g/2oz (½ cup) grated Cheddar cheese

salt and freshly ground black pepper

You can serve these for a spicy breakfast, brunch or supper. If wished, make the tomato and chickpea mixture in advance. You can also use it as a filling for tacos or quesadillas.

1 Heat half the olive oil in a heavy-based frying pan (skillet) set over a low heat and cook the sliced onion, stirring occasionally, until meltingly soft and golden brown. Season with salt and pepper, and stir in the chilli powder.

2 Meanwhile, in another frying pan (skillet), cook the diced onion in the remaining oil with the chilli and garlic over a medium heat for 6–8 minutes until tender. Add the chopped tomatoes and chickpeas and cook over a very low heat for 15 minutes or so until reduced to a thick mixture. Stir in the spinach and as soon as it turns bright green and wilts, remove from the heat and stir in the coriander. Season to taste.

3 Heat the tortillas on a griddle pan or in a low oven and spread with the chickpea mixture. Top with the avocado, fried onions and grated Cheddar.

OR YOU CAN TRY THIS...

– For an authentic flavour, copy the Mexicans and cook the onions in lard, not oil.

– Spice it up by adding an extra chilli (a fiery Scotch bonnet if you're feeling adventurous) or stirring more chilli powder into the fried onions.

– If you're really hungry, top with a fried egg or add some diced chorizo to the tomato and chickpea mixture.

DINNERS

CHICKPEA PILAF WITH GARLIC LABNEH

SERVES: 4 | **PREP:** 15 MINUTES | **COOK:** 30 MINUTES

225g/8oz (1 cup) basmati rice (dry weight), washed well
pinch of saffron
5 tbsp olive oil
2 onions, sliced
1 tbsp cumin seeds
2 tbsp crushed coriander seeds
½ tsp ground cardamom
pinch of dried chilli flakes
1 aubergine (eggplant), cut into chunks
2 green or yellow (bell) peppers, deseeded and cut into chunks
1 x 400g/14oz can chickpeas, rinsed and drained
60ml/2fl oz (generous ¼ cup) vegetable stock
sea salt and freshly ground black pepper
25g/1oz pine nuts, toasted
cooked fresh spinach or green beans, to serve (optional)

For the garlic labneh:
225g/8oz (1 cup) labneh
1 garlic clove, crushed
grated zest of 1 lemon
4 tbsp finely chopped dill

Popular in Lebanon and throughout the Middle East, labneh is a really thick and creamy strained yoghurt. It is sold in many delis and good supermarkets.

1 Cook the rice according to the instructions on the packet, adding a pinch of saffron.

2 Heat half the olive oil in a frying pan (skillet) and cook the onions slowly over a low heat, stirring occasionally, for about 10 minutes until really soft and golden. Stir in the cumin and coriander seeds, cardamom and chilli and cook for 1 minute. Remove from the pan and set aside.

3 Add the remaining oil to the pan and cook the aubergine and peppers for about 5 minutes until the aubergine is tender and golden and the peppers are softened. Add the chickpeas and return the spicy onions to the pan. Pour in the vegetable stock, then cover the pan and cook over a very low heat for 5–10 minutes until all the liquid has evaporated. Season to taste.

4 While the vegetables are cooking, mix together all the ingredients for the garlic labneh in a serving bowl.

5 Break up the cooked rice with a fork and transfer to a serving bowl. Add the vegetable and chickpea mixture and fork through gently. Top with the garlic labneh, then sprinkle with toasted pine nuts. Serve with cooked spinach or green beans if liked.

OR YOU CAN TRY THIS...

– Stir some currants or raisins into the pilaf before serving and sprinkle with chopped dill.
– Instead of pine nuts, scatter with fresh pomegranate seeds.
– Add some shredded cooked chicken to the rice and vegetables.
– Swirl some hummus round the edge of the serving plates and spoon the pilaf into the middle.

SPICED MEXICAN BEEF & CHICKPEA CHILLI

SERVES: 4 | **PREP:** 10 MINUTES | **COOK:** 45 MINUTES

2 tbsp sunflower oil
1 large red onion, diced
1 red (bell) pepper,
   deseeded and chopped
2 garlic cloves, crushed
500g/1lb 2oz (2¼ cups)
   minced (ground) beef
   (max 5% fat)
2 tsp chilli powder
1 tsp ground cumin
1 tsp paprika
good pinch of ground
   cinnamon
2 x 400g/14oz cans chopped
   tomatoes
1 tbsp tomato purée (paste)
210ml/7fl oz (generous
   ¾ cup) beef stock
1 bay leaf
1 x 400g/14oz can chickpeas,
   rinsed and drained
salt and freshly ground
   black pepper
 handful of coriander
   (cilantro), chopped
boiled rice, sour cream and
   tomato salsa, to serve

For the tortilla chip topping:
75g/3oz lightly salted tortilla
   chips, roughly crushed
75g/3oz (¾ cup) grated
   Cheddar cheese

**A really warming supper on a cold evening for everyone who loves
spicy food. And it tastes just as good, if not better, the following day,
so you can make it in advance or freeze it.**

1 Heat the oil in a large heavy-based saucepan over a low–medium
   heat and cook the onion, red pepper and garlic for 6–8 minutes,
   stirring occasionally, until softened.

2 Stir in the beef and spices and cook, stirring occasionally, until
   browned all over. Add the tomatoes and tomato purée and mix
   well. Add the stock and bring to the boil.

3 Reduce the heat to a simmer and add the bay leaf and chickpeas.
   Cook gently for about 30 minutes until the beef is cooked, the
   vegetables are tender and the liquid has reduced and thickened.
   Remove the bay leaf and season to taste with salt and pepper.

4 Divide the chilli among 4 shallow serving bowls and scatter
   the coriander, crushed tortilla chips and Cheddar over the top.
   Serve immediately with boiled rice and accompanying bowls
   of sour cream and salsa.

OR YOU CAN TRY THIS...
– Make this hotter with a diced fresh chilli or a pinch of dried chilli flakes.
– Add some drained canned kidney beans or black beans.
– Serve with thick Greek yoghurt rather than sour cream – it's much
   lower in fat and calories.
– Scatter some diced avocado over the top.

SPINACH & CHICKPEA SPANAKOPITA

SERVES: 6–8 | **PREP:** 20 MINUTES | **COOK:** 45–50 MINUTES

1.5kg/3lb spinach, washed and trimmed
2 tbsp olive oil, plus extra for brushing
2 onions, chopped
2 garlic cloves, crushed
1 small bunch of dill, chopped
1 small bunch of flat-leaf parsley, chopped
250g/9oz feta cheese, crumbled
100g/3½ oz (1 cup) grated kefalotiri or Pecorino
1 x 400g/14oz can chickpeas, rinsed and drained
grated zest of 1 lemon
freshly grated nutmeg
3 medium eggs, beaten
300g/10oz packet (or about 12 sheets) filo (phyllo) pastry
salt and freshly ground black pepper

TIP: While you work with the filo pastry, cover the pack with a damp cloth to prevent it drying out and cracking.

Enjoy this classic Greek pie as a main course, or cut it into small pieces and serve with pre-dinner drinks.

1 Preheat the oven to 190°C, 375°F, gas mark 5.

2 Put the spinach into a large saucepan over a medium heat and cover with a lid. Cook for 2–3 minutes, shaking the pan a few times and stirring the spinach, until it wilts. Drain in a colander and press down on the spinach with a small plate to extract all the excess water. Put the spinach on a piece of kitchen paper (towel) and cover with more kitchen paper. Press down lightly and set aside to cool.

3 Heat the olive oil in a large frying pan (skillet) and cook the onions and garlic for about 10 minutes until soft and golden. Remove from the pan and cool.

4 Roughly chop the spinach and place into a large bowl with the cooled onions, chopped herbs, cheeses and chickpeas. Add the lemon zest and nutmeg and stir in with the beaten eggs. Season with salt and pepper – not too much salt as the feta is quite salty.

5 Lightly brush a deep 30 x 20cm (12 x 8in) ovenproof dish with olive oil. Place a sheet of filo pastry in the dish and brush with a little oil. Add more sheets in the same way, so you end up with 6 layers. Spoon the spinach mixture into the dish to cover the filo pastry evenly, and level the top. Cover with a sheet of filo pastry, brushing it lightly with oil, and then add 5 more sheets in the same way.

6 Brush the top with olive oil and bake in the oven for 30–35 minutes until crisp and golden brown. Serve lukewarm, cut into squares.

OR YOU CAN TRY THIS...

– Instead of cooking the onions and garlic, add 2 bunches of finely chopped spring onions (scallions) to the spinach mixture.

GREEK CHICKPEAS WITH GREENS & LEMON RICE

SERVES: 4 | **PREP:** 15 MINUTES | **SOAK:** OVERNIGHT | **COOK:** 2 HOURS*

250g/9oz (1¼ cups) dried
   chickpeas
90ml/3fl oz (generous
   ¼ cup) olive oil
1 bunch of spring onions
   (scallions), finely sliced
2 garlic cloves, crushed
1 chilli, diced
1 tsp ground cumin
1 tsp paprika
4 tomatoes, skinned and
   chopped
1kg/1lb 2oz spinach, washed,
   trimmed and chopped
1 small bunch of dill, finely
   chopped
juice of 1 large lemon
salt and freshly ground black
   pepper

*this includes cooking the dried
 soaked chickpeas

On the Greek mainland and the islands this healthy, nutritious dish is made with spinach or whatever greens and wild herbs are available and in season. It can be served warm with rice or grilled (broiled) fish, lamb or chicken, or cold as part of a meze.

1 Soak the chickpeas in water overnight and cook as per the instructions on page 12.

2 Make the lemon rice: heat the olive oil in a heavy-based pan and cook the onion gently over a low–medium heat until tender. Add the rice and cook for 1–2 minutes, stirring all the time. Stir in the paprika and then add the chicken stock, lemon juice and rind and bring to the boil. Reduce the heat, cover with a lid and simmer gently for 20 minutes until the rice is cooked and has absorbed all the stock. Add the herbs and fluff up with a fork.

3 Meanwhile, heat the olive oil in a large heavy-based saucepan and cook the spring onions and garlic over a low heat, stirring occasionally, for about 10 minutes, until tender.

4 Stir in the chilli and spices and cook for 1 minute. Add the tomatoes and cook gently for 5 minutes. Stir in the cooked chickpeas and spinach. Don't worry that the spinach will fill the pan – it will wilt in the heat and turn bright green and then you can mix it into the chickpeas. Season to taste with salt and pepper, and stir in the chopped dill and lemon juice.

5 Serve immediately with the lemon rice in shallow bowls.

For the lemon rice:
2 tbsp olive oil
1 small onion, finely
    chopped
225g/8oz (1 cup) long-grain
    rice (dry weight)
1 tsp paprika
480ml/16fl oz (2 cups)
    chicken stock
1 long strip of lemon rind
    and juice of 1 lemon
handful of parsley or dill,
    chopped

OR YOU CAN TRY THIS...
– Use canned chickpeas instead of dried and you can prepare and
  cook this dish in a fraction of the time.
– Flavour the chickpeas and greens with chopped feathery fennel
  fronds or fennel herb, or add chopped flat-leaf parsley or chives.
– Use vegetable rather than chicken stock to cook the rice.

ITALIAN CHICKPEAS WITH ROASTED TOMATOES & BURRATA

SERVES: 4 | **PREP:** 15 MINUTES | **COOK:** 25 MINUTES

300g/10oz baby plum
  tomatoes, halved
4 tbsp fruity olive oil
2 garlic cloves, crushed
1 tsp dried oregano
1 large onion, diced
2 celery sticks, diced
1 x 400g/14oz can chickpeas,
  rinsed and drained
1 small bunch of flat-leaf
  parsley, finely chopped
juice of 1 lemon
1 tbsp red wine vinegar
300g/10oz fine green beans,
  trimmed and halved
200g/7oz burrata cheese
balsamic vinegar, for
  drizzling
salt and freshly ground
  black pepper

Burrata is a semi-soft fresh cheese, usually made from buffalo's milk, with an outer skin of mozzarella. Inside it's really creamy and makes a delicious topping for this warm chickpea salad. It's available in most supermarkets and Italian delis. If you can't get it, use a good mozzarella instead.

1 Preheat the oven to 170°C, 325°F, gas mark 3.

2 Arrange the halved tomatoes in a large roasting pan and drizzle them with half the olive oil, 1 garlic clove and the oregano. Season with salt and pepper. Roast in the oven for 20–25 minutes until tender.

3 While the tomatoes are roasting, heat the remaining oil in a large frying pan (skillet) and cook the onion, celery and the remaining garlic clove over a low–medium heat, stirring occasionally, for 8–10 minutes until really tender. Stir in the chickpeas and warm through for 3–4 minutes. Add the parsley, lemon juice and red wine vinegar. Season to taste.

4 Meanwhile, cook the green beans in a pan of boiling water for 3–4 minutes until just tender but still a little crisp when you bite into them. Drain and refresh under running cold water. Drain and pat dry with kitchen paper (towels).

5 Stir the roasted tomatoes, their garlicky oil and the green beans into the warm chickpeas and divide among 4 serving plates. Tear the burrata into pieces and scatter over the top. Drizzle with balsamic vinegar and serve.

OR YOU CAN TRY THIS...
– Use torn mozzarella or crumbled feta instead of burrata.
– Add some diced carrot to the onion and celery.
– Mix in some stoned (pitted) olives, capers or diced chilli.
– Instead of parsley, add chopped coriander (cilantro) or mint, torn basil or snipped chives.

PANEER, SPINACH & CHICKPEA CURRY

SERVES: 4 | **PREP:** 10 MINUTES | **COOK:** 25 MINUTES

2 tbsp vegetable oil
300g/10oz paneer, cubed
1 large onion, thinly sliced
2 garlic cloves, crushed
2.5cm/1in piece fresh root
    ginger, peeled and diced
2–3 tbsp curry paste
1 tbsp black mustard seeds
1 x 400g/14oz can chopped
    tomatoes
2 x 400g/14oz cans
    chickpeas, rinsed
    and drained
250g/9oz baby spinach leaves
juice of ½ lime
250g/9oz (generous 1 cup)
    basmati rice (dry weight)
salt and freshly ground
    black pepper
natural yoghurt, to serve

Paneer is a fresh unsalted Indian curd cheese that holds its shape well when cooked. You can fry it in ghee or oil, or cut it into chunks and thread them onto skewers before grilling (broiling). It's often added to vegetarian curries with spinach and chickpeas or potatoes.

1 Heat half of the vegetable oil in a large heavy-based saucepan over a medium heat. Add the paneer and cook for 5 minutes, turning it frequently, until golden brown all over. Remove from the pan with a slotted spoon and drain on kitchen paper (towels).

2 Add the remaining oil to the pan and cook the onion, garlic and ginger, stirring occasionally, for about 5 minutes until tender and golden. Stir in the curry paste and mustard seeds and cook for 1 minute.

3 Add the chopped tomatoes and chickpeas, cover the pan and cook for 8–10 minutes until reduced. Stir in the spinach and cook, uncovered, for 4–5 minutes until it wilts and turns bright green. Stir in the lime juice and fried paneer cubes, then season to taste.

4 Meanwhile, cook the rice according to the instructions on the packet.

5 Divide the curry among 4 serving plates and top with a spoonful of yoghurt. Serve with the rice.

OR YOU CAN TRY THIS...
– Sprinkle with chopped coriander (cilantro) and serve with cucumber raita (see page 88) and naan bread.
– Add some cubed potatoes or butternut squash.
– For a more authentic version, make your own curry paste by grinding toasted cumin, coriander and fenugreek seeds with fresh chillies in a spice grinder.

CHICKPEA & VEGETABLE TAGINE WITH DATES & SEEDS

SERVES: 4 | **PREP:** 15 MINUTES | **COOK:** 35–40 MINUTES

2 tbsp olive oil
1 onion, thinly sliced
3 garlic cloves, crushed
1 small aubergine
  (eggplant), cubed
1 tsp cumin seeds
1 tsp coriander seeds
½ tsp ground cinnamon
good pinch of ground ginger
2–3 tsp harissa
2 x 400g/14oz cans chickpeas,
  rinsed and drained
3 carrots, sliced
1 yellow (bell) pepper,
  deseeded and cut into
  chunks
4 tomatoes, diced
125g/4oz (½ cup) stoned
  (pitted) dates
300ml/½ pint (1¼ cups)
  water
1 tsp runny honey (optional)
1 preserved lemon, rinsed,
  skin only, thinly sliced
handful of flat-leaf parsley,
  chopped
salt and freshly ground black
  pepper
Greek yoghurt and steamed
  couscous, to serve

This Moroccan sweet-and-sour-flavoured tagine is the perfect way to warm up on a cold winter's day. The dates, carrots and honey enhance the sweetness while the preserved lemon adds a sour note.

1 Heat the olive oil in a large heavy-based saucepan and cook the onion, garlic and aubergine over a low–medium heat for about 8 minutes until tender and golden. Stir in the seeds, ground spices and harissa and cook for 1 minute.

2 Add the chickpeas, carrots, pepper, tomatoes and dates and stir well. Pour in the water and bring to the boil. Reduce the heat to a simmer, cover the pan and cook gently for 20–25 minutes until all the vegetables are tender and the liquid has reduced and thickened.

3 Season to taste with salt and pepper, then sweeten with a little honey, if wished. Stir in the preserved lemon and parsley.

4 Serve with a spoonful of Greek yoghurt on a bed of steamed couscous.

OR YOU CAN TRY THIS...

– Instead of dates, try stoned (pitted) prunes or dried apricots.
– Experiment with different vegetables: cauliflower florets, courgette (zucchini) or pumpkin.
– Use chopped mint or coriander (cilantro) instead of parsley.
– If you don't have cumin and coriander seeds, add a teaspoon each of the ground spices.
– Sprinkle with toasted pine nuts just before serving.

TIP: You can steam the couscous in a covered steamer pan or muslin (cheesecloth)-lined colander set above the pan of simmering tagine.

CARIBBEAN CHICKPEA CURRY WITH COCONUT RICE

SERVES: 4 | **PREP:** 15 MINUTES | **COOK:** 35 MINUTES

2 tbsp coconut oil

1 large onion, chopped

1 red (bell) pepper, deseeded and chopped

3 garlic cloves, crushed

2.5cm/1in piece fresh root ginger, peeled and diced

1 red chilli, diced

2 tbsp curry paste

1 small bunch of coriander (cilantro)

3 sweet potatoes, peeled and cut into chunks

1 x 400g/14oz can chickpeas, rinsed and drained

350g/12oz cherry or baby plum tomatoes, halved

240ml/8fl oz (1 cup) vegetable stock

300ml/½ pint (1¼ cups) reduced-fat coconut milk

450g/1lb spinach, washed and trimmed

juice of 1 lime

salt and freshly ground black pepper

This delicious curry can be made in advance and reheated or even frozen for a later date.

1 Make the coconut rice: heat the oil in a heavy-based saucepan and cook the onion, stirring occasionally, over a medium heat for about 5 minutes until starting to soften and turn golden. Stir in the rice and when all the grains are glistening with oil, pour in the stock and coconut milk. Stir in the salt and bring to the boil.

2 Reduce the heat to a bare simmer, cover the pan and cook for 15–20 minutes until the rice is tender and all the liquid has been absorbed.

3 Meanwhile, make the curry: heat the coconut oil in a large saucepan and cook the onion, red pepper, garlic, ginger and chilli over a low–medium heat, stirring occasionally, for 6–8 minutes until tender. Stir in the curry paste and cook for 1 minute.

4 Chop the coriander stalks (reserving the leaves) and add them to the pan with the sweet potatoes, chickpeas, tomatoes and stock. Bring to the boil, cover the pan, reduce the heat and cook very gently for 20 minutes until the liquid has reduced and the sweet potato is tender.

5 Add the coconut milk and spinach and cook for a few more minutes until the spinach turns bright green and wilts into the curry. Chop the coriander leaves roughly and stir into the pan with the lime juice. Season to taste with salt and pepper.

6 Divide the coconut rice among 4 serving plates and spoon the curry over the top.

For the coconut rice:
1 tbsp olive oil
1 onion, chopped
225g/8oz (1 cup) long-grain
   rice (dry weight)
480ml/16fl oz (2 cups)
   vegetable stock
300ml/½ pint (1¼ cups)
   coconut milk
good pinch of salt

OR YOU CAN TRY THIS...

– Instead of serving this
  with rice, spoon it into
  a split warmed pitta
  or flatbread. Or eat
  with naan bread and
  poppadoms.
– Vary the vegetables:
  use butternut squash,
  pumpkin or aubergine
  (eggplant) instead of
  sweet potatoes.

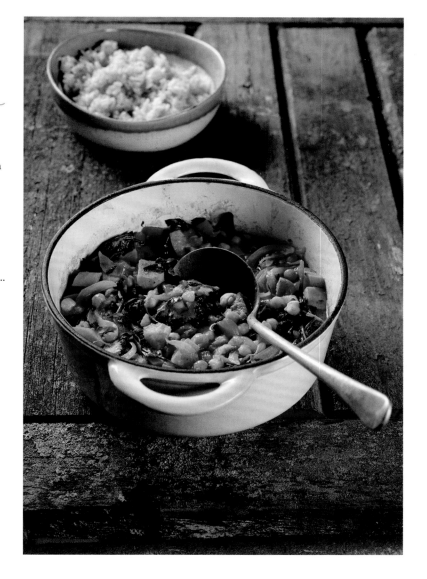

SAUTÉED CHICKEN & FALAFELS WITH HUMMUS

SERVES: 4 | **PREP:** 20 MINUTES | **SOAK:** OVERNIGHT | **STAND/CHILL:** 1–2 HOURS
COOK: 15 MINUTES

400g/14oz skinned chicken
    breast fillets
2–3 tbsp olive oil
2 garlic cloves, thinly sliced
1 quantity hummus
    (see page 14)
handful of salad leaves
juice of 1 small lemon
seeds of ½ pomegranate
salt and freshly ground
    black pepper

These golden-brown falafels are a wonderful fresh green inside when you cut them. Why not make double the quantity of mixture and freeze half for another meal?

1 Make the falafels: put the chickpeas into a bowl and cover with plenty of cold water. Leave to soak overnight.

2 Drain the chickpeas and pat dry with kitchen paper (towels). Blitz them briefly in a food processor with the spring onions, garlic, spices and herbs. Don't process for too long – you want the mixture to be slightly lumpy and crumbed rather than too smooth and puréed. Stir in the baking powder and salt. At this point you can transfer the falafel mixture to a bowl and put it, covered, in the refrigerator for 1–2 hours before cooking. This will allow it to rest and firm up.

3 Take 2 tablespoons of the mixture and, using your hands, shape into a small ball. Repeat with the remaining mixture.

4 Fry the falafels in batches in oil in a deep frying pan (skillet) until crisp and golden. Drain on kitchen paper (towels) and keep warm.

5 To cook the chicken, heat the olive oil in a frying pan (skillet) over a low–medium heat for 10–15 minutes, adding the garlic towards the end to prevent it browning, until the chicken is golden brown on the outside and cooked right through. Season with salt and pepper.

6 Smear the hummus around 4 serving plates and arrange the garlicky chicken, falafels and salad leaves in the centre. Squeeze over the lemon juice and scatter with the pomegranate seeds.

For the falafels:
250g/9oz (1¼ cups)
   dried chickpeas
4 spring onions
   (scallions), chopped
3 garlic cloves, crushed
1 tsp ground cumin
1 tsp ground coriander
½ tsp ground cinnamon
¼ tsp ground allspice
pinch of grated nutmeg
1 small bunch of flat-leaf
   parsley, chopped
1 small bunch of coriander
   (cilantro), chopped
½ tsp baking powder
good pinch of salt
sunflower oil, for frying

OR YOU CAN TRY THIS...
– Serve with roasted vegetables, spicy lamb or griddled prawns
   (shrimp) instead of chicken.
– Make the falafels hot and spicy by adding diced fresh chilli
   or chilli powder.

ROASTED CHICKPEA FAJITAS WITH GRIDDLED VEGETABLES

SERVES: 4 | **PREP:** 15 MINUTES | **COOK:** 25–35 MINUTES

2 x 400g/14oz cans
   chickpeas, rinsed
   and drained
1 tbsp rapeseed oil, plus
   extra for brushing
1 tbsp chilli powder
2 tsp ground cumin
1 tsp ground coriander
1 tsp smoked paprika
2 large red onions, thinly
   sliced
2 red, green or yellow (bell)
   peppers, deseeded and
   thinly sliced
1 large ripe avocado, peeled,
   stoned (pitted) and diced
juice of 1 lime
1 small bunch of coriander
   (cilantro), chopped
4 large or 8 small soft
   tortillas
salt and freshly ground
   black pepper
natural Greek yoghurt and
   tomato salsa, to serve

The roasted chickpeas used here can also be served as a healthy snack, or you could griddle extra vegetables and halve the amount of chickpeas in the fajitas, serving the remainder with pre-dinner drinks.

1 Preheat the oven to 190°C, 375°F, gas mark 5.

2 Put the chickpeas into a bowl with the oil and ground spices and stir well until all the chickpeas are coated with the spicy mixture.

3 Spread them out on a baking tray (cookie sheet) and roast in the oven for 25–35 minutes, turning once or twice, until golden brown and crunchy.

4 Meanwhile, lightly oil a ridged griddle pan and place over a medium heat. Cook the onions and peppers for 8–10 minutes, turning occasionally, until tender and slightly charred.

5 While the vegetables are cooking, toss the avocado in the lime juice and chopped coriander. Warm the tortillas on a griddle or in a low oven.

6 Mix the roasted chickpeas with the griddled vegetables and avocado. Season to taste with salt and pepper. Divide them among the tortillas. Serve with the yoghurt and salsa for everyone to add and then roll up or fold over the tortillas, tucking in the ends.

OR YOU CAN TRY THIS...
– Add some shredded griddled chicken to the mixture.
– Sprinkle with grated Monterey Jack or Cheddar cheese before rolling or folding.
– Serve with harissa, sweet chilli or hot pepper sauce.
– Instead of diced avocado, top with guacamole.

CHICKPEA BURRITOS

SERVES: 4 | **PREP:** 20 MINUTES | **COOK:** 35–40 MINUTES

2 tbsp olive oil
1 large red onion, chopped
3 garlic cloves, crushed
1 red (bell) pepper, deseeded and diced
1 yellow (bell) pepper, deseeded and diced
1 jalapeño chilli, diced
1 tsp smoked paprika
½ tsp ground cumin
pinch of cayenne pepper
350g/12oz ripe tomatoes, chopped
1 x 400g/14oz can chickpeas, rinsed and drained
handful of coriander (cilantro), chopped
4 large soft tortillas
1 small bunch of spring onions (scallions), chopped
50g/2oz (½ cup) grated Monterey Jack or Cheddar cheese
salt and freshly ground black pepper
sour cream and guacamole, to serve

Burritos are more Tex-Mex than real Mexican food but they taste great, make a healthy family supper and are normally a crowd-pleaser!

1 Preheat the oven to 180°C, 350°F, gas mark 4.

2 Make the filling: heat the olive oil in a frying pan (skillet) over a low heat. Add the onion, garlic, peppers and chilli and cook gently, stirring occasionally, for 6–8 minutes until softened. Add the spices, tomatoes and chickpeas and simmer for 10–15 minutes until thickened. Stir in the coriander and season to taste with salt and pepper.

3 Spoon a little of the filling into the centre of each tortilla – don't use it all. Sprinkle with the spring onions and then fold each tortilla around the filling like a parcel, folding in the sides to seal it. Arrange the burritos, seam-side down, in an ovenproof dish.

4 Pour the remaining filling over the top and sprinkle with the grated cheese. Bake in the oven for 15 minutes until hot and the cheese has melted and is golden brown and bubbling.

5 Serve the burritos immediately with some sour cream and guacamole.

OR YOU CAN TRY THIS...
– Add some shredded cooked chicken or diced chorizo to the chickpea filling.
– Serve with 0%-fat Greek yoghurt instead of sour cream.
– Instead of guacamole, just mash a ripe avocado with a little lime juice.

ROAST COD WITH SPINACH, CHILLI & CHICKPEAS

SERVES: 4 | **PREP:** 10 MINUTES | **COOK:** 20 MINUTES

4 large cod fillets (about 175g/6oz each)
grated zest and juice of 1 lemon
pinch of dried chilli flakes
4 tbsp extra-virgin olive oil
1 large red onion, thinly sliced
2 garlic cloves, crushed
1 tsp cumin seeds, crushed
good pinch of paprika
1 x 400g/14oz can chickpeas, rinsed and drained
120ml/4fl oz/½ cup fish or vegetable stock
300g/10oz spinach, washed and trimmed
salt and freshly ground black pepper

This is such a simple, healthy dish and it's really easy to cook. Haddock, sea bass, monkfish (anglerfish) or other white fish fillets work really well, too.

1 Preheat the oven to 180°C, 350°F, gas mark 4.

2 Wash the cod fillets and pat dry with kitchen paper (towels). Arrange them on a non-stick baking tray (cookie sheet), skin-side down, and sprinkle with the lemon zest and juice, chilli flakes and half the olive oil. Season with salt and pepper.

3 Cook the cod in the oven for 15–20 minutes until the flesh is thoroughly cooked. Check after 10 minutes and if it looks dry on the outside, cover with some foil to keep it moist.

4 Meanwhile, cook the onion and garlic in the remaining oil in a saucepan over a low–medium heat, stirring occasionally, for 5 minutes. Stir in the cumin seeds and paprika and cook for 1 minute.

5 Add the chickpeas and stock and simmer, covered, over a low heat for 5–10 minutes until reduced. Stir in the spinach and cook for about 2 minutes until it wilts and turns bright green.

6 Divide among 4 warm serving plates and arrange the cod fillets on top. Serve immediately.

OR YOU CAN TRY THIS...
– For more heat and spice use cayenne pepper instead of paprika.
– Shredded spring greens or kale can be substituted for the spinach but will take longer to cook.
– Add a spoonful of tomato purée (paste) or some chopped tomatoes to the spinach and chickpeas.

HARISSA PRAWNS (SHRIMP) & CHICKPEAS

SERVES: 4 | **PREP:** 10 MINUTES | **COOK:** 25 MINUTES

2 tbsp olive oil
1 onion, finely chopped
2 garlic cloves, crushed
2–3 tsp harissa
1 x 400g/14oz can
    chopped tomatoes
pinch of sugar
few basil leaves, torn
1 x 400g/14oz can chickpeas,
    rinsed and drained
450g/1lb raw peeled tiger
    prawns (jumbo shrimp)
juice of 1 lemon
1 small bunch of flat-leaf
    parsley, chopped
salt and freshly ground
    black pepper
steamed or boiled rice,
    to serve

A really easy and economical supper dish that you can rustle up quickly when you get home from work. And nearly all the ingredients are store-cupboard staples – keep a bag of frozen raw prawns (shrimp) in the freezer and defrost before using.

1 Heat the olive oil in a large frying pan (skillet) over a low–medium heat and cook the onion and garlic for 6–8 minutes until tender. Stir in the harissa and cook for 1 minute.

2 Add the tomatoes, sugar, basil and some seasoning and cook gently for about 10 minutes until reduced and thickened. Add the chickpeas and cook for 2–3 minutes to warm them through.

3 Add the prawns and cook for about 3 minutes, turning them once or twice, until pink on both sides. Stir in the lemon juice and parsley and check the seasoning.

4 Serve the curry on a mound of steamed or boiled rice.

OR YOU CAN TRY THIS...

– Use canned crabmeat or frozen *fruits de mer* instead of prawns.
– Substitute basil or coriander (cilantro) for the parsley.
– Use Thai or Indian curry paste instead of harissa.

SPICED MACKEREL WITH CARROT & CHICKPEA MASH

SERVES: 4 | **PREP:** 15 MINUTES | **COOK:** 20–25 MINUTES

juice of 1 lime
1 tbsp curry paste
4 tbsp 0%-fat Greek yoghurt
4 large fresh mackerel fillets
2 tbsp oil
1 large onion, thinly sliced
1 red chilli, deseeded and shredded
1 tsp cumin seeds
1 tsp black mustard seeds
½ tsp ground turmeric
salt and freshly ground black pepper

For the cucumber raita:
½ cucumber, deseeded and diced
250g/9oz (1 cup) 0%-fat Greek yoghurt
4 spring onions (scallions), finely chopped
1 garlic clove, crushed
grated zest and juice of ½ lime

For the carrot and chickpea mash:
600g/1¼lb carrots, sliced
1 x 400g/14oz can chickpeas, rinsed and drained
½ tsp ground cumin
½ tsp ground turmeric
1 small bunch of coriander (cilantro), chopped

Despite the lengthy list of ingredients, this is a quick and easy supper to prepare and make. The cooling raita counteracts the spicy mackerel, onions and mash.

1 Mix the lime juice, curry paste and yoghurt in a bowl. Add the mackerel fillets and turn them in the yoghurt marinade. Cover and leave in the refrigerator to marinate while you make the raita and mash.

2 Mix all the raita ingredients together in a bowl and season to taste with salt and pepper. Cover and chill in the refrigerator.

3 Make the carrot and chickpea mash: cook the carrots in a saucepan of lightly salted boiling water for 10–15 minutes until tender. Drain well and mash with a fork or blitz briefly in a blender. Crush the chickpeas coarsely with a potato masher and add to the carrots with the spices and coriander.

4 While the carrots are cooking, heat the oil in a frying pan (skillet) and cook the onion over a medium–high heat for about 5 minutes, stirring occasionally, until tender and golden. Add the chilli and cook for 1 minute, then stir in the seeds and turmeric. Season to taste.

5 Remove the mackerel fillets from the marinade and cook under a hot grill (broiler) for 2–3 minutes on each side until the skin is crisp and golden and the flesh is cooked and tender.

6 Serve the mackerel and onion on top of the spicy carrot mash with a spoonful of cucumber raita.

OR YOU CAN TRY THIS...

– Substitute another oily fish, such as herring or salmon fillets.
– Try using mashed swede (rutabaga) or pumpkin instead of carrots.

SALMON & SPICY CHICKPEAS WITH GREENS

SERVES: 4 | **PREP:** 15 MINUTES | **COOK:** 15 MINUTES

2 tbsp olive oil, plus extra
    for oiling
1 large onion, diced
2 garlic cloves, crushed
1 red chilli, diced
1 tbsp tahini
1 x 400g/14oz can chickpeas,
    rinsed and drained
juice of 1 lemon
handful of flat-leaf parsley,
    chopped
4 salmon fillets
salt and freshly ground
    black pepper
harissa, to serve

For the stir-fried greens:
2 tbsp groundnut oil
2 garlic cloves, thinly sliced
1 tsp grated fresh root ginger
pinch of dried chilli flakes
350g/12oz spring greens
    or kale, washed and
    shredded
grated zest of 1 lemon

Chickpeas add a satisfying crunch to this spicy supper. If you're not a fan of hot food, leave out the chilli.

1 Heat the olive oil in a frying pan (skillet) and cook the onion, garlic and chilli over a low–medium heat for about 5 minutes, stirring occasionally, until tender. Stir in the tahini and cook for 1 minute.

2 Add the chickpeas and cook for 5 minutes until they are warmed through and the onion is really soft and golden. Stir in the lemon juice and parsley. Season to taste with salt and pepper.

3 Meanwhile, cook the salmon in a lightly oiled non-stick frying pan (skillet) or on a griddle pan until the skin is crisp and golden and the flesh is cooked and opaque.

4 Meanwhile, heat the groundnut oil in a wok set over a high heat. Stir-fry the garlic, ginger and chilli for 30 seconds without burning them. Add the greens or kale and lemon zest, and stir-fry for 2–3 minutes until bright green and just tender (it should retain a little crispness and 'bite'). Season to taste.

5 Serve the salmon on top of the chickpeas with the stir-fried greens and a little harissa on the side.

OR YOU CAN TRY THIS...

– Instead of salmon, try sliced griddled chicken or king (jumbo) prawns.
– Tenderstem or purple sprouting broccoli is delicious stir-fried in this way. Just steam or blanch it first for 2 minutes.

FETA FALAFEL BURGERS

SERVES: 4 | **PREP:** 15 MINUTES | **COOK:** 20 MINUTES

3 tbsp olive oil
1 large onion, finely
    chopped
2 garlic cloves, crushed
2 x 400g/14oz cans
    chickpeas, rinsed
    and drained
150g/5oz feta cheese,
    broken into pieces
2 tomatoes, diced
1 small bunch of flat-leaf
    parsley
grated zest of 1 lemon
1 medium egg, beaten
4 wholemeal rolls or seeded
    burger buns
shredded lettuce leaves and
    sliced tomato
4 tbsp tzatziki (see page 22)
freshly ground black pepper

TIP: Don't add salt to the
burger mixture – the feta
is quite salty already.

These are packed with nutrients and fibre, making them a really
healthy choice. If wished, you could make them smaller and roll them
into balls before shallow-frying and serving with salad in a wrap or
pitta-bread pocket.

1 Heat 2 tablespoons of the olive oil in a frying pan (skillet) and cook
the onion and garlic over a low–medium heat for 10 minutes until
softened but not coloured.

2 Transfer to a blender or food processor and add the chickpeas, feta,
tomatoes, parsley, lemon zest and some of the beaten egg. Blitz to a
thick paste that you can shape into burgers. If it's too dry, add more
egg or diced tomato. Season with black pepper.

3 Divide the mixture into 4 equal-sized portions and, using your
hands, shape each one into a burger.

4 Spray a large non-stick frying pan (skillet) lightly with oil and place
over a medium heat. When it's hot, add the burgers and cook for
8–10 minutes, turning them over halfway, until lightly browned
on both sides and heated through.

5 Split the rolls or burger buns in half and fill each one with a burger,
some lettuce and sliced tomato and a spoonful of tzatziki.

OR YOU CAN TRY THIS...
– Use sunblush or dried tomatoes instead of fresh ones.
– If the mixture is too thick, slacken it with a squeeze or two of
   lemon juice.
– Use basil or coriander (cilantro) instead of parsley for a more
   aromatic flavour.
– Serve with hot salsa or mango chutney instead of tzatziki.

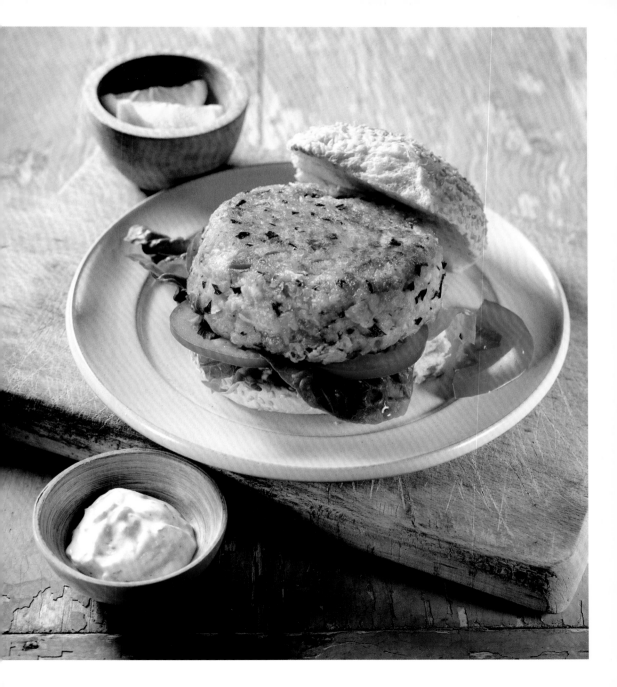

HUMMUS WITH LAMB & CARAMELIZED ONIONS

SERVES: 4 | **PREP:** 10 MINUTES | **COOK:** 20 MINUTES

25g/1oz (scant ¼ cup) pine nuts
4 tbsp olive oil
2 onions, thinly sliced
1 garlic clove, crushed
2 tsp ground cumin
½ tsp ground allspice
½ tsp ground cinnamon
1 tsp dried chilli flakes
350g/12oz (1½ cups) minced (ground) lean lamb
1 tbsp pomegranate molasses
1 quantity hummus (see page 14)
handful of flat-leaf parsley, chopped
salt and freshly ground black pepper
lemon quarters and warm pitta bread, to serve

In the Levant hummus is often served topped with spiced lamb, either minced (ground) or cut into small pieces. Don't overcook the lamb – it should still be slightly pink, juicy and succulent.

1 Heat a small frying pan (skillet) over a medium–high heat. Add the pine nuts to the hot pan and toast them, tossing them occasionally, for 1–2 minutes until golden brown and fragrant. Remove immediately (don't let them burn) and set aside to cool.

2 Heat the olive oil in a large heavy-based frying pan (skillet) and cook the onions and garlic very slowly over a low heat for about 15 minutes until tender, golden brown and starting to caramelize.

3 Stir in the spices and chilli flakes and cook for 1 minute. Add the lamb and cook for 3–4 minutes, stirring occasionally, until lightly browned but still a little pink. Stir in the pomegranate molasses and season to taste.

4 Smear the hummus round 4 serving plates in a circle. Pile the lamb and onions into the centre and scatter with the parsley and toasted pine nuts. Serve immediately with lemon quarters and warm pitta bread.

OR YOU CAN TRY THIS...
– Make the lamb more aromatic with some dried oregano or za'atar, freshly grated nutmeg, smoked paprika and fresh mint or basil.
– Add some whole chickpeas to the lamb mixture.

CHICKPEA & CHORIZO STEW

SERVES: 4 | **PREP:** 15 MINUTES | **COOK:** 45–50 MINUTES

2 tbsp olive oil
2 red onions, chopped
3 garlic cloves, crushed
2 celery sticks, diced
1 tsp smoked paprika
300g/10oz chorizo,
    cut into chunks
120ml/4fl oz (½ cup) white
    vermouth or wine
180ml/6fl oz (¾ cup)
    chicken stock or water
1 x 400g/14oz can
    chopped tomatoes
1 bay leaf
2 x 400g/14oz cans
    chickpeas, rinsed
    and drained
handful of flat-leaf parsley,
    chopped
freshly ground black pepper
sour cream or yoghurt,
    to serve
pinch of dried chilli flakes,
    to serve (optional)

This comforting stew will warm you up on a cold day. You can make
it go further to feed more people by serving it with boiled rice or pasta
noodles, such as tagliatelle or pappardelle.

1 Heat the olive oil in a heavy-based saucepan over a low–medium heat.
   Add the red onions, garlic and celery and cook for 8–10 minutes,
   stirring occasionally, until softened.

2 Stir in the paprika and chorizo and cook gently for 2–3 minutes
   before adding the vermouth or wine. Turn up the heat and cook
   vigorously for a few minutes, then add the stock or water and
   tomatoes. Bring to the boil, then reduce the heat to a simmer.

3 Add the bay leaf and chickpeas and cook gently for 25–30 minutes
   until the liquid reduces to a rich, spicy red sauce. Season to taste
   with salt and pepper.

4 Ladle into 4 shallow bowls and sprinkle with parsley. Serve topped
   with a spoonful of sour cream or yoghurt and some chilli flakes
   (if using).

OR YOU CAN TRY THIS...
– Add some diced red or green (bell) pepper or a hot chilli.
– Instead of white wine or vermouth, use sherry or red wine.
– Use fresh tomatoes instead of canned.
– Spicy fresh Toulouse or Merguez sausages can be substituted
   for the chorizo.

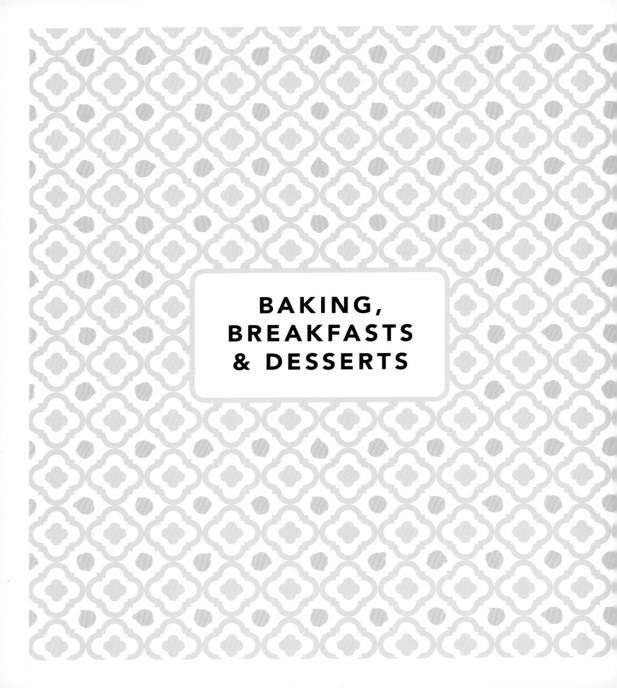

BAKING, BREAKFASTS & DESSERTS

FARINATA

SERVES: 4 | **PREP:** 10 MINUTES | **STAND:** 30 MINUTES | **COOK:** 30–40 MINUTES

250g/9oz (scant 2 cups) gram flour (chickpea flour)
large pinch of salt
550ml/18fl oz (2¼ cups) water
2 tbsp olive oil
2 sprigs of fresh rosemary, leaves stripped and finely chopped
vegetable or olive oil, for cooking
8 rashers (slices) streaky bacon, rind removed
4 sprigs of cherry tomatoes on the vine
freshly ground black pepper
maple syrup, for drizzling

These thick Italian pancakes originated in Genova and are made with chickpea flour. You can make the batter in advance and leave it to stand. Serve them for a weekend breakfast or delicious brunch with crispy bacon, griddled tomatoes and maple syrup.

1 Preheat the oven to 200°C, 400°F, gas mark 6.

2 Sift the gram flour into a large bowl. Add the salt and gradually whisk in the water until you have a smooth batter. Stir in the olive oil and chopped rosemary and leave to stand for at least 30 minutes (or up to 2 hours).

3 Set a 20cm (8in) ovenproof frying pan (skillet) over a medium–high heat. Add enough oil – about 2 tablespoons – to cover the base of the hot pan and pour in one-quarter of the batter. When it starts to bubble (after about 30 seconds), pop the pan into the oven for 4–5 minutes until the pancake is browned underneath.

4 Remove and carefully flip the pancake over before returning to the oven for 4–5 minutes to cook the other side. The pancake should be golden brown and crisp on the outside but slightly custardy inside. Slide out of the pan onto some kitchen paper (towels) on a plate. Keep warm while you cook the remaining pancakes in the same way.

5 Meanwhile, grill (broil) the bacon and cherry tomatoes on a griddle pan or under a hot grill (broiler).

6 Serve the hot pancakes cut into wedges with the bacon and tomatoes. Grind some black pepper over the top and drizzle with maple syrup.

OR YOU CAN TRY THIS...
– Sprinkle the cooked pancakes with grated cheese or dot with diced Taleggio and place in the oven for 2–3 minutes until it melts.
– Serve with spicy sausages, fried red (bell) peppers and onions or a spoonful of guacamole, hummus or salsa.
– Vary the herbs: try chopped sage, flat-leaf parsley or chives.

SMASHED CHICKPEA, CHILLI & SPRING ONION QUESADILLAS

SERVES: 4 | **PREP:** 20 MINUTES | **COOK:** 20 MINUTES

1 x 400g/14oz can chickpeas,
 rinsed and drained
1 red chilli, finely diced
4 spring onions (scallions),
 thinly sliced
few sprigs of coriander
 (cilantro), chopped
175g/6oz (1¾ cups)
 Cheddar or Monterey
 Jack cheese, grated
oil, for brushing
8 x 20cm/8in flour tortillas
salt and freshly ground
 black pepper
sour cream, to serve

For the avocado salsa:
1 ripe avocado, peeled,
 stoned (pitted) and diced
2 juicy tomatoes, diced
½ red onion, diced
1 red chilli, diced
1 garlic clove, crushed
few sprigs of coriander
 (cilantro), chopped
juice of 1 small lime

These quesadillas are so easy to make and can be eaten as a snack, party food or even for a weekend brunch with salad or griddled vegetables. We have served ours with an avocado salsa but you could substitute guacamole or drizzle them with some sweet chilli sauce.

1 Make the avocado salsa: mix all the ingredients together in a bowl and set aside while you make the quesadillas.

2 Coarsely mash the chickpeas in a bowl. Add the chilli, spring onions, coriander and grated cheese and mix well together. Season to taste with salt and pepper.

3 Lightly brush a non-stick frying pan (skillet) with oil and place over a medium heat. Put a tortilla in the hot pan and cover with one-quarter of the chickpea mixture, leaving a thin border around the edge. Put another tortilla on top and cook for about 3 minutes until golden brown and crisp underneath.

4 Carefully turn over the quesadilla and cook the other side for 2–3 minutes until golden brown and the cheese melts. Remove from the pan and keep warm while you cook the remaining quesadillas in the same way.

5 Serve them cut into wedges with sour cream and the avocado salsa.

OR YOU CAN TRY THIS...
– Instead of grated hard cheese, use diced mozzarella or salty feta.
– Serve with a regular tomato salsa and add the diced avocado to the chickpea filling.
– For more substantial quesadillas, add shredded chicken, diced ham or ready-to-eat tofu to the chickpea mixture.
– Sour cream is quite high in calories and fat, so if you're weight conscious, serve with 0%-fat Greek yoghurt instead.

AQUAFABA FRENCH TOAST

SERVES: 4 I **PREP:** 10–15 MINUTES I **COOK:** 12 MINUTES

120ml/4fl oz (½ cup)
aquafaba (liquid from
1 x 400g/14oz can)
120ml/4fl oz (½ cup)
almond (or other nut)
milk
1 tsp vanilla extract
pinch of ground cinnamon
oil, for frying
4 large thick slices of crusty
white or seedy bread
salt and freshly ground
black pepper
maple syrup, for drizzling
sliced bananas or berries,
to serve

Aquafaba is the drained liquid from canned chickpeas that can, amazingly, be used as a vegan dairy-free replacement for eggs. Instead of throwing it away, you can whisk this virtually odourless and tasteless liquid into stiff peaks and use it to make meringues, muffins, cakes and mayonnaise. As a general guide, you need 3 tablespoons aquafaba to replace one whole egg; 2 tablespoons per white; and 1 tablespoon per yolk.

1 Whisk the aquafaba with the milk, vanilla extract, cinnamon and seasoning in a large bowl until you have a really frothy batter. Use an electric whisk to get the maximum volume and make it easier on your arms. Pour the batter into a shallow dish.

2 Lightly oil a large non-stick frying pan (skillet) and place over a medium heat.

3 Dip one or two slices of bread into the batter to coat them on both sides. Gently shake off the excess and arrange the slices in the hot pan.

4 Cook for 3–4 minutes until golden brown and crisp underneath, then turn the bread over with a metal spatula and cook the other side. Remove and keep warm while you cook the remaining French toast in the same way.

5 Serve the hot French toast drizzled with maple syrup with some sliced banana and berries.

OR YOU CAN TRY THIS...

– Dust with ground cinnamon and drizzle with runny honey.
– Instead of fruit, top with crispy bacon and serve with griddled tomatoes.
– Add some snipped chives or a spoonful of chia seeds to the batter.
– Try cooking the French toast in coconut oil.
– Use soya milk or any dairy-free nut milk to make the French toast.

PROVENÇAL SOCCA

SERVES: 4 | **PREP:** 15 MINUTES | **STAND:** 1–2 HOURS | **COOK:** 40 MINUTES

250g/9oz (scant 2 cups) gram flour (chickpea flour)
large pinch of salt
550ml/18fl oz (2¼ cups) water
2 tbsp olive oil
2 sprigs of fresh rosemary, leaves stripped and finely chopped
pinch of ground cumin
vegetable or rapeseed oil, for cooking
1 red onion, thinly sliced

For the roasted pepper and rocket (arugula) topping:
2 roasted (bell) peppers, sliced (or bottled)
4 small handfuls of rocket (arugula)
balsamic vinegar, for drizzling

For the giant couscous and sunblush tomato topping:
8 tbsp cooked giant couscous
60g/2oz sunblush tomatoes, roughly chopped
4 tbsp canned chickpeas, rinsed and drained
few sprigs of coriander (cilantro), chopped
squeeze of lemon juice

Lacy-edged golden socca pancakes, or 'pizzas', are a speciality of Nice. They are almost exactly the same as the Ligurian farinata but are often served topped with melted mozzarella, roasted peppers or tomatoes and salad leaves.

1 Preheat the oven to 200°C, 400°F, gas mark 6.

2 Sift the gram flour into a large mixing bowl. Add the salt and gradually whisk in the water until you have a smooth batter. Stir in the olive oil, chopped rosemary and the ground cumin and leave to stand for 1–2 hours.

3 Heat some of the vegetable or rapeseed oil in a 20cm (8in) ovenproof frying pan (skillet) over a medium heat. Add the red onion to the hot pan and cook for 8–10 minutes, stirring occasionally, until cooked and tender.

4 Tip the onion into the batter and stir well. Pour one-quarter of the batter into the hot pan and place over a medium–high heat. As soon as it starts to bubble, pop the pan into the oven for about 4 minutes until the pancake is browned underneath.

5 Use a spatula to flip the pancake over and return to the oven for about 4 minutes to cook the other side. The pancake should be golden brown and crisp on the outside but slightly custardy inside. Slide out of the pan onto some kitchen paper (towels) on a plate. Keep warm while you cook the remaining pancakes in the same way.

6 Eat the pancakes warm and cut into wedges, or serve like a pizza with one of the suggested toppings.

OR YOU CAN TRY THIS...

– Smear some home-made or bottled tomato sauce over the pancakes and dot with mozzarella. Bake or grill (broil) until hot and melted.
– Add some crushed garlic to the red onion while it's cooking.

CHICKPEA TORTILLA NACHOS

SERVES: 4–6 | **PREP:** 20–25 MINUTES | **COOK:** 20 MINUTES

250g/9oz (2 cups) gram
   flour (chickpea flour)
1 tsp baking powder
1 tsp sea salt
1 tsp paprika
1 tsp coarsely ground
   black pepper
pinch of crushed
   chilli flakes
60ml/2fl oz (¼ cup)
   vegetable or coconut oil
60ml/2fl oz (¼ cup)
   warm water

You can store these home-made tortilla chips for up to 14 days in an airtight container. Eat them as a snack or transform them into an inviting mountain of nachos – irresistible.

1 Preheat the oven to 190°C, 375°F, gas mark 5.

2 Put the flour, baking powder, salt, paprika, pepper and chilli flakes into a large bowl. Stir in the oil and warm water until you have a slightly sticky dough. If it's too crumbly, add some more water.

3 Roll out the dough as thinly as possible between 2 sheets of baking parchment. Remove the covering sheet of parchment and cut into triangles (tortilla chips).

4 Carefully, slide the baking parchment with the nachos on top onto a large baking tray (cookie sheet) and bake in the oven for 10–15 minutes until crisp and golden brown. Remove and cool. Increase the oven temperature to 200°C, 400°F, gas mark 6.

5 Put the tortilla chips onto a non-stick baking tray (cookie sheet). Mix the tomatoes, chilli, spring onions and avocado with the lime juice, then sprinkle over the tortillas, with the black beans. Scatter the grated cheese over the top and pop into the hot oven for at least 5 minutes until the cheese melts. Alternatively, use an overhead grill (broiler).

6 Sprinkle the nachos with coriander and serve immediately with salsa and sour cream (or yoghurt).

For the topping:
4 ripe tomatoes, deseeded
    and chopped
1 red or green chilli,
    thinly sliced
bunch of spring onions
    (scallions), sliced
1 ripe avocado, peeled,
    stoned (pitted) and diced
juice of 1 lime
1 x 400g/14oz can black
    beans, rinsed and drained
125g/4oz (1 cup) grated
    Cheddar or Monterey
    Jack cheese
1 small bunch of coriander
    (cilantro), chopped
fresh salsa and sour cream
    (or Greek yoghurt),
    to serve

OR YOU CAN TRY THIS...

– Vary the topping with the following: red kidney beans, chickpeas,
  diced red onion, toasted pumpkin seeds and guacamole.
– Use diced mozzarella instead of grated hard cheese.

SPICY CHICKPEA PANCAKES WITH RICOTTA & SPINACH FILLING

SERVES: 4 | **PREP:** 15 MINUTES | **STAND:** 30 MINUTES | **COOK:** 10 MINUTES

250g/9oz (scant 2 cups) gram flour (chickpea flour)
½ tsp ground turmeric
1 tsp salt
400ml/13fl oz (generous 1½ cups) cold water
1 garlic clove, crushed
sunflower oil, for frying
chutney, pickles or raita, to serve

For the ricotta and spinach filling:
400g/14oz baby spinach leaves
250g/9oz (generous 1 cup) ricotta
1 small red chilli, diced
grated zest of ½ lemon
200g/7oz (¾ cup) canned chickpeas, rinsed and drained
salt and freshly ground black pepper

These crisp golden pancakes are best made paper-thin before wrapping them around the ricotta and spinach filling.

1 Put the flour, turmeric and salt into a large bowl and whisk in the cold water until you have a smooth batter. It should have the consistency of cream. If it's too thick, add a little more water. Stir in the garlic and leave to stand for 30 minutes.

2 Meanwhile, make the filling: put the baby spinach leaves with 1–2 teaspoons water into a large pan set over a medium heat and cover with a lid. Cook for about 2 minutes, shaking the pan occasionally, until the leaves turn bright green and wilt. Drain in a colander, pressing down with a saucer or plate to extract the moisture.

3 Chop the spinach and mix with the ricotta, chilli, lemon zest and chickpeas. Season to taste with salt and pepper.

4 To cook the pancakes, place a large heavy-based frying pan (skillet) over a medium heat. Add a little sunflower oil – just enough to thinly cover the bottom of the pan. When it's hot, add sufficient batter to cover the base (3–4 tablespoons). Tilt the pan to swirl the batter around evenly. Cook for about 30 seconds or so until bubbles appear on the surface and the underside is cooked and golden, then flip the pancake over and cook the other side. Remove and keep warm while you cook the remaining pancakes in the same way.

5 Divide the filling among the pancakes and fold over or roll up. Serve warm with chutney, pickles, raita or even some natural yoghurt.

OR YOU CAN TRY THIS...
– Use a different filling: curried chicken or vegetables work well.
– Flavour the pancake batter with diced chilli, chopped spring onions (scallions), roasted mustard or onion seeds or chopped herbs.

PANELLE

SERVES: 8 | **PREP:** 25 MINUTES | **CHILL:** 2 HOURS (OR OVERNIGHT) | **COOK:** 15–20 MINUTES

2 tbsp olive oil, plus extra
    for greasing and frying
250g/9oz (2 cups) chickpea
    flour (gram flour)
good pinch of sea salt
    crystals
freshly ground black pepper
960ml/1¾ pints (4 cups)
    water
Parmesan shavings, lemon
    wedges and rocket
    (arugula) salad drizzled
    with balsamic vinegar,
    to serve

These Sicilian chickpea fritters are surprisingly easy to make. To get them really crisp and golden outside (but still soft inside) we suggest frying them in the traditional way, but to save calories you can bake them in a medium–hot oven.

1 Lightly oil a 25cm/10in square baking tin (pan).

2 Put the chickpea flour, sea salt and a generous grinding of black pepper into a large bowl.

3 Bring the water to the boil in a saucepan and gradually whisk it into the seasoned flour. You should end up with a smooth mixture without any lumps.

4 Transfer to the saucepan and bring to the boil, then remove from the heat and stir in the 2 tablespoons of olive oil. Transfer to the prepared baking tin and level the top. Cover and chill in the refrigerator for at least 2 hours (overnight if you like) until firm.

5 When you're ready to cook the panelle, cut it into thin slices, squares or triangles. Heat some oil to a depth of 5mm/¼in in a deep frying pan (skillet) over a medium heat and when it's really hot cook the panelle, a few at a time, for about 2 minutes until crisp and golden underneath. Turn them over and cook the other side. Keep warm on a plate lined with kitchen paper (towels) while you fry the rest in the same way.

6 Eat piping hot sprinkled with Parmesan shavings. Serve with the lemon wedges and a rocket salad drizzled with balsamic vinegar.

OR YOU CAN TRY THIS...
– Scatter with chopped flat-leaf parsley or mint and squeeze a little lemon juice over the top.
– Top each panelle with a dot of tapenade or drizzle with green pesto.

CHOCOLATE ESPRESSO & CHICKPEA FUDGE CAKE

SERVES: 8 | **PREP:** 15 MINUTES | **COOK:** 30–40 MINUTES

150g/5oz (generous ½ cup) unsalted butter, softened, plus extra for greasing
200g/7oz plain (semisweet) chocolate (minimum 70% cocoa solids)
2 tbsp strong espresso coffee
150g/5oz (generous ½ cup) caster (superfine) sugar
1 x 400g/14oz can chickpeas, rinsed and drained
4 medium eggs, separated
icing (confectioner's) sugar, for dusting
crème fraîche and your favourite summer berries, to serve

OR YOU CAN TRY THIS...

– Instead of espresso, flavour the cake with grated orange zest or a few drops of vanilla extract.
– Serve with ice cream, Greek yoghurt or even some mascarpone cheese.

Don't worry if this cake slumps as it cools; it is meant to be squidgy and soft inside, similar to a brownie. The chickpeas replace the traditional flour, making it gluten-free. For the best results, you need a food processor or food mixer or, at the very least, a good electric whisk.

1 Preheat the oven to 180°C, 350°F, gas mark 4. Grease a 23cm/9in loose-bottomed cake tin (springform pan) with butter and line the bottom with baking parchment.

2 Break the chocolate into small pieces and place them in a heatproof bowl set over a saucepan of simmering water. When the chocolate melts, remove from the heat and stir well. Add the espresso coffee.

3 Beat the sugar and butter together in a food mixer or processor until light and fluffy. Beat in the chickpeas and keep whisking until the mixture is smooth. Beat in the egg yolks, one at a time, then gradually beat in the melted chocolate.

4 In a clean, dry bowl, beat the egg whites until they form stiff peaks. Fold them gently into the chocolate mixture in a figure-of-eight movement with a metal spoon until thoroughly incorporated.

5 Pour the cake mixture into the prepared tin and cook in the oven for 30–40 minutes until well risen. The cake should spring back when you press it gently with your finger. Remove from the oven and leave in the tin to cool.

6 When the cake reaches room temperature, remove it from the tin and dust with sifted icing sugar. Serve still slightly warm and cut into slices with crème fraîche and summer berries.

AQUAFABA PAVLOVA

SERVES: 6–8 I **PREP:** 25 MINUTES I **COOK:** 1½–2 HOURS I **COOL:** 30–45 MINUTES

120ml/4fl oz (½ cup)
  aquafaba (liquid from
  1 x 400g/14oz can)
225g/8oz (1 cup) caster
  (superfine) sugar
1 tbsp cornflour (cornstarch)
1 tsp cider vinegar

For the topping:
300ml/½ pint (1¼ cups)
  double (heavy) cream
3 tbsp coarsely grated plain
  (semisweet) chocolate
300g/10oz fresh raspberries
  or strawberries

You only need the drained liquid from one can of chickpeas to make a pavlova. It's a great dessert for entertaining and your guests will be surprised when you tell them it's made with chickpea brine, not eggs!

1 Preheat the oven to 140°C, 275°F, gas mark 1. Trace a 23cm/9in circle on a sheet of baking parchment and use to line a baking tray (cookie sheet).

2 Pour the aquafaba into the bowl of an electric mixer (or a deep mixing bowl if using a hand-held whisk). Whip the aquafaba for 3–5 minutes until fluffy and soft peaks form. Start on a slow speed and gradually increase it to high.

3 Thoroughly mix the sugar and cornflour in a small bowl and then start adding it, about 2 tablespoons at a time, to the aquafaba, whisking on a high speed until all the sugar has been added. Add the cider vinegar and keep whisking until the meringue is glossy with stiff peaks that hold their shape. You'll know when it is ready because when you lift the beaters out the meringue will stay in place and not drop off.

4 Spoon the meringue onto the circle on the baking parchment, spreading it out to the edges and making a slight hollow in the centre.

5 Put the meringue into the oven and reduce the heat to 130°C, 250°F, gas mark ½. Bake for 1½–2 hours (until crisp on the outside and dry on top), then turn off the oven, open the door slightly so it's ajar, and leave the meringue inside for another 30–45 minutes until cool.

6 Just before serving the pavlova, whip the cream until it forms soft peaks and holds its shape. Spread it over the top of the pavlova and sprinkle with the grated chocolate. Top with the berries and serve cut into slices.

OR YOU CAN TRY THIS...

- Use arrowroot instead of cornflour in the meringue.
- Flavour the meringue with grated lemon or orange zest or vanilla.
- Vary the topping and use thick Greek yoghurt or mascarpone instead of cream; instead of berries try passionfruit, kiwi fruit or mango; lemon curd and bitter kumquats.
- Sprinkle with toasted flaked almonds or chopped pistachios.

INDEX